The Naked Truth

Exposing the Deception of Adventism

By Hazel Holland

Copyright © 2010 Hazel Holland
All rights reserved.

ISBN: 143926662X
ISBN-13: 9781439266625

Explanation of Painting on Front Cover

The picture on the front cover, **The Naked Truth**, has been taken from various parts of the water color (above) that the author painted to illustrate a prophetic dream she had on April 11, 1996. After painting the mountain of children, as she had seen it in the dream, she was impressed to paint the mountain again, but this time, to superimpose a face on the mountain. Thinking that she was painting a warrior bride rising up in intercession for the mountain of children held captive by fear, she later realized that she had painted the "Naked Truth" behind Adventism's stronghold. This book is an unraveling of that truth.

(All the illustrations used in this book were painted by the author).

The mountain of children as seen in the dream.

Table of Contents

Acknowledgements vii

Forward ix

Introduction: The Release of the Captives xv

PART I: THE DREAM - Exposing Adventism's Package

Chapter 1: The Dream: Exposing Adventism's Package 1

PART II: THE DREAM - Exposing Adventism's Package
(The Interpretation)

Chapter 2: A New Church Experiment 11

Chapter 3: The Central Pillar 19

Chapter 4: Hidden Bondage Revealed 29

Chapter 5: Say to this Mountain, Move! 43

Chapter 6: The "Rest" that Remains 59

PART III: THE VISION - In the School of the Spirit

Chapter 7: The Vision – In the School of the Spirit 81

PART IV: THE VISION - In the School of the Spirit
(The Interpretation)

Chapter 8: I Saw His Glory 87

Chapter 9: Exposing a Sacred Cow 101

Chapter 10: Receiving the Father's Heart 119

Chapter 11: Sounding a Clear Call 135

Chapter 12: Epilogue–Adventism's Ancient Stronghold 153

Appendix A: Chapter 9 165

Appendix B: Assisted Suicide—A Word to Evangelicals 181

Bibliography 187

Acknowledgments

I want to express my deepest appreciation to all my spiritual brothers and sisters who have lifted me up in prayer over the past ten years as I have endeavored to be obedient to the Spirit of the Lord in the completion of the manuscript for this book. I am indebted to Dr. Cherry Brandstater who willingly volunteered her editing skills during the last few months of completing the writing for this book.

My heartfelt thanks goes out to my spiritual sons and daughters from La Sierra University who have faithfully prayed for me, and encouraged me through difficult times to dwell in the Secret Place of the Most High and rest in the shadow of His wings. One of them in particular is Ramone Romero who volunteered his editing skills in the early phase of organizing some of the chapters.

I also wish to express my indebtedness to many Christian authors whose thoughtful insights into God's Word repeatedly sent me back to the Scriptures to dig for more truth. A book entitled, "Sabbath in Christ," by Dale Ratzlaff, particularly helped me. I have used some of his research and borrowed a number of his concepts.

Finally, I want to express my love and thanks to my son, Rob, who has had a difficult time accepting and understanding the call of God upon my life. God has used him in many ways to birth in me a greater compassion and love for all His children who are sometimes afraid of the way the Holy Spirit is moving in these last days.

I am reminded of Rob's final words in a dream that God gave me back in 1995. In the dream as we were both looking up into the night sky a huge cross of light appeared in the heavens. I quickly realized that Rob couldn't see it, but before I could say anything the cross of light turned into a large wooden cross with a huge knot in the center of it. The words that escaped from his lips caused me to be overcome with the joy of the Lord as I heard him exclaim, "Now I see!"

My prayer is that each one of you will come to "see" and accept the incredible gift of God's love that has been given to each of us in Jesus Christ. May the Spirit reveal to you that although our world is but a speck in a universe of billions of galaxies, you are and forever will be His first love!

Hazel Holland

Forward:
SETTING THE RECORD STRAIGHT

Then the angel said to me, "Write: 'Blessed are those who are invited to the wedding supper of the Lamb!'" And he added, "These are the true words of God." At this I fell at his feet to worship him. But he said to me, "Do not do it! I am a fellow servant with you and with your brothers who hold to the testimony of Jesus. Worship God! For the testimony of Jesus is the spirit of prophecy."
Revelation 19:9-10

God is setting the record straight about the "spirit of prophecy"—prophecy comes to testify about Jesus! Prophecy is given as a witness that Jesus Christ is everything God has said He is—our salvation, our righteousness, our wisdom, our holiness, our redemption (1 Corinthians 1:30). Christ is the testimony of God, and this is God's testimony: "God has given us eternal life, and this life is in His Son. He who has the Son has life; he who does not have the Son of God does not have life." (1 John 5:11-12)

"The testimony of Jesus is the spirit of prophecy." How is it that these simple words have caused so much confusion in various corners of the Body of Christ? This verse has been cited more than any other to support the claims of prophets, to give credibility and authority to a prophet's words: "You had better listen to what our prophet says because it's the 'spirit of prophecy' and that is the 'testimony of Jesus'... so these are the very words of Jesus on this subject."

This complete misreading of Scripture makes the prophet the center and Jesus the supporter, and is often used to justify any less-than-

Scriptural teaching. When we remove the words "spirit of prophecy" from their context and put them at odds with the rest of the New Testament witness, it displaces Jesus from His rightful place as the center of all things and redirects the spotlight onto the prophet. Prophecy is supposed to tell people about Christ. The good news is about *Him*—all prophets must gladly fade into the background as they point people to the Savior (See Acts 10:25-26, 36, 43).

The "spirit of prophecy" is not some special elite spirit—there is *one* Holy Spirit, and prophecy is merely *one of His gifts* (1 Corinthians 12:4-11). We set ourselves up for idolatry and spiritual deafness when we divide the Holy Spirit by isolating any one of His gifts above the others or revere someone for having the special "spirit of prophecy". The word "spirit" in Greek can also mean "essence, inner life, disposition, state of mind, power, or wind." Revelation can thus read, "The testimony of Jesus is the *essence* of prophecy." This usage of "spirit" is not new to us: we say charitable acts in December show the "spirit" of Christmas. In the same way, the "spirit" of prophecy is to testify *about Christ*, and this has always been the refreshing passion of the *one* Holy Spirit (John 14:26, 16:14). This Spirit lived in the prophets of old, in Christ and in the apostles—and now this same Spirit lives in you and me.

The promise of the New Covenant is "they will **all** know Me" (Hebrews 8:11). Jesus said, "The Spirit of truth... lives with **you** and will be in **you**. I will not leave you as orphans; I will come to **you**. Before long, the world will not see Me anymore, but **you** will see Me... on that day **you** will realize that I am in My Father, and **you** are in Me, and I am in **you**." Jesus boldly promised to show Himself to each of us and make His home inside of each of us (John 14:17-23). He said He would continue to reveal His Father to us (John 17:26) and sing praises to His Father in the midst of our meetings (Hebrews 2:12).

So why do we seek after prophets to explain the Bible to us or to give us a word from the Lord? Have we forgotten that the Lord is longing to speak to us Himself and that hearing from Him for ourselves is our Covenant inheritance? Could it be that we have not been taught how to hear the Spirit? Are we still waiting for the "latter rain" outpouring of the Spirit even though Peter said the "last days" began at Pentecost (Acts 2:16-18)? Do our images of prophets and the prophetic still operate under the model of the Old Covenant?

If we have not understood the title deed of our inheritance—the *New* Covenant—we will find ourselves taking our cues from the Old Covenant template of the prophetic. We'll expect a prophet to be like Moses who acted as an intermediary between the people and God, and thereby miss the awesome privilege of having God speak directly to us. The angel's words of Revelation are spoken to stop us from bowing down to prophets and to keep us focused on Jesus: "You must worship *God*! The spirit and essence of all prophecy is to testify *about Jesus*," to reveal the truth about Christ, what He has done, and all that is freely given in Him! (1 Corinthians 2:12)

As many have noted, the best cure for the abuse of the gifts of the Spirit is not to suppress their use, but rather to let God use them properly. Over-emphasizing prophecy *and* prohibiting prophecy both bring damage to the Body of Christ. Paul wrote, "When you come together, everyone has a hymn, or a word of instruction, a revelation, a tongue or an interpretation. *All of these must be done for the strengthening of the church*" (1 Corinthians 14:26). When God's Spirit is allowed to express Himself in a group and it is understood that all gifts are given to testify about Jesus, the results are healing and freedom. I began to learn this in practical, personal experience in a small group, in the school of the Spirit…

My first contact with Hazel Holland came in the fall of 2000 when I read a prophecy she had posted on the Internet. At 21 years of age, I had grown up Adventist and had already been a missionary to Japan, yet I had felt many troubling things in the church but was unable to fully recognize them without feeling guilty. From a young age I had been told, "No church is perfect," and "You shouldn't criticize God's church." But when I read what God had shown to Hazel, I finally understood that He had seen all His children's pains (including mine!) and was very concerned about what was happening to all of us.

A few days later, I cautiously went to meet Hazel and test her beliefs. She spoke the Gospel I knew from the book of Romans—that we are saved by faith in Christ. But when I tested her on the Sabbath question, she said something shocking to me: *If we are to be saved by keeping Sabbath in the end-times, then we are saved by our good works instead of by faith in Christ!* For the first time in my life, the Gospel was allowed to interpret the Adventist end-time beliefs. I knew I had truly heard the Gospel, but I was frightened of going through this turning point because the Sabbath was my insurance in the "last days." Was God now calling me to walk where there seemed to be no ground beneath my feet, to step out over the chasm trusting that He would catch me?

I went to visit Hazel again, and this time I brought all my friends. A Thursday night prayer meeting was born. As the meetings continued, several of us began to move in gifts of the Holy Spirit that we had never recognized before. Yet the most wonderful thing about the meetings was not the gifts—granted, they were exciting, but they were never the point. I eagerly desired the gifts when I first arrived, but the Lord wanted me to first be reconciled with my natural father and have peace with him. God used Hazel and others to help me "un-freeze" my emotions and release my bitterness. He taught me how to choose to forgive those who had hurt me and find healing at the foot of the Cross.

At the meetings, I learned firsthand that when we allow the Spirit of God to move through us freely, He will use His gifts as aides to help uncover root problems in our hearts. I sometimes would arrive at the meetings in with an emotional, physical or spiritual pain, but unable to identify the reason behind it. As the group began to pray for me and wait on the Lord together, God would give a picture, vision, impression or word to someone, which in turn would shed light on what was troubling me. I always knew when something was from God because I felt the inner witness of the Spirit—His true words always "resonated" in my own spirit. The gift of prophecy functioned in the same way, usually through Hazel and occasionally through others. As a result of the ministry of the Holy Spirit in and among us, countless wounds were healed.

Likewise, when any of us received dreams or visions, we brought them to God and He answered in the same manner. Before taking the dream to the group, I would first pray and wait on God personally for understanding (if I forget to do this and took the dream straight to the group, God always reminded me to come to Him first next time). Without fail God brought discernment and understanding like an unveiling process as we waited on Him together—and His interpretations usually came through more than one individual. The Lord seems to prefer to disperse His revelations among each person in a group instead of giving the burden of full understanding to just one member. I believe this is part of "carrying each other's burdens" (Galatians 6:2)—He gives us brothers and sisters through whom He will speak to us and bless us.

As we freely allow Him to do that, we better understand Him and what His heart is for us.

The Naked Truth is based on a dream and subsequent vision the Lord gave Hazel Holland in 1996. While most of the interpretation was given to Hazel, some insights and understanding were received by those of us with whom she shared the book for prayer, similar to how He brought understanding through many people in the prayer meetings at her home. This book has been "given birth" as the result of the prayers of many. He seems to take delight in giving interpretations one piece at a time until a whole picture emerges, so that in the whole process we are dependent on Him for understanding, and when the picture is finished our eyes are fixed on Him alone, the Revelator of all things, and Himself the great Revelation, Himself our salvation. We will be happy in the end if the focus is on the burden on the Lord's heart instead of on the vessels through whom He conveyed it.

Why did the Lord give this dream and vision to Hazel Holland? What message does He want to convey to His children? In these last days, I believe God is raising up prophets in order to reset our faith and practice to the finished work of His Son—the spirit and heart of prophecy. "Prophecy" in Hebrew also means "burden," and I pray that you may hear the burden of God's heart as you read the pages of this book. Its contents may initially surprise and even disturb you, but He has promised that His burden is light and above all that as we lay down our heavy burdens He will give us rest in Himself.

Ramone R. Romero
June 2006
Osaka, Japan

When we believe in Him, we will trust our very lives to His good work and enter into His "rest".

Introduction
RELEASING THE CAPTIVES

"When the Lord brought back the captives to Zion, our mouths were filled with laughter... our tongues with songs of joy."
Psalm 126:1

Several years ago as I was praying for people God had placed on my heart, I was suddenly overcome with great joy. The weeping I had experienced as I sought God's heart on their behalves was replaced by a tidal wave of exuberant laughter that felt strangely warm and wonderful. It was like nothing I had ever known before.

Immediately the Lord directed me to turn to Psalm 126. As I read the following verses I sensed that God was giving me a foretaste of the anointing of joy that will come upon the bride of Christ as the final harvest comes in.

"When the Lord brought back the captives to Zion, we were like men who dreamed. Our mouths were filled with laughter, our tongues with songs of joy. Then it was said among the nations, 'The Lord has done great things for them.' The Lord has done great things for us, and we are filled with joy. Restore our fortunes, O Lord like streams in the Negev. Those who sow in tears will reap with songs of joy. He who goes out weeping, carrying seed to sow, will return with songs of joy, carrying sheaves with him" (Psalm 126:1-6).

Many months later I realized that God had also given me these verses of Scripture as a prophetic word for this book. He was giving me a foretaste of His joy in order to encourage me to stand at my post as a "watchman on the walls" of the church, particularly a Seventh-day Adventist (SDA) Church in Redlands, California (see Isaiah 62:6-7). He had called me to pray and intercede for the "release of captives" that He had shown me in a vivid prophetic dream in the spring of 1996. Although weeping would last for a night, I knew abundant joy was coming in the morning.

At times over the past twelve years when I was tempted to lose hope of getting this book finished, I would remember this Scripture and I would be driven to spend more time on my face seeking God's heart. In some of my most difficult moments of discouragement, it seemed like the oil of joy would be poured over me again, and I would be filled with that same exuberant laughter as I remembered that "the joy of the Lord is my strength" (Nehemiah 8:10). The Lord *is* going to bring back the captives to Zion. Many hurting, broken and discouraged people who have been in bondage to old covenant teachings will be delivered and set free. By the power of His Spirit God will fill their mouths with exuberant laughter, and loose their tongues with songs of great joy.

Although I previously knew nothing about intercession, God began to teach me through His Word how He wants to release the life-birthing energies of the Holy Spirit through our prayers of intercession in order to bring into being the desires of His heart.[1] As I daily submitted myself to His love and immersed myself in His Word, God began to give me more of His heart of compassion and love for His children, especially His SDA children.

I was amazed to discover that in the New Testament *every* believer is called to be a priest. Every believer is called to come before God on behalf of someone else as an intercessor. Intercession is not a special gift that God gives a chosen few. No. It is the privilege of every believer in Jesus Christ to intercede as we experience the heart of God toward those for whom He calls us to pray.

Somehow through our intercession, God's Spirit is released to shatter the strongholds of the enemy that continue to dull and blind many people's minds and hearts to the gospel of Jesus Christ. People who formerly walked in "darkness" are now being called to walk as children of light (1 Peter 2:9; Ephesians 5:8).

Down through the ages the Scriptures reveal how God has continually sought to find intercessors through whom He could share the secrets of His heart for His often-wayward children. Through many prophetic voices that have spanned centuries of time, God has consistently sought to guide, instruct, encourage and warn His people. As we read and study the prophetic revelations of the Bible we see that they not only reflect, at least to some extent, the age in which they were written, but we also see the impact they have had on the affairs of men and nations as God has shown us how He desires intimate contact and personal communion with all His children.

When Jesus Christ came in fulfillment of the prophetic words of the Old Testament prophets, He changed the course of human history. Through His life and death He made it possible for mankind to be restored to unbroken fellowship and communion with His Maker. The veil of sin that prevented our direct access to the Father has now been removed by the obedience of the One Man, Jesus Christ.

Before Jesus Christ returned to His Father in heaven as our High Priest and Intercessor, He promised to give us the Holy Spirit who would be with us and in us forever (John 14:16-17). He also promised to give us spiritual gifts for the common good of the Church in order to build up, edify, encourage and even warn, when necessary, the body of Christ (1 Corinthians 12, 14). Instead of communicating with His people through certain chosen vessels as He did in the Old Testament, God would now maintain personal and intimate contact with *all* His children through His Spirit.

Long ago God spoke through the prophet Joel that He would actively seek to communicate His will to His children living in the "last days" by pouring out His Spirit on all flesh, especially by the release of the prophetic gift. Visions, dreams, trances and visitations all have biblical precedents, and are established ways that the Lord uses to speak to His people (Joel 2:28-29).

Furthermore, it is the unanimous witness of the New Testament writers that the time period following the death of Jesus Christ was the "last days."[2] These men and women who were moved by the Holy Spirit at Pentecost believed that the "last days" was a time period that began in the first century. Therefore, since the Bible states that the "last days" began in the first century, doesn't it follow that the message for **these** "last days" is the same message preached in the first century by the apostles and first century disciples?

Jude affirms that the genuine and full gospel of Jesus Christ was "once for all entrusted to the saints" (Jude 3). Paul declared it to be the full counsel of God (Acts 20:27), and cursed anyone who would preach a different gospel from the gospel preached by the apostles and first century disciples of Christ (Galatians 1:6-9).

Because there has been such a dramatic increase in prophetic revelations being given to many Christians over the last several years, isn't this then a direct fulfillment of this same promise and a sign that we are *still* living in the "last days?" Seeing the prophetic voice being restored to the body of Christ and crossing denominational walls challenges many believers cherished comfort zones, especially those within the SDA church.

You may ask, "But when it comes to dreams and visions how can I discern the true from the false? Didn't Jesus warn us that in the last days there would be many false prophets" (Matthew 24:24)?

Yes He did. The very fact that the Lord warned us that there would be false prophets at the end of the age definitely implies that there will also be true ones. Remember the parable of the weeds? In this parable the Lord taught us that whenever He sows wheat in a field the enemy comes along and sows tares in the same field (Matthew 13:24-30). Satan will always try to bring confusion by counterfeiting everything that God is doing.[3]

Obviously, God is allowing this because He wants us to be able to distinguish the true from the false. From the very beginning of time God has been committed to allowing His children to choose between the true and the false, between good and evil. Instead of rejecting all prophetic experiences as being from the enemy, we must learn how to discern the true from the false.

If we do not want to be deceived by false prophecy, we must know what is true. The answer is not to reject all prophecy, but to know *His* voice.[4] The Scriptures tell us that His sheep *know His voice* so well they can distinguish it from the voice of a stranger (John 10:3-5). Once we *know* God's voice, we can avoid falling into some of the same pitfalls and errors of the leaders in Christ's day by choosing to know *both* the Scriptures and the power of God (Matthew 22:29).[5]

Once we know *His* voice we will begin to see that the diversity within the body of Christ is akin to the diversity in the twelve tribes of Israel. It is all right to be a member of a different tribe, a different denomination—a different body—as long as we understand that we are *all* a part of the same holy nation. God is calling for unity in diversity, *not* conformity. We as believers in the body of Christ are being called to be *one in the Spirit* (John 17) so that we can be conformed to the image of God's Son. We are being called to minister as a nation of priests unto the Lord as we worship the Father in Spirit and in Truth (John 4:24).

After receiving this vivid dream that was immediately followed by an equally vivid vision, I began diligently searching God's Word for myself in order to understand the interpretation. As a result of my study over the past ten years, not only have I come face to face with the radical teachings of the new covenant gospel, but I have also come to the firm conclusion that this everlasting gospel that was "once and for all delivered to the saints" is clearly a different message from the one I had understood growing up in the SDA church. Perhaps some of you reading these words right now are being shaken loose from your own particular comfort zones. I hope so.

Although I grew up believing SDAs had a unique message to deliver to the world in these "last day," I began to see that the message being proclaimed, though unique, unfortunately was not founded upon God's Word. The more I studied the writings of Paul in Romans and Galatians, and the more I read the book of Hebrews, the more I began to realize that I was studying myself right out of Adventism. I discovered that the uniqueness of the SDA message represented error and stood in stark contrast to the Good News of the new covenant gospel of Jesus Christ and His finished work on the cross.

Furthermore, I began to understand more clearly how the symbolic imagery in the dream I was given supports the witness of the New Testament Scriptures regarding the importance of relinquishing our hold on the old order of things now that the new has come (see Hebrews 8:13). The New Testament Scriptures also tell us that Jesus is God's final Word. We are to listen to Him. (Matthew 17:5). So when He foretells in the book of Hebrews "everything that can be shaken will be shaken," I believe Him. We can know that God is faithful and will keep His word.

Again the symbolic imagery in this dream supports the witness of Scripture by revealing that God is going to shake everything that can be shaken that is not grounded on Him. Apparently Adventism's foundational truths are going to be shaken, because they are *not* built upon the Solid Rock of Jesus Christ as many of us have been led to believe. God will expose the error of the SDA church's unique teachings that are supported by Ellen White's writings (see Fundamental Beliefs of

Seventh-day Adventists, No. 17)[6], because they are based on religious performance (being focused on trying to obey the Ten Commandments, especially the 4th) rather than faith in the new covenant gospel. As this generational spiritual bondage to old covenant law is exposed (which Paul calls, "a body of death"), I saw that it would cause a spiritual earthquake in the hearts and minds of many of Adventism's members.

God's purpose in shaking us loose from our comfort zones that we so tenaciously cling to is to show us that "we are not children of the slave woman" any longer because we are no longer under old covenant law. Mount Sinai must bow to the foot of the cross! We are either disciples of Moses, who represents the old covenant law, or we are disciples of Jesus, who is the author of the new covenant gospel. We can no longer be disciples of both (See John 9:28-29). For in Christ we have been set free from this yoke of slavery, IF we choose to believe!

In the spring of 2000 another one of my comfort zones was shaken when I was told by the leadership of the SDA church that I was a member of in Redlands, California that since I could not control the manifestations of the Holy Spirit that would come upon me during corporate worship services, I was no longer welcome to worship in the main sanctuary. With many tears and much sadness I went to worship and intercede in the prayer room during times of corporate worship. I so much wanted God's heart to be poured out on this body of people whom I dearly loved. Thankfully, there were always one or two friends who joined me in intercession during these times, so I was never alone.

After spending a couple of months in the prayer room, the Lord spoke to my heart early one morning as I was interceding at home for the leadership of my church and told me that my time was up. I struggled and wept and agonized with God over this word because I didn't want to leave the comfort and security of my Adventist church family that I had come to love and been a part of since 1989. I told God that I was willing to continue intercession in the prayer room indefinitely during times of corporate worship if He was calling me to continue to serve in that way. But He was not.

Leaving the comfort zone of my church in 2000 was heart-breaking for me. I knew that if its leadership no longer wanted me to be a part of the corporate body during times of worship, it was highly unlikely that a more conservative Adventist congregation would accept the manifestations of the Spirit on me.

After being led by the Spirit to fellowship with various church bodies outside of the SDA denomination, I gradually came to understandings of scripture that caused me to see the need to remove my name from membership in the Adventist church. I could no longer belong to, believe in, support or encourage others to follow what I had come to consider an erroneous belief system. Leaving the familiarity of my spiritual heritage in 2002 was a heart-wrenching decision I never thought I would be called to make.

So I was surprised when the Holy Spirit urged me to return to this same SDA church in the fall of 2004 after being away for four years. Since a positive change had taken place in the church's leadership, I knew God was calling me back as an intercessor. I knew I was being called back to stand in the gap alongside other intercessors and pray for the release of this body of believers from old covenant teachings and erroneous understandings of scripture that continued to prevent them from entering into the freedom of the new covenant gospel and the fullness of the Spirit.

The struggle to let go of historic Adventist truths that are *not* founded upon God's Word will be tough for some, but necessary if this particular SDA church is to go where God is leading it. Only as we obey the call of the Holy Spirit to fix our attention upon the finished work of Jesus Christ on our behalf will we fulfill the prophetic destiny God has corporately placed upon this body—to become a catalyst for change that will expose the "naked truth" behind Adventism's stronghold, and release many of God's captive children from the bondage of works into the freedom of God's good work in Jesus Christ.

The dream I received on April 11, 1996 was followed by an equally vivid vision that emphasized how God wants to draw our attention away from the old order of things to the new—the *finished work* of Jesus Christ on our behalf. The Father wants us to *know* that in the new covenant gospel it's Christ's "good" work that He is looking at, not ours. When we *believe in Him,* we will trust our very lives to *His good work* and enter into *His* "rest."

For those who have trusted in the bondage of "good" works that are motivated by old covenant teachings, my prayer is for the freedom to lay the shame and guilt down at the foot of the cross and enter into the joy of *His* "good" work.

I believe the Holy Spirit is bringing together several voices at this time to awaken this particular SDA church in Redlands, California to the need for action in throwing off the yoke of bondage. And I believe that the anointing to fulfill the prophetic destiny of this congregation depends, in large part, on the response of the leadership and people to heed the call, perhaps the warning, to stand on the truth of the Scriptures without mixture and without fear.

I want to challenge all who read the prophetic message contained within these pages, to prayerfully examine and study God's Word and come to understand that the Good News of the new covenant is *not* about us—it's about Him! "Truth" is more than a system of belief within a particular denomination. Truth is a Person. And to know the Truth is to fall in love with the Person of Jesus Christ. This is the time to move. This is the time to lay down all of the excuses and all of the fears and all of the rationalizations and do what many know in their hearts has been needed for many decades. It's curtain time—time for the veils to be lifted.

Endnotes: Introduction

[1] Dutch Sheets, *Intercessory Prayer: The Lightning of God*, Course Syllabus (Published by Dutch Sheets, 1986) 33.
[2] See Hebrews 1:1-2; 1 Peter 1:20; 1 John 2:18; James 5:11; Jude 17-18.
[3] Rick Joyner, *The Call* (Whitaker House, 1999) 13.
[4] Ibid., 15.
[5] Ibid., 17.
[6] Fundamental Beliefs of Seventh-day Adventists, No. 17 says, "One of the gifts of the Holy Spirit is prophecy. This gift is an identifying mark of the remnant church and was manifested in the ministry of Ellen. G. White. As the Lord's messenger, her writings are a continuing and authoritative source of truth which provide for the church comfort, guidance, instruction, and correction. They also make clear that the Bible is the standard by which all teaching and experience must be tested."

The cartoon-like video pictured hundreds of terrified children who were clinging frantically to a tall, steep, pyramid-shaped "mountain."

Chapter 1: The Dream
EXPOSING ADVENTISM'S PACKAGE

"He will bring to light what is hidden in darkness and will expose the motives of men's hearts."
I Corinthians 4:5

It was on April 11, 1996 in Riverside, California that I received this revelation that is the main focus of this book. God spoke to me through this dream that occurred while I was asleep, and it was immediately followed by a vision, a series of vivid images appearing while I was awake and very aware. The setting of this dream is a Seventh-day Adventist (SDA) church I attended in Redlands, California.

Bottleneck and Packages

I dreamed that I looked up from where I was sitting on the front row of the church, and discovered that I was alone. A fleeting sense of embarrassment washed over me as I turned around in my seat and saw a large group of people standing at the back of the church. From my position it appeared that most of the congregation had already left their seats and were forming a bottleneck at the entrance to the church sanctuary as they all tried to leave at the same time. However, a dozen or so people were still making their way up the aisles from the front section to join the people in the back.

The distance between the people congregated in the back and myself made me feel awkward. Since I didn't like the feeling of being isolated from the others, I quickly got up to join them. As I slowly walked up the aisle I wondered what could have happened to cause such a large bottleneck of people to form at the main entrance to the sanctuary.

Another thing I observed that seemed strange about the people around me slowly making their way to the back was that I recognized none of them. I also noticed that the remaining people moving up the aisles appeared to be carrying packages under their arms or in their hands.

At first I wondered if they were carrying reading materials related to Prayer Ministry. Since I was a leader in one of the Prayer Ministry teams of our church at the time, I considered the possibility that I had forgotten to pick up copies of printed materials for the rest of my team. Then I thought these packages might be gifts or rewards that people had earned for faithful service. Perhaps certain people were being recognized for their sacrifice of time in the work of the church.

But as I neared the back of the church I saw that the last half a dozen rows on either side of me were jammed full of people, trying to make their way out into the main aisles towards the back. These people were carrying similar packages under their arms or clutching them in their hands as I had seen the others do. In fact all the packages appeared to be the same size, and wrapped similarly.

As I stood waiting for the rows of people to move into the aisle, I noticed that no one appeared to be interested in anything going on around them, but seemed to be self-contained and very much *"wrapped up"* in themselves. With their eyes fixed in a cold blank stare each person looked straight ahead as they moved forward along the rows towards the aisles. They appeared to be trapped in a code of silence and isolation. No one was talking to a neighbor or sharing with a friend. In fact, the lack of interaction in this body of people spoke with an eloquence that words could not match. In the warm and friendly church that I was use to this silence and guarded behavior was most unusual.

Although these people appeared to be in close proximity to one another, I sensed they were far away by the look of cool indifference in the robotic stares of those closest to me. I tried to speak to a couple of people nearby about the packages they were clinging to, but they just ignored my overtures as if there was a wall between us that prevented them from hearing or answering my question. Instinctively I thought that perhaps I had offended them by asking about the packages that I saw them carrying. I didn't understand why everyone appeared to be so guarded and afraid.

This was *not* the church that I belonged to. The inside looked the same, but where had all the friendly, loving and familiar faces gone? Who were these people that I didn't recognize or know? I felt as if I had just been dropped into a cold and unfriendly congregation where the climate of love that I had previously known had suddenly grown cold. It seemed that I was the misfit who had failed to learn how to play by these new rules. Everyone else seemed to know them except me.

As I continued to observe the people crowded together around me, they reminded me of a flock of sheep. Although there appeared to be no "shepherd" giving them directions, they all continued to press in tightly, pushing and shouldering their way towards the main doors of the church sanctuary. They looked as if they were following some hidden internal command. It was as if invisible sheepdogs were biting at their heels, herding them together, and trying to get them to conform and line up.

Handed a Package

As I waited wondering how long it would take for this bottleneck of people to move so I could leave the sanctuary, I suddenly saw a familiar face to my right. Archie, who I had gotten to know several years earlier in an incest survivors group, was headed in my direction. Like a salmon struggling to swim upstream, he maneuvered his way through the sluggish stream of human traffic, seemingly oblivious to the cold wall of human indifference that stood between us.

As soon as he reached me, he abruptly thrust a brown paper package into my hand. Immediately I became aware that I could now *hear* the indistinct chatter of people talking in hushed tones around me. Finally I felt that I belonged and was no longer isolated.

"Thank you!" I said curiously as I took hold of the flexible package. I was taken by surprise. Was this what I had seen others carrying just moments earlier? It seemed that the other packages were more colorful than this one, but I couldn't remember exactly how. Perhaps Archie had run out of colorful wrapping paper. Anyway, the outside wrapping wasn't what was important. The contents of the package and the thoughtfulness of the giver were what counted.

Then the idea crossed my mind that perhaps Archie had collected some magazines for the children in my special education classroom. However, as soon as I made a move to start to open the package, Archie laid his hand on the package and cautioned, "Not now! Don't open it here! Later!"

"Oh, Okay!" I responded gently. I sensed the tension and embarrassment, even shame in his voice, and the awkwardness of the moment for him. How could I assure him that I wasn't offended by the plain outer covering of his "gift?" It didn't detract from its contents. I knew his sincerity. I wanted to assure him that I appreciated his thoughtfulness, but he quickly turned to leave by the same way he had come, disappearing into the nameless sea of faces before I could say anything.

Where to go with it?

Momentarily I felt comforted by the fact that I had been thought of by a friend. There was at least one person in this unfriendly church who was willing to acknowledge my presence. But I wished he hadn't left so quickly. I had questions that needed answers. Perhaps he could help me. I saw how he had struggled to push his way through this multitude of indifferent and joyless faces in order to give me this "gift." That made it all the more valuable as far as I was concerned.

I stood there for a moment, holding the lightweight package in my hands as I looked again at the bottleneck of people in front of me, hoping to see a quicker way around them. Suddenly I realized that the door to the church sanctuary was closed. We were all standing in front of a shut door!

As I turned and looked to the left, I noticed an empty row of seats leading towards the outside aisle. Perhaps I would be able to find another way around the bottleneck of people I mused as I walked to the end of the row and turned right. I noticed up ahead of me a smaller set of doors that led into the multi-purpose room. If I could leave through them I could make my way into the church lobby, and perhaps bypass this entire herd of people.

However, I was suddenly stopped from pursuing my goal when I turned around to take one last look at the empty rows of chairs. Instantly I was thrown forward and immediately found myself sprawled across the top of an empty desk that was now standing in the aisle.

Momentarily stunned by this sudden turn of events, I lay there on my stomach, stretched across the top of the empty desk, both of my hands stretched out in front of me, desperately clutching the now torn package, trying to keep the exposed contents from falling to the floor.

Contents Exposed

Since the "gift" had ripped open "accidentally," I decided to take a quick peek and view the contents. As my fingers quickly flipped through the stack of twenty or so magazines, I noticed there were no pictures inside, but what appeared to be tedious columns of undecipherable print. But what really caught my attention was the same cartoon-like illustration that appeared on the outside front cover of each magazine. It was more like a video than a still picture and it caused me to be filled with great joy and laughter.

However, the only thing I *could* remember about this cartoon-like illustration when I woke up from the dream was that I had seen a tall mountain of "something" that had to do with being "freed from debt." It would be sixteen months later before I would be shown the details of this "mountain" again in an open vision, and another year before God would show me the "mountain" a third time in order to remove the remaining "veil" that covered my own mind.

This cartoon-like video pictured hundreds of terrified children, shabbily dressed in tattered and torn clothing, clinging frantically to a tall, steep, pyramid-shaped "mountain." This "mountain" was like an island, completely surrounded by the surging blue waters of the ocean. The caption written in large, bold letters across the base of it said, **"SAY TO THIS MOUNTAIN, MOVE!"** Suddenly a violent earthquake hit this "mountain" of children! As the mountain began to shake and quake it leaned towards the right.

Initially I was horrified to see the multiple layers of children's dead bodies that formed this human "mountain." The children who were alive were not only seen clinging frantically to one another, but also to the partially exposed remains of children who had died trying to climb this "mountain." They were all shaking and crying out in terror as they tried to prevent themselves from slipping down the sides of this "mountain" into the surging blue waters of the ocean below.

Judging by the frantic expressions on their faces, and the strange contortions that they were putting their bodies through in order to avoid falling into the sea, it was obvious that none of them had any intention of loosening their grip on this "mountain." Some of the children tumbling down the sides of the mountain were seen grasping at others as they tried to break their rapid descent towards the sea below. In the process of doing this they caused others to lose their footing and begin to slip also.

At the Foot of the Mountain

My attention was drawn to the growing number of frightened children in the sea at the foot of the "mountain." Suddenly I noticed that not only was the "mountain" shaking, but also it was slowly sinking, causing the frightened children to further lose their footing. I noticed that the children who were clinging to the base of the mountain and had their "feet in the water," appeared to be less frightened than those above them who were feverishly climbing over the dead remains of others in their attempt to avoid falling into the sea. However, those who had only their "feet in the water" *still* clung tenaciously to the partially exposed bodies of children who had died trying to climb this "mountain."

The second group of children who were knee-deep in the water appeared to be less scared than those who had only their "feet in the water." But they were not free of the "mountain" either. They were holding on to the children, who had only their "feet in the water," who in turn were clinging to the partially exposed body parts of slave children who had died trying to climb this "mountain."

The third group of children who were waist-deep in water appeared to be less afraid than the other two groups, but somewhat apprehensive. If they ventured out further from the "mountain" they would be in "over their heads" and unable to maintain further contact with the other children or return to the familiar security of the "mountain."

Although the fourth group of children who were immersed in the water over their heads seemed to be the least afraid of all, they still clung anxiously to other children around them as they began to tread water and thrash around in order to stay afloat. As soon as these children recognized that they could no longer feel the sides of the "mountain" under their feet and had to swim in order to stay afloat, they began to swim back towards the mountain in order to grab a hold of other children who were still standing in the water up to their knees or waists.

In spite of the fact that all of the children floundering around in the ocean at the foot of the "mountain" had been immersed in the "sea" to some level, they were still afraid to totally let go of the "mountain" or one another. By holding on to one another they formed human chains through the water that helped them maintain contact with the partially exposed remains of the children who had died trying to climb this "mountain of death."

Children at the Top

After watching the behavior of the children at the foot of the mountain, my eyes were drawn to the terrified children who continued to scramble up the sides of the "mountain," because they realized that the "mountain" was slowly sinking into the sea. I noticed that the children nearest the top seemed the most ill prepared of all to survive the shaking of this massive earthquake. Because the "mountain" was shaped like a tall pyramid, the top was very narrow. So when the top of the "mountain" began to sway dangerously back and forth and reel from side to side "like a wave of the sea, blown and tossed by the wind" the children at the top hung on for dear life to the partially exposed remains of those beneath them.

As I was wondering how long these children at the top would survive this roller coaster ride before being thrown into the blue "sea," two of them lost their grip, and were thrown clear of the mountain. They were seen somersaulting through the air, headed straight for the open blue sea. The incredulous look of joy on their faces was in stark contrast to the looks of fear that held the others captive. Their mouths were held wide open as if they were shouting and laughing, and their wide-eyed expressions of surprise made me laugh, too.

Exposed, But No Shame!

As I glanced out across the church, I was surprised to see Archie seated at a desk next to the *center pillar* of the church with his head buried in his arms. Archie's pose was unlike the way he normally behaved. It reminded me of the way my special education students often behaved when they felt inadequate, frustrated or hopeless about the task that lay in front of them. Feeling overwhelmed with shame or guilt, I had often seen them bury their heads in their arms, afraid to face the negative remarks and cutting comments that too often would come out of the mouths of their insensitive peers.

Hearing my laughter caused Archie to cautiously lift his head just above his arms, and look towards me with an "is-it-safe-for-me-to-expose-my-real-self" grin on his face. I smiled back, knowing that he had seen me peek at his "package" of magazines. He appeared to be both relieved and surprised by my sudden outburst of laughter. Then quite unexpectedly, both of us were overcome with laughter at the same time.

Struggle to hold on

Just moments before the back half of the church had been jammed full of hundreds of people. Now everyone had disappeared. What's more, the door of the church sanctuary that had been "shut" was now open and two people appeared to be coming through the now "open door."

But what amazed me even more than the deserted church was the fact that the many rows of seats had been instantly replaced by neatly arranged rows of desks, like the one Archie was seated at, and I was draped over.

Realizing suddenly how strange and unladylike I must look, I began struggling to regain my composure and stand up without dropping Archie's "gift" on the floor. But the package that had been light in my hands suddenly became heavier with every move that I made. As I tried to get a firmer grip on it, the brown paper began to rip again, exposing the entire contents, and making it even more difficult to hold. With increasing difficulty, I finally made it to my feet.

When I thought I had the magazines under control, I took a step forward to my right, erroneously believing that I could manage their growing weight. Not only had the outer wrapping fallen off by now, but also the magazines continued to increase in weight, slipping and sliding around in my arms like a writhing snake! I tried to take another step forward, still endeavoring to maintain my balance, and prevent the slippery "gift" from getting away.

Letting go

Suddenly, the magazines became like lead in my arms, forcing me to bend over double. I felt as if a millstone was hanging around my neck, dragging me down to the ground. As the weight of the package became impossible to hold on to any longer, I was "forced" to let it go. Instantly the magazines flew forward with lightning speed, coming to rest beneath the foot of the cross that hung on the north wall in front of me. Although I was bent forwards, that same unseen hand that had thrown me forwards on to the desk, now threw me backwards on to the floor.

Just as soon as I hit the floor I was filled with indescribable joy and laughter. Now that the *weight* was gone I felt *light* and *free*. As I lay there on my back, glued to the carpet with my arms outstretched, waves of laughter continued to roll over me. I became aware that I was resting in the awesome presence of God. I could have stayed there forever. I knew a few of my friends had experienced this "laughter in the Spirit" a number of times, but this was still a relatively new experience for me.

As I lay there resting in this new freedom and joy, I soon became aware I was not the only one laughing. Someone else was being filled with the joy of the Lord in the direction of the center pillar! Then a few moments later a couple of other voices broke out in laughter a short distance behind me in the direction of the now "open door."

This fear of deception prevents many from laying aside previously held opinions and teachings to search the Scriptures for themselves to discover Truth.

Chapter 2
A NEW CHURCH EXPERIMENT

"It is impossible that no offenses should come..."
Luke 17:1

I would like to share a little background as to how this Seventh-day Adventist (SDA) church I attended in Redlands, California came into being. Hopefully this will aid in understanding under what circumstances God chose a SDA church as the setting for this dream.

Initially, this church was a new kind of church "experiment" within the SDA denomination that began around 1988. The very reason it exists today is that throughout the past twenty years many Adventists fled traditional SDA churches in search of an Adventist church that emphasized God's redeeming grace rather than old covenant law. From its outset the leadership chose to place a special emphasis on God's redeeming grace expressed solely in the Person of His Son, Jesus Christ—an emphasis that many believers found lacking in other SDA churches.

Finding a church that emphasized *grace* instead of *law* attracted many wounded and broken people. The abused, misused, rejected and dejected were the "poor" who had the good news of the gospel preached to them and many received it with open arms. Tired of being judged on the basis of their external behaviors, and unable to conform any longer to the human standards that others set before them, many people came to this fellowship with deep inner shame that cried out for healing. Since distinctive Adventist doctrines were not emphasized in this church setting, believers from various other denominations felt comfortable worshiping God and enjoying meaningful fellowship with their Adventist friends.

So, for many weary travelers like me, this church became a safe haven, a place where wounded people could finally begin to experience wholeness in Christ. Spiritual healing became evident as bondages were released into God's healing presence, and many people began to express themselves in demonstrative worship. Though casual visitors may not have seen this, for many hurting and broken people, this church became a welcome oasis in a dry and thirsty desert.

However, this church's emphasis on God's grace has not been equally appreciated or understood by all. Neither has this church's emphasis on expressive worship that flows from the hearts of grateful believers who have experienced God's grace in their personal lives. Over the years many people have grown "tired" of the "by grace alone, through faith alone" message and left. Some have wanted to move *beyond* the cross and go back to certain *distinctive* Adventist doctrines that made them feel more comfortable. Others have become offended by the worship music, expressing their distress over the loudness of the beat, the unfamiliar words, or the praise dancing that stretched them beyond their comfort levels. Eventually many of them also left.

Offended by the Spirit

Seeing the numbers of worshipers begin to diminish over the years caused great concern among the leadership. That concern was heightened when the Holy Spirit began to show up and move on people. As the Spirit began to descend upon those who "disrobed" before God it became offensive to those who did not.

The image of King David removing his kingly robes in order to dance before the Lord because of His deep recognition of the presence of a King greater than he comes to mind. Remember how his wife was offended by his behavior? In a similar way, often the offended were those who chose to hold onto their dignity while their brothers and sisters "disrobed" before God.

So when many began to receive God's healing touch they recognized they were in the presence of Deity, so their dignity had to go. As they chose to become "naked and unashamed" before God, He began to fill their brokenness with the fragrance of agape love.

As a result of becoming open to the Spirit, various manifestations of the Spirit began to occur most often during worship services and ministry times. Prophetic gifts began to be displayed. More and more believers began to receive visions and dreams. Words of knowledge began to flow, along with the healing gifts and the gift of tongues. Some were delivered spontaneously from demonic strongholds during worship services.

However, some saw certain behaviors such as enthusiastic praise, involuntary shaking, weeping, laughter or other unusual manifestations as very disruptive to corporate worship. Could it be that the offended were more concerned for things to be "in order" than they were to experience God's presence for themselves? It is safe to promote the presence of the Holy Spirit verbally, but when He actually shows up the unpredictable results become a source of fear and offense for those unwilling to appear foolish or out of control.

Spirit of Control

In an effort to try to reduce the numbers of offended people, the leadership began trying to accommodate those who voiced their discontent by trying to control this move of the Spirit. Instead of embracing the Holy Spirit's presence when He came to reveal His agenda, the former leadership began rejecting the manifestations of His presence as the work of the flesh or the deceptions of the enemy.

As I read about past revivals in church history and saw how people in positions of leadership within the church sometimes fell into the trap of trying to control the work of the Holy Spirit, it appeared that some in the leadership at this church were following in their footsteps. Because they were not completely invested in the move of the Spirit themselves they were more concerned that some may not understand things such as speaking in tongues and so made restrictive parameters for the use of the gifts that SDAs traditionally have not accepted as valid.

Current advances in expressive worship, not only within this church, but also within many churches in various denominations in the body of Christ today are nothing new. Lively and challenging worship has always characterized Christian renewal and revival. History reveals that Methodists during the time of the Wesleyan Revival were accused of being so passionate and enthusiastic in their worship that the more staid observers found it shocking. Established religionists of the day saw their fervor as a kind of plague. Many of them were enthusiastic about worship in ways that caused offense. Noting the occurrence of visions and revelations that occurred during this time period, a bishop wrote, "The pretending to revelations and extraordinary gifts of the Holy Ghost is a horrid thing, a very horrid thing!"

The potent worship of Spirit-filled Christians that disturbed the complacency of the intellectual mind during the Methodist Revival of the 1740's will continue to disturb the complacency of the ones who value mind above spirit today. Many will become offended at the freedom others have *in* Christ, and will resist it and seek to control it if they have become blinded to the truth that without the Spirit we are most "pitiful, poor, blind and naked" (Rev. 3:17).

The problem is that when fleshly methods are used to try to control the behavior of another, it results in fear. Granted there will always be some of these negative responses in any move of God because the enemy seeks to counterfeit what God is doing. But after applying the "fruit" test, God's gift of discernment should make it clear who is revealing the heart of the Father, who is revealing a human agenda and who is deceived by the enemy.

Is it possible that as the Holy Spirit began to fall upon members of this congregation, He challenged many of the cherished beliefs and secret motives in the hearts of all? Many people became offended and didn't recognize this move of the Spirit, because they were afraid of having the true conditions of the heart exposed. They didn't want to undress and become naked before God. They didn't want to look at their brokenness and confess that they were less than perfect and in need of restoration and healing just like the rest of humanity.

Suddenly the influence and control of the previous leadership of this church was threatened as the Spirit began to assert *His* ownership and *His* influence over the congregation by coming in unexpected and unusual ways. He began to challenge certain erroneous beliefs and teachings that were an affront to the gospel of Jesus Christ. It is reminiscent of how the cherished beliefs and secret motives in the hearts of the Pharisees in Jesus day were most certainly challenged when the multitudes began following Jesus instead of them. Their influence and control over the people was severely threatened.

Spirit of Fear

Other believers resisted this move of the Holy Spirit because they feared it was the false revival they had been warned about in Ellen White's writings that would happen in the last days. This fear caused them to question this move of God because they feared being deceived by the enemy. This fear of deception has kept many Adventists from recognizing the Spirit when He appears in ways that they have not been taught to expect. This fear of deception prevents many from laying aside previously held opinions and teachings to search the Scriptures for themselves to discover Truth. Lacking a strong personal assurance of salvation, and not clearly understanding the ministry of the Holy Spirit, many people judged this move of the Spirit to be false. This fear is understandable and is present, not only among SDAs but also within many mainline Christian churches as well.

Having head knowledge, but lacking experiential heart knowledge of the Person, who *is* Truth, prevents many from being able to rise above the dry bones of religion and become worshippers of the Truth Giver. Only the Spirit of God can breathe life into dry bones and cause them to come to life (Ezekiel 37:5). Only the Holy Spirit can give us the heart of the Father and cause us to be born from above by the wind of God (John 3:3-8, The Message Bible).

God reminds us in His Word that He is eager to give us all good things needed for our spiritual health, and He will never give one of His children a stone when asked for bread. "If you know how to give good gifts to your children, how much more will our Father in heaven give the Holy Spirit to those who ask Him" (Luke 11:11-13).

No matter what we've been taught, the Scriptures tell us that God won't allow a deceptive spirit to impersonate the Holy Spirit when we come seeking and asking in Jesus' name. We must exercise our faith and believe that God the Holy Spirit is more powerful and strong than Satan and his deceptive spirits. Don't the Scriptures tell us that His sheep *know His voice* so well they can distinguish it from the voice of a stranger (John 10:3-5)?

Instead of becoming fearful when others express their devotion to God in untraditional ways, a conscious decision to remain open to the Holy Spirit's coming in unexpected and unfamiliar ways will be rewarded with unexpected intimacy with the Lord. Scripture reveals that

God's "chosen people" rejected Jesus' first coming because He didn't come in the manner they were expecting. Everything about Christ's teachings offended most of the spiritual leaders of His day.

In a similar way, the former pastor of this church along with many members rejected this first move of the Spirit because He didn't come in the manner they were expecting. Sadly, after several years of resisting and trying to control the work of the Spirit, the former leadership gradually wandered away from the truth of the gospel, and eventually resigned in 2004.

Failure to Recognize the Spirit

When new leadership came in the fall of 2004, there was an immediate openness to the Holy Spirit in the church. The gifts and manifestations of the Spirit that had been an offense to the previous leadership were embraced and valued by the new. As a result of the new leadership obeying the voice of the Spirit, He began moving again upon the congregation in unusual and unexpected ways. Would the church pass the test this time and not offend the Spirit of Truth by resisting Him as He came the second time around?

Gamaliel's recommendations are just as applicable today as they were to the religious leaders of his day who were attempting to control the apostle's teachings, and were similarly disturbed and offended by their manifestations of the Holy Spirit (Acts 5:34-39). He told them, "Consider carefully what you intend to do to these men… Leave these men alone! Let them go! For if their purpose or activity is of human origin, it will fail. But if it is from God, you will not be able to stop these men; you will only find yourselves fighting against God."

Acts 14 tells how Paul was held in awe one day by the same crowd of people who threw stones at him the following day. Paul and Barnabas had healed a man crippled from birth in Lystra and the people who witnessed this miracle could hardly be restrained from worshiping them until Jews from Antioch and Iconium showed up and began to "poison the minds of the people." Suddenly the crowd that had hailed them stoned Paul and left him for dead. The very next day Paul and Barnabas left the city. How sad that Lystra missed her day of visitation because she failed to recognize the move of the Spirit through Paul and Barnabas.

I think this story from Acts illustrates two common reactions in the church to God's Spirit/and or the miraculous—one is to worship the manifestation, the other is to stone it. In the midst of this battle isn't the Holy Spirit imploring with God's heart for us *not* to resist Him?

Even though the previous leadership resisted the Spirit and departed from the truth of the gospel, God still had core people who continued to pray and intercede that God's purposes would still be fulfilled in this church. While many were eagerly waiting for Christ's Second Coming, many failed to recognize Him when He did come to awaken hearts to the truth of the new covenant gospel and the fullness of the Spirit. Although it was tragic that many who failed to recognize the time of visitation resisted the first move of God, God allowed the church to retake the test. Apparently He still wants to use this particular church as a spiritual womb in which to birth spiritual children.

One understanding of Galatians 4:27 could be: "Rejoice and be glad oh barren woman. Cry aloud—you who bear no children in the flesh. For greater will be the children you bear in the Spirit than she who has a husband."

I believe God chose this particular SDA church (whose membership consisted of SDAs and non-SDAs) to become a catalyst for revival, not only within Adventism, but also in the marketplace, because of the many broken and hurting people who came and found a safe place to heal from their wounds. But this revival can only happen as we continue to choose to fall on the Rock and be broken and let the Holy Spirit reveal to us the spiritual bondage we've been carrying for years. He wants to lift the veils from our eyes that have prevented us from fully entering into the freedom of the new covenant gospel and the fullness of the Spirit.

Just like the dream portrays, discovering the "truth" will cause a spiritual earthquake among the laity of the SDA church.

Chapter 3
THE "CENTRAL PILLAR"

*"See to it that no one misses the grace of God and that
no bitter root grows up to cause trouble and defile many."*
Hebrews 12:15

One of the signs of Christ's soon return described in Matthew 24:10-13 is that *"Many* will be offended... the love of *many* will grow cold..." Jesus has warned us that not just a few, but *many* will become offended. Who are these people who will become offended? Are they professed Christians, or people in the world?

Several years ago as I was reading John Bevere's book, "The Bait of Satan," I came across his comments on this passage of Scripture. The Greek word for "love" in this verse is *agape*. Although there are several Greek words for *love* in the New Testament, *agape* is the type of love that is spoken of here by Jesus. It is the unselfish and unconditional love that Jesus demonstrated for us when He died on the cross and forgave us our sins. Agape love gives even when it is not received or returned. Agape love gives regardless of the response. Therefore, "the many" Jesus refers to in this passage of Scripture are *Christians* who have become offended and whose *agape* has grown cold.[1]

Immediately, the Spirit impressed me that there was a connection between these verses of Scripture, and the growing bottleneck of people I had seen in the dream. As I reflected on the dream that began with people standing with their backs to me in front of the closed door to the church sanctuary, I realized that I had no way of knowing who they represented or how *long* they had been standing there. For seven years

I had assumed that they were members of this particular church, but now I realized that God had been showing me a picture of past generations of Adventists.

Then it became evident that I, along with the remaining people in this church who had left their seats to join those already standing in the back, represented this present generation of Adventists. As I stood behind both the present and past generations of Adventists I wondered why the people nearest the door appeared to be "stuck" and unable to move forward. I could see the looks of frustration on the faces of those closest to me as they tried unsuccessfully to push their way towards the entrance through the dense and seemingly endless crowd of faces. Soon it became evident that no one was going anywhere unless someone *opened* the closed door of the church. Surprisingly no one seemed to notice that it was *shut*.

It was as if the people standing closest to the "shut door" had formed a wall of fear in front of it that prevented those behind them from "seeing" that it was shut. Although the past generations of Adventists did not budge from their rigid position in front of the "shut door" this present generation of Adventists were not so willing to stand still.

Suddenly the veil was lifted from my eyes as I saw that the people standing in the back of the church closest to the *shut door* represented past generations of our spiritual forbearers who became "stuck" after they embraced the "Shut Door" theory.[2] I knew that most people in this present generation of Adventists who had left their seats to join those in the back had little, if any, knowledge of past generations of Adventists and their "shut door" mentality.

Most certainly the dream conveyed that this present generation of Adventists seen standing behind past generations of Adventists was completely unaware that the door to the church was *shut*. That probably meant that many of them were not aware of the theological errors that had arisen out of the 1844 Disappointment that had caused this "door" to become "shut" in the first place. In that case, this present generation of Adventists would probably not know that they were also "stuck" and unable to move forward because they had unknowingly embraced theological errors that had been handed down to them from their spiritual forefathers.

"The Door is shut!"

Briefly, the theological error that our forefathers embraced which "shut" the door of the SDA church to the rest of the world and isolated them from other Christians was this: when Jesus didn't come in 1844 as they expected, they still insisted that their message had been right. They still believed probation had ended, and they still hoped Christ would come and expected Him any day. They stopped trying to convert sinners and ceased praying for them[3] because they insisted, "The door is shut!"(Matthew 25:1-13).

This "shut door" teaching that early Adventists embraced was based on the parable of the ten virgins in Matthew 25:1-13. In the parable a loud cry rang out at midnight announcing to the ten sleeping virgins that the bridegroom [Jesus Christ] had arrived for the marriage feast. Our spiritual fathers believed that this parable was fulfilled on October 22, 1844 when the Bridegroom came to the "marriage supper" and only the "wise virgins" went into the marriage supper with Him. Of course the "wise virgins" were only those Adventist believers who had participated in William Miller's 1844 movement. All who rejected the 1844 message were the "foolish virgins" who were left outside. In fact the rest of the world was "shut out"—eternally lost because probation had closed.

Ellen White, one of the founding leaders of the Adventist church, adds her own testimony by saying, "After the passing of time of expectation in 1844, Adventists still believed the Savior's coming to be very near; they held that… the work of Christ as man's intercessor before God had ceased."[4]

For seven years after 1844 the term "shut door" appeared over and over again in articles written by Ellen White, and others. It was the central theme of their arguments so much so that they were called, "The Door Shutters." Until the autumn of 1851 all SDAs held to this theory, including Ellen White.[5]

Reinterpretation of 1844

After 1851 Adventists abandoned the "shut door" theory they had once promoted for seven years by replacing it with a reinterpretation of the 1844 Disappointment so that all could get in—at least *conditionally*.⁶ However, they tried to hide the original "shut door" theory they had promoted for seven years and replaced it with a reinterpretation of the 1844 Disappointment to apply to a change in the ministration of Jesus Christ in the heavenly sanctuary. Much evidence of its having once been taught as a teaching within the SDA church was carefully covered up and continues to be covered up to this very day. It has never been openly acknowledged and honestly renounced.

Instead of returning to Earth on October 22, 1844, they understood Jesus Christ to have passed from the Holy Place into the Most Holy Place of the heavenly sanctuary at that time. They stressed that one must follow Him in there by faith in order to be saved. They believed that Jesus was now "shut in" with His special people, preparing them and purifying them through a series of tests and trials. They taught that Christ was testing His children on certain points of truth, such as the Sabbath, and that their work for the salvation of the lost was finished."⁷

Ellen White believed that praying to Christ anywhere else but the Most Holy Place was equivalent to being lost! She says, "They [speaking of people in the other churches they considered Babylon] have no knowledge of the move made in heaven, or the way into the Most Holy, and they cannot be benefited by the intercession of Jesus there… They offer up their useless prayers to the apartment which Jesus left."⁸

Wouldn't you agree that this theory is about as bad as the "shut door" theory? Instead of admitting they were wrong about the date, they *covered up* their theological mistake with another theological error.

According to this new theory, in order to find salvation, now, a sinner must understand the change Jesus made up in heaven in 1844 as He began a work of judgment. Since only SDAs knew about this work of judgment and the rest of the Christian world was ignorant about this change, they must be warned.

A keynote of Adventism ever since its inception has been, "Fear God and give glory to Him, because the hour of His judgment has come" (Revelation 14:7). This work of judgment, which they believe began in 1844, was an investigation into the lives of all who professed to be righteous, starting from the beginning of time. As soon as the lives of the righteous dead had been examined, they believed that God would begin His investigation into the lives of the righteous living.

The outgrowth of this false teaching of an Investigative Judgment [more recently known as the pre-Advent judgment], and the need for the sanctuary in heaven to be cleansed from the record of our sins, has been to rob many believers in the Adventist church from their assurance of salvation. Never knowing when our names would come up before God caused many of us growing up in the church to live lives of desperation and fear. To this day, the same reticence to expose the error and release the people from the bondage of that heritage persists even in this particular SDA church. Somehow saying "we were wrong" will not come off of the lips of the shepherds in the areas of error that constitute the very heart of Adventism for fear of toppling the whole house. And so the falsehood continues to fester. The reasons given are professed love and kindness or not wanting to join the ranks of dissenters who have made their identity that of criticizing Adventism. And so the people are left clinging to the mountain that is sinking into the sea. Adding truth to a sinking, putrid mountain does not cause the people to let go of the previous distortions of the gospel.

Immediately I began to understand the look of fear and shame I had seen on Archie's face as he sat crouched next to the center pillar of the church. It was the same fear that many of us in Adventism have had over the years. Secretly we hoped we would be caught doing something "good" when our name appeared before the judgment seat of Christ. Although we secretly hoped that our years of "good works" would count for something, we never could be sure that we were saved.

Again this picture seemed to match with Archie's behavior as he buried his head in his hands feeling overwhelmed with shame, afraid to face the negative consequences of his *inability to perform* the "good works" that he thought God expected of him. Our soul ties with the traditional teachings of the denomination are like taproots that go down very deeply.

Christians in other denominations who were confident of their salvation were not to be trusted. After all, didn't we have the "truth?" How could they possibly be so confident when they didn't have a true understanding of the Sabbath: Adventism's one, great, untouchable *good work*? How could they possibly be so confident when they didn't have a true understanding of the investigative judgment? Immediately, we judged their works as shallow and their faith suspect, because for most Adventists the Sabbath is their insurance policy in the investigative judgment.

Unfortunately this confusion over the gospel comes from regarding Ellen White's writings as a "continuing and authoritative source of truth"[9] Although many theologians, pastors and administrators within the SDA church know that there is no biblical support for this doctrine of an Investigative Judgment, they [for the most part] quietly go about their business trying to keep from making waves. Why? Because Ellen White strongly endorsed it, calling it the "**central pillar of Adventism**."[10]

It has become evident to me that after much reading and research into Ellen White's writings, she never fully understood that faith in Christ's finished work alone is enough for salvation. She believed that churches that rejected the 1844 sanctuary truth became "Babylon" even though they continued to have faith in Jesus Christ. She believed and taught that Satan deceived them and their prayers were useless.[11] Furthermore, she taught that Christians should never be taught to say, "I am saved." She believed we could only know we are saved *after* the Second Coming of Christ.[12] She taught that we are *not* saved by faith alone, but we must live a life of "perfect obedience" before God's promises would be fulfilled to us.[13] And yet the members of this SDA church that I use to attend continue to hear quotations and receive written teachings in prayer ministry that base their validity on quotations from this woman who has brought "a ministry of death" to the church.

Although I'm sure that many SDAs today reject the investigative judgment doctrine, along with these confusing and erroneous views of the gospel (as I did long before I left Adventism), because they clearly go against New Testament Scriptures such as 1 John 5:13 that says, "I write these things to you… so that you may *know* that you have eternal life", they still choose to remain in a denomination whose leadership refuses to deal honestly with the church's continuing conflict over the nature of the gospel.

Perhaps some hope that eventually the corporate leadership of the church will choose to admit this erroneous teachings of an investigative judgment, and repent of their prideful mentality that has often said, "Sure, that is how righteousness by faith is used by the Apostle Paul and the Reformers, but we Adventists have chosen to use it to include both justification and sanctification."[14]

Sadly this erroneous unbiblical teaching of an investigative judgment has never been publicly confessed, repented of or renounced by the corporate leadership of the SDA Church, nor, lamentably by the leadership of this Adventist church I use to attend. For then wouldn't it become evident that Ellen White is not a "continuing and authoritative source of truth?" Then we would be forced to admit that we have been wrong on this *"central pillar of Adventism."* So in order to try to prevent this from happening there has been a huge cover-up of the truth about Ellen White's writings (that began to be exposed at the 1919 Bible Conference) that has been perpetuated by the leadership of the denomination for over a hundred years. And the resistance to confronting the problems at this Adventist church that I use to attend flies in the face of endeavors to teach truth. One does not add truth to a foundation of wood and hay and stubble. The faulty foundation must be plowed away and replaced with solid footings or the building, however glorious, will not stand.

The life-and-death struggle that the Adventist church is engaged in within its own ranks over the real nature of the gospel is sometimes missed by evangelical Christians. But the evangelical community should know that the Adventist church has gone to great pains to assure "apostate Protestants" (that's how early Adventists viewed other denominations, and that mindset is still very much alive within Adventism today) that God has raised up the Adventist church to correct the misunderstanding of the Reformation gospel so that the Protestant world can be halted in its slide toward Roman Catholicism.[15] However, the Protestant, and the evangelical community in particular is hardly going to listen to the SDA Church expound on the supposed errors of the Reformation gospel when Adventism itself cannot agree on what the true gospel is! Besides, what hope do SDAs have of trying to influence evangelical Protestants who claim the Reformers with their *Sola Scriptura* (the Bible alone) as their forefathers?[16]

It had taken seven years of "waiting" on the Lord before I realized this "shut door" theory that eventually was replaced by the investigative judgment doctrine was being revealed in the dream. Now I began to see the connection between the "shut door" mentality of our forefathers, the "shut door" of this SDA church that I had witnessed in the dream, and the look of fear and shame I had seen on Archie's face as he struggled to press through the cold stares and guarded behavior of this present generation of Adventists.

Clearly we are looking at a generational cover-up of some of the errors and theological mistakes that appear in Ellen White's writings. Ellen White and the leadership of the early SDA church endorsed unbiblical teachings that continue to prevent people from having an assurance of salvation or to move forward into the present leading of the Holy Spirit. Not wanting to face openly the evidence that her writings are frequently not in harmony with Scriptural teaching, many leaders within the SDA church have continued to this day to suppress the truth and pass unbiblical teachings down to the next generation. Fear that the entire denomination would collapse if they admit she was wrong in many areas, or that leaders have been wrong in the way they have handled her works, has resulted in a huge *cover-up* that is now many layers thick.

Will many of us become offended too, and our love for Jesus Christ grow cold when we realize that the erroneous teachings of Adventism have been covered up by the corporate leadership of the denomination, and disguised in neat little packages that have been handed down to us from generation to generation as a "package deal?" Just like the dream portrays, discovering the "truth" (that is hidden inside the wrapped packages that people are seen holding onto in the dream) will cause a spiritual earthquake among the SDA laity. As many finally come to see that the **"central pillar of Adventism"** must be replaced by the solid footings of the **"central article of Reformation theology"**—the gospel of justification by faith, will they gladly choose to embrace Christ's finished work on their behalf? I pray they will decidedly choose to trust in the doing and dying of Jesus Christ alone as their basis of acceptance with God.

Endnotes: Chapter 3

[1] John Bevere, *The Bait of Satan: Living Free from the Deadly Trap of Offense* (Charisma House, 2004) 10.
[2] D. M. Canright, *Life of Ellen G. White Seventh-day Adventist Prophet—Her False Claims Refuted* John Bevere, *The Bait of Satan: Living Free from the*

Deadly Trap of Offense (Charisma House, 2004) 10. (Cincinnati, Ohio: The Standard Publishing Company, 1919). 60.

[3] Ibid.

[4] Ellen G. White, *The Great Controversy* (Mountain View, California: Pacific Press Publishing Association, 1950) 268.

[5] Canright 10.

[6] Ibid., 77.

[7] Dirk Anderson, *White Out* (Life Assurance Ministries Publications, Glendale, AZ, 1999) 23-24.

[8] Canright 78.

[9] *The Fundamental Beliefs of Seventh-day Adventists, No. 17* (Review & Herald Publishing Association, 1980). See also: (http://www.adventist.org/beliefs/fundamental/index.html).

[10] White, *The Great Controversy*, 409.

[11] White, *Spiritual Gifts, Vol. 1*, (Washington, D.C, Review & Herald Publishing Assn, 1945) 140, 172, 173.

[12] White, *Review and Herald,* (Washington, D.C: Review & Herald Publishing Assn., 1890) 06-17.

[13] White, *Testimonies for the Church, Vol. 2* (Mountain View, California: Pacific Press Publishing, Association 1882) 148.

[14] Geoffrey J. Paxton, *The Shaking of Adventism* (Wilmington, Delaware: Zenith Publishers, 1977) 149.

[15] Ibid., 151.

[16] Ibid., 156.

Although Adventist's true message has been disguised over the years by its attractive outer packaging, now the dark inner contents of that "package" are being exposed.

Chapter 4
HIDDEN BONDAGE REVEALED

"Nothing in all creation is hidden from God's sight. Everything is uncovered and laid bare before the eyes of Him to whom we must give account."
Hebrews 5:13

As I thought about the dream, I remembered the determined look I had seen on Archie's face as he unexpectedly appeared in the dream. When he cautiously maneuvered his way towards me, struggling to press through the cold stares and guarded behavior of the people around him (representing this present generation of Adventists), I was taken back to the Sabbath when he was asked by the former leadership to preach the sermon at church.

I remember how Archie publicly *"came out of hiding"* by openly addressing the church body on the pain he had suffered as a child, growing up as an incest survivor. No pretty paper, fancy ribbons, or colorful bows could change the ugliness of the shame and pain that he endured as a victim of this generational sin. It had been well over ten years since Archie and I *graduated* from the same church related incest survivors group. God had brought about deep inner healing in both of our lives, as well as in the lives of many others in that group.

As I further reflected on Archie's story and remembered my own, I was reminded that incest survivors become trapped in self-destructive life styles in order to drown out their feelings of fear, shame and unworthiness. We often have a difficult time breaking free from these cycles of powerlessness. God's love becomes so distorted in our minds by earlier betrayals of trust that fear and shame torment us into believing we will never again be able to trust another human being, let alone trust in a caring and loving God. Consequently, the massive offense that we carry and the bitterness that we feel, become tools in the hand of the enemy to keep us in captivity. As a result, the wounding of incest and the accompanying addictions serve to reinforce the fact that its pain is so deeply imbedded in the soul that no one can see the full extent of the bruising—no one except the Lord.

In my own family incest began in the environment of emotional neglect and emptiness that were a normal part of everyday life. Rigidity, coldness and fear-induced loyalty were the weapons that the enemy used to keep me from stopping the abuse once it began. However, beyond its obvious sexual connotation, incest in essence is an abuse of the *legitimate authority* that a parent or guardian has over a child. It is a generational family dysfunction, passed down through the generational genes, destroying trust and distorting the healthy parent-child relationship.

For example, in the normal order of things, a parent or guardian is in the position of exercising control and authority over a child by virtue of age, knowledge and experience. The parent is presumed to know better than the child does what is right and wrong, what is safe and unsafe—essentially what is good for the child. Until the child is old enough to be accountable for his or her own decisions, choices and behavior, the parent or guardian stands in the place of God for the child.

Following this line of reasoning we begin to see that parental authority becomes abusive when the parent uses the position of power to satisfy selfish wants or needs at the expense of the child. Because the child is dependent upon the parent or parent figure, the child becomes the victim. Since the victim has generally been taught to admire, trust and respect the one who has abused him, the victim unknowingly becomes a collaborator in the abuse cycle. The conflicting emotions of love and hate, courage and fear, trust and distrust, towards the offending parent leave an indelible mark of fear and shame on the child as the child is forced to deny his or her own reality.

Spiritual Incest

I have no wish to dwell on a repulsive subject such as incest. But God used the disgusting behavior of Hosea's wife to teach a spiritual lesson. God chose the prophet Hosea to represent His faithful and forgiving love to us—His bride. He is pictured in this beautiful, prophetic, love story as our Husband—the relentless pursuer who buys back His unfaithful wife. So here, too, I believe the Holy Spirit is revealing that the generational sin of incest that Archie's presence in the dream represents is a **symbol** of a **greater spiritual sin** that exists within Adventism, and no doubt the larger body of Christ.

Just as incest was a generational sin, passed down through the generational genes on both sides of my biological family, so *spiritual incest* is a generational sin passed down through the denominational genes of the SDA church. As incest is the abuse of parental authority, *spiritual incest* is the abuse of spiritual authority exercised by spiritual parents and those in authority over us in the church. Another way of saying this is, "Spiritual abuse is the misuse and abuse of spiritual authority by church leaders who set themselves up as gate keepers, using religious performance rather than faith in Jesus as the criterion for accepting or rejecting their followers."[1]

For the purposes of this book I am dealing specifically with the generational sin of spiritual incest in the SDA church. In fact generational spiritual incest has been the best-kept secret within the SDA church for the past one hundred and fifty years. Understanding our spiritual roots and the process our spiritual forbearers used to arrive at their system of beliefs will help us understand why this present generation of Adventists shown in the dream is behaving like incest victims.

As we look at our church history it will become crystal clear how our spiritual forbearers set themselves up to become not only victims but also perpetrators of spiritual incest, and why this cycle of spiritual abuse continues to be experienced in the lives of many of its members to this day. Let me explain.

The Cycle of Spiritual Incest

This generational cycle of spiritual abuse actually began before 1844 with the Millerites. William Miller's message latched onto a natural part of us that wants to be the hero that spreads a crucial message from God. Unfortunately the message of Christ's Second Coming being imminent overtook the gospel. The fruit of this message was bad from the very start.

Because the Father is the only one who knows when Christ is coming again our founders (the beginning generation of SDAs) assumed illegitimate authority by proclaiming the day when Christ would come. They took His name and proclaimed it as if from His mouth, when it was not. When our founders, including Ellen White, assumed illegitimate authority they became the "abusive parents" and started the cycle of spiritual abuse.

First of all, after abandoning the "shut door" heresy and then covering it up, they quickly replaced it with a reinterpretation of the 1844 Disappointment to apply to a change in the ministration of Jesus Christ in the heavenly sanctuary. Having staked all they believed upon their assertion that the end of the world would come on that date, they adamantly refused to admit they had been wrong, both about the date and their "shut door" mentality. They isolated themselves from other Christians by refusing to fellowship with those they considered part of "fallen Babylon," and branded those Adventists who expressed any doubts about Ellen White's visions as "rebels" or in the "dark." As a result of making these kinds of judgments their hearts became a breeding ground for arrogance and spiritual pride. In fact it is still taboo to openly identify the error in Ellen White's writings without being branded as a troublemaker.

Refusing to deal with the bitterness of the Great Disappointment and confess their mistakes and repent of their errors our spiritual forbearers only added fuel to the fire by adding another unbiblical teaching to the already shaky foundation of Adventism. When the Investigative Judgment and the Cleansing of the Sanctuary doctrines replaced the "shut door" teaching, Ellen White, claiming to be an inspired prophet of God, placed her stamp of approval upon these changes. Thus, for the past one hundred and fifty years, these heresies that she condoned have continued to be taught and passed down from generation to generation. They have been maintained very largely by deception on the part of her defenders and supporters—namely the corporate leadership of the SDA church.

It becomes obvious that to jettison these heresies from Adventism's "package" means to call into question the prophetic "gift" of Ellen White. Having to admit that Ellen White taught error regarding these foundational teachings requires one to critically examine whether her claims to "inspiration" can be trusted at all.

The second reason our spiritual forbearers set themselves up to become, not only victims, but also perpetrators of spiritual abuse is that they sought God's stamp of approval through the "prophetic revelations" of Ellen White and used her visions and dreams to explain biblical truth instead of letting the Bible interpret itself. In essence they began to value a "gift" they could see rather than the enigmatic God whom they could not comprehend. They traded Spirit for flesh and were taught to fear the True Spirit as deception thereby grieving the One who could keep them from falling.

Thirdly, our forbearers made Ellen White's words a test of faith and fellowship in the SDA church instead of placing their faith in God's final Word—Jesus Christ. Her interpretation of the Bible came to be preferred to the point where her writings were seen as being inspired on the same level as the Bible.[2] As a result of these heresies I believe they "shut the door" of their hearts to the voice of the Spirit when they began to rely more on human wisdom than God's to build the Adventist Movement.

Nowhere in the Bible is there an example of a prophet's taking advantage of his gifting to enrich himself. Yet that is exactly what our spiritual parents Ellen and James White did. In essence, James White took advantage of his position in the church to benefit himself and his family financially, and his wife helped him by her revelations.[3]

The Whites began their ministry penniless[4] but "as soon as they became leaders, they commercialized their work, and managed to supply themselves well… They always had the best of everything, and plenty of it. Everywhere they went they required to be waited upon in the most slavish manner. At an early camp meeting in Michigan they sent their son Edson out in the camp crying, "Who has a chicken for mother? Mother wants a chicken." Mrs. White dressed richly, and generally had a number of attendants to wait on her."[5]

One of the most unfortunate characteristics of Ellen White's life and writings is that she always made God responsible for her mistakes and errors. An example of this is when she promised to explain her mistakes and blunders in 1905 and said that God would help her to do it. But then in 1906 she turned around and said that God told her not to attempt to do this.[6]

However, her worst deception was to pass off messages from sources other than God as words directly from "her accompanying angel" or "the Lord" Himself when, in fact, they are clearly in direct opposition to the clear word of Scripture. Her claim to be an inspired prophet of God continues to be largely maintained through deception and cover-up on the part of her defenders and supporters—and passed down from generation to generation of SDAs.

In conclusion, not only did our spiritual parents refuse to admit their theological errors; they also blamed God for them or covered them up. On top of that they misused and abused their position of spiritual authority as leaders within the SDA church by setting themselves up as gatekeepers, using fear, shame and religious performance as the criteria for accepting or rejecting their spiritual children.[7]

Outward Appearance of "Packages"

Being an incest survivor myself I am all too familiar with the need to cover-up one's real inner feelings of shame and powerlessness by presenting to the world an attractive outer "package" in order to be accepted. Initially, I remember experiencing feelings of shame and rejection in the dream when I discovered others around me were carrying attractive packages and I had none. It wasn't until Archie handed me his unattractive brown package that my feelings of shame vanished. Suddenly I felt accepted and a part of the group. In fact the former guarded and fearful behavior of the people around me in the dream vanished as they chatted among themselves. I was unable to "see" the bondage people were in as long as I held on to the package.

I am reminded that when I first received Archie's "gift" I was very thankful and meant to hold on to it. In fact I clung desperately to it even after it was torn open and was in danger of falling to the ground, because I still believed it to be a "gift" that I should treasure and pass on to my "children." Having witnessed the "struggle" that Archie had gone through as he endeavored to push his way through the bottleneck of people to reach me made the "gift" seem all the more valuable.

Perhaps my appreciation of this "gift" speaks of how many of us initially receive the "package" of Adventism. As a third generation Adventist I know I initially felt that the special truths of Adventism had been handed down to me as a "gift" that I was fortunate and privileged to have received. Therefore, it was my responsibility to become a good steward and take care of this "package" I had received and pass it on.

In a million years I would never have dreamed of discarding this "gift" or letting it fall to the ground or of throwing it *away*. That is why I was so horrified and dismayed in the dream when I was thrown headfirst across the top of a desk and the "package" was ripped open. Abruptly I was stopped from pursuing my goal when I ran headfirst into the Stumbling Stone. As Adventism has pursued its own "vision" over the years hasn't it also continually tripped over the Stumbling Stone?

As I looked back on my early religious training, I realized that the spiritual emphasis in many SDAs homes, schools and churches has been on outward performance. What other people would think about our behavior was considered far more important than the attitudes within our own hearts. Was that why all of the packages I had seen people carrying [except Archie's] appeared to be wrapped in different colored paper?

In the hope of disguising the darkness of the inner contents of the "package" that people were seen carrying, the corporate leadership of the SDA church has covered up the true nature of the "package" contents by making the outer covering appear attractive and desirable. In fact each generation of SDAs has tried to package Adventism's message in such a way as to make it even more desirable and more attractive than the generation before them. However, the attractive packaging does not change the nature of what is inside the "package."

Remember the plain brown paper package that Archie hands over to me is very unattractive. No matter how hard we try to make Adventism's package attractive to others, from God's perspective Adventism's "package" can never be dressed up to look like anything but filthy rags!

Spiritual Pornography

I'm sure most of us are aware that pornographic magazines are generally disguised in plain, brown paper wrappings so that the sexually explicit nature of the materials will be hidden from those who might be offended. I believe the Lord is using this powerfully imagery to shock SDAs and wake them up so they will see their spiritual blindness.

The flimsy brown paper that covered Archie's package of magazines conceals a graphic picture of the naked truth about the SDA church—truth that has gotten generations of SDAs "stuck" and prevents them from moving forward. What is this painful "truth" that God is uncovering that caused the congregation to instantly disappear the moment the front cover of the magazines was exposed?

From God's perspective, Adventism's "package" of "righteousness" is a more formidable enemy of the new covenant gospel than many of us realize. Although Adventism's true message has been disguised over the years by its attractive outer packaging, now the dark inner contents of that "package" are being exposed.

The imagery portrayed on the front covers of the magazines reveals that SDAs are in bondage to the law of sin and death. God sees their "good works" that are the result of trying to obey old covenant law (including the Ten Commandments) as a package of pornographic magazines! That's right. When we try to add our "good works" to what Jesus Christ has already done for us through His finished "good work" on the cross we are perverting the new covenant gospel of Jesus Christ and are guilty of spiritual pornography. The next chapter will throw further light on what God is telling us through this graphic imagery.

So the fear and shame I had seen in Archie's eyes in the dream mirrored the same fear and shame I have experienced numerous times in my life when I have "stumbled" and the "package" of Adventism was torn open, and I was forced to look at some of Adventism's dirty laundry. Nagging questions would be raised in my mind as a result of questioning the biblical accuracy of Ellen White's writings, and unique teachings that were founded on her words rather than God's Word.

Over the passage of time I began to feel it my Christian duty to try to resolve some of these conflicts I had, as to the biblical accuracy of some of Adventism's "special truths" or find some logical reason to ignore them. Actually without even realizing it, I was a victim of spiritual incest, unknowingly passing on a "package" of spiritual pornography to the next generation. By remaining silent and not expressing my concerns and growing fears over the value of Adventism's "gift," I had actually participated in helping to cover up the hidden spiritual pornography in Adventism's "package." Just as our forbearers denied their "shut door" errors, I participated in similar denial by not wanting to face my growing fears that perhaps Adventism's "package" was not such a good "deal" after all.

I believe we are seeing similar denial portrayed in the dream by the people around Archie. Not wanting to face their growing fears about Adventism's "package," they are seen holding on to it tightly as if their very lives depended on it. Although shame and fear are evident on Archie's face, he chooses to let go of Adventism's "package" and pass it on to me. I, in turn, perceive it to be a "gift" and plan to pass it on to my classroom of "handicapped children."

Here we see evidence in the dream of spiritual incest being passed on, not only from one generation to the next, but also from one unsuspecting incest victim to the next within the same generation. Not until the "package" was torn open and the true nature of its contents seen, was the generational cover-up finally exposed.

Because we have been taught to admire, trust and respect our "spiritual parents" (the founders of the SDA church, including Ellen White), we are also faced with conflicting emotions of love and hate, courage and fear, trust and distrust towards them whenever we begin to question their spiritual authority. Recognizing that the corporate leadership of the SDA church in every generation has continued the role of the "spiritually abusive parent" in order to keep this cycle of abuse going is sobering.

Unknowingly our spiritual forbearers passed on this cycle of spiritual incest to us (their spiritual children). In turn, we have been forced to hide and cover up our feelings of fear, shame and betrayal, deny our own reality, and became collaborators in this cycle of generational spiritual incest.

Covering up painful feelings is part of what all incest survivors learn to do in order to deny reality and cope with life's disappointments. Archie chose drugs and alcohol as the tool to numb his pain, and I chose addictive relationships to numb mine. Being familiar with the symptoms of abuse that victims of incest exhibit, I recognized that the generations of Adventists huddled together at the back of the church were behaving like they had been abused. Our denominational history reveals that victims of spiritual incest often become abusers. Most abusers have likely been victims.

Like incestual parents, we may feel bad about this and realize that we have a deep problem, but we are afraid of admitting this to our "family." We're afraid of speaking of it and confessing it to them. Why? Because not only will we probably lose our position of authority and influence in our "family," but most of all we are afraid of losing our "family." If we admit the errors and our complicity in perpetuating them we're afraid they'll turn tail and leave us.

This has been strongly evidenced by this particular SDA church's rationalization for not clearly stating the truth. The trumpet will not make a clear sound as long as there is a putrid mixture. There is a very subtle deception that staying in the system will give a platform for leading other Adventists into more freedom while there is a refusal to identify and proclaim the problems even to its own members. There has not been teaching or acknowledgement of the errors that still grip the hearts of the members of this church. How can this particular SDA church then possibly lead the way to freedom?

The parallel becomes clear. In the corporate SDA church, I believe the leadership in every generation has been afraid of admitting the errors and abuses incorporated in the foundation of Adventism by our "spiritual parents." Why? Because if they do, they'll not only lose their spiritual authority and institution, but they're afraid that they'll lose their family—the members, the congregations, and all those who have looked up to them as their "head" (parent, head of the family, the person who knows what is correct) in the SDA church.

The dream vividly portrays this truth. When I fell across the desk and the "package" was ripped open and its contents displayed, instantly everyone, (except Archie) in the church who had been holding on to their packages vanished from sight.

Those of us who have experienced incest at the hands of a biological parent or parental figure can relate to the pain involved by that betrayal of trust. But it is quite another thing for us to experience betrayal at the hands of our "spiritual parents." The very people whom we placed our trust in to lead us closer to God, we discover have betrayed us.

Freedom through Forgiveness

The good news is that we don't have to continue this generational cycle of spiritual incest by passing on Adventism's "gift" to the next generation. Spiritual incest will continue to be generational *only* as Adventism's children continue to "shut the door" of their hearts and minds to the Spirit of Truth. This cycle of spiritual abuse will be broken when we choose to release our "packages" at the foot of the cross and receive the truth of the gospel and give permission and encouragement to those entrusted to our care to do the same.

We are being called by the Spirit to release the "package" of Adventism's legacy at the foot of the cross, but this will not happen without a struggle. Remember in the dream how I tried to hang on to the ripped "package?" As it became heavier and heavier it became like a millstone around my neck. Finally, I was forced to release it, and *all* the contents of the "package" went flying to the foot of the cross.

It will be difficult to confess our sin of being collaborators in this vicious cycle of generational spiritual incest. But God is calling us now, not only to repent of our blindness, but also to choose to forgive our "spiritual abusers"—both from the past and the present.

As I reflected again on Archie's story, I was reminded that it was only when Archie *chose* to receive God's unconditional love, acceptance and forgiveness for *himself,* that he was freed to extend this gift of God's grace to his abusers. The root of bitterness and the spirit of offense that had almost destroyed him were torn down when he chose to forgive those who had hurt him—distant relatives—his own flesh and blood. Only then did the process of healing in his fractured life really begin.

In a similar way, this present generation of Adventists is being called to extend the gift of God's grace to their spiritual abusers—not only Adventism's founding parents, but also the past and present leadership of the corporate SDA church. By using their positions of power and spiritual authority the present-day leadership of the SDA church continues to perpetuate the lies and deception in our history by covering up the theological mistakes and errors of past generations. In order to remain free from bitterness we must choose to forgive them and release them from judgment as we safely leave their motives with God while not justifying the errors.

Trying to "save face" and walk away from this cycle of spiritual incest smelling like a rose is not going to happen for the victim or the abuser. Perhaps we can find the necessary compassion within our own hearts to in some way identify with the struggles our forbearers went through as they found themselves at odds with the rest of the Christian world who rejected them and their erroneous "shut door" teaching.

Because our SDA beliefs have become such an integral part of the very fabric of our lives, many Adventists no doubt will continue to "shut the door" of their hearts and minds and remain victims rather than face the painful truth of what their "offending parent" has done. But for those who want to become survivors, free from the bondage of spiritual abuse, the cross of Jesus Christ is the only answer!

As you begin to identify with the miracle of God's healing grace in Archie's life, I pray that it will mirror your own. Although Archie was treated unjustly as a child and held prisoner for many years by his own bitter memories as an adult, he became free through choosing to forgive himself, along with his abusers. No longer seeing himself as a victim trapped in his past feelings of shame and unworthiness, he became free to share his story of recovery from incest through the healing power of forgiveness. He moved from the darkness of despair into the light of God's healing love. I pray this miracle will be repeated in your life too as you choose to release the spiritual bondage that you have unknowingly been clinging to at the foot of the cross.

Endnotes: Chapter 4

[1] Ken Blue, *Healing Spiritual Abuse* (InterVarsity Press, October 1993) 25-26.
[2] Dale Ratzlaff, *The Truth about Seventh-day Adventist Truth* (Life Assurance Ministries, 2000) 6. "In recent years much new evidence has surfaced which demonstrates the many problems associated with the writings of Ellen White. In order to keep these as "inspired writings," SDAs have had to liberalize their concept of inspiration to allow for such things as massive plagiarism which was denied, historical errors, suppressed visions, inaccurate statements, and contradictions to the Bible."
[3] Canright 125.
[4] White, Testimonies, Vol. 1, p. 75.
[5] Canright 125.
[6] Ibid., 185
[7] Blue 25-26.

The incredulous look of surprised joy on the faces of the two children who had been thrown from the "mountain" stood out in stark contrast to the looks of fear and terror that held the other slave children captive.

Chapter 5
SAY TO THIS MOUNTAIN, "MOVE!"

"I tell you the truth, if you have faith and do not doubt... you can say to this mountain, 'Go throw yourself into the sea,' and it will be done."
Matthew 21:21-22

During corporate worship at church on Saturday morning, July 31, 1999, the Spirit began to draw my attention to the words of the song we were singing, "Though the mountains fall, they fall into the sea..." Immediately He began focusing my attention on the human mountain of children I had seen caricatured on the front covers of the magazines in this dream. I felt an agony in my spirit as I experienced the cry of the Father's heart of agape love for those terrified children who were so afraid of falling into the sea below them.

A Spiritual Kingdom

Later as I was reading my Bible I noticed that the words of this song, "Whom have I but You?" are taken from Psalm 46:1-3. Here the psalmist David boldly proclaims: "God is our refuge and strength, an ever-present help in trouble. Therefore we will not fear, though the earth give way and the *mountains fall into the heart of the sea*, though its waters roar and foam and the mountains quake with their surging."

God was using the words of this song to specifically draw my attention to a *spiritual* application of these words. In the Scriptures, nations, kingdoms and governments are sometimes symbolically represented as mountains (Joshua 14:12a). In prophetic dreams and visions, a mountain can also symbolize a spiritual kingdom.

An example of this is found in the dream God gave Nebuchadnezzar. The statue he saw was smitten by a rock that became a *mountain* that "filled the whole earth" *(Daniel 2:35)*. Here God gave a prophetic word to King Nebuchadnezzar that *His* kingdom, unlike man's kingdoms, would be an everlasting kingdom—like a mountain that would fill the whole earth. Eventually, "the *government* will be on His shoulders [instead of man's shoulders]... Of the increase of His government and peace there will be no end" (Isaiah 9:6-7).

In other words, a mountain can represent a temporal kingdom or God's kingdom—God's body here on earth as illustrated by the following Scripture: "Those who trust in the Lord are like Mount Zion, which cannot be shaken, but endures forever" (Psalm 125:1). With that in mind, I want to focus attention again on the front covers of the magazine where cartoon-like children wearing ragged and tattered clothing were seen clinging frantically to another "mountain."

Unbelief Revealed

When I saw the details of this "mountain" for the second time, I saw the same words I had seen sixteen months earlier inscribed in large bold letters across the foot of it, **"Say to this Mountain, Move!"** Immediately, the Spirit brought the following verses of Scripture to my mind as I watched the blue sea lapping at the foot of the "mountain." Speaking to His disciples privately after they had asked Him why they failed to heal the demonized boy, Jesus replied, "If you have faith as small as a grain of mustard seed, you can **say to this mountain**, **'Move from here to there'** and it will move. Nothing will be impossible for you'" (Matthew 17:20-21).

As we take a closer look at the context of these verses of Scripture we find that a crowd had gathered at the foot of the Mount of Transfiguration to witness the disciples drive out a demon from a suffering boy. When the disciples failed to cast out the demon, the father brought his son to Jesus to be healed. Addressing the crowd that undoubtedly included the scribes and Pharisees, Jesus rebuked them, saying, "O unbelieving and perverse generation... How long shall I stay with you? How long shall I put up with you? Bring the boy here to Me" (verse 17).

Although Jesus words sound harsh to us, I believe He was not only addressing *their* unbelief, but a *whole generation* who had all the evidence in front of them that Jesus was their Messiah, but they still chose *not* to believe. By choosing to hold on to their erroneous beliefs and traditions, they chose to remain in unbelief—in a passive state of perversity.

In a similar way, I believe God is addressing this present generation of SDAs. By choosing to cling to Adventism's "package" that has been passed down to us from our forbearers, we remain in a passive state of unbelief. We are afraid to open it and face what is inside. Although many individuals, over the years, have opened their "package" and released it at the foot of the cross, as a generation of SDAs we have not. By our actions in the dream we continue to cling to erroneous teachings that prevent us from fully entering into the freedom of the new covenant gospel.

Just as the disciples had been trusting in *themselves* to drive out the demon instead of trusting in *Jesus,* have we been guilty of trusting in our "hidden lists" of Adventist agenda (found inside the "package")? As unbelief prevented the disciples from being able to receive God's power that would bring freedom and release to the suffering boy, has *unbelief* prevented many of us from receiving God's healing grace that alone can bring freedom and release us from the bondage we have been holding on to?

Exposing Barrenness

After the Spirit brought the previous verses of Scripture to my mind, He prompted me to read the following verses with this "mountain" in mind. "I tell you the truth, if you have faith and do not doubt, not only can you do what was done to the fig tree, but also you can say to *this* mountain, 'Go throw yourself into the sea,' and it will be done." (Matthew 21:21; See also Mark 11:22). Let's look at the context of this passage in order to see what Jesus is saying and what conclusions we might draw that could apply to this "mountain" of terrified children.

Early in the morning, the day after Jesus cleansed the temple for the last time, He and His disciples were on their way back to Jerusalem, when He saw a fig tree beside the road. Probably He was hungry so He walked over to the tree anticipating He would find fruit.

Instead He found nothing but leaves. Immediately He cursed the barren fig tree, and instantly it withered right before his disciple's eyes. They were amazed and wanted to know how the fig tree withered so quickly.

I believe the barrenness of the fig tree represents hypocrisy, particularly the hypocrisy of the religious leaders of Christ's day. Jesus exposed their barrenness and lack of faith when he addressed the pretense of their religion in the temple. Their lack of good fruit became obvious as they ran to hide from the One who knew their every thought.

Just as figs are to be expected on a fig tree that has leaves, isn't Christ telling us that He looks for the fruit of religion to be seen in the lives of those who make a profession of it? Having a form of godliness but lacking Holy Spirit power produces the dead works of barrenness.

I believe God is revealing to this present generation of SDAs, clinging tightly to Adventism's "package," that we are holding on to the dead works of barrenness. He is bringing a spiritual earthquake in order to rip open our "packages" so we can choose to be freed from the spiritual bondage that has kept us cringing in fear for generations.

Isn't Jesus perhaps saying to this present generation of SDAs, "Come learn a lesson from the fig tree while there is still time (Matthew 24:32)? God's wrath was unleashed on a tree instead of a human being, because God's wrath was poured out upon Jesus Christ when He suffered for our sins and bore the curse for us. But if we choose to continue to cling to our "dead works of barrenness" instead of releasing them at the foot of the cross, we will be overcome with the weight of our offenses, and they will become a curse for us, like a millstone around our necks (as Archie's ripped package became to me) that will eventually crush us.

Mount Sinai

In order to further understand what God is saying through this symbolic picture on the magazine covers, let us take a careful look at another passage of Scripture—a powerful allegory that Paul wrote to the Galatians regarding two women who represented two covenants. Paul wrote this letter to the Christian churches in the Roman province of Galatia, because they were being misled by Judaizing teachers who wanted to put them back "under the law" (Galatians 4:21). Does this "human mountain" of terrified children in anyway relate to the "covenant from Mount Sinai that bears children who are to be slaves" (Galatians 4:24)?

Tell me, you who want to be under law, are you not aware of what the law says? For it is written that Abraham had two sons, one by the slave woman [Hagar] and the other by the free woman [Sarah]. His son by the slave woman was born in the ordinary way, but his son by the free woman was born as the result of a promise.

These things may be taken figuratively, for the women represent two covenants. One covenant is from Mount Sinai [old covenant] and bears children who are to be slaves: This is Hagar. Now Hagar stands for Mount Sinai in Arabia and corresponds to the present city of Jerusalem, because she is in slavery with her children. But the Jerusalem that is above is free, and she is our mother. For it is written:

"Be glad, O barren woman, who bears no children (in the flesh); break forth and cry aloud, you who have no labor pains; because more are the children of the desolate woman (born by the power of the Spirit) than of her who has a husband."

Now you, brothers, like Isaac, are children of promise. At that time the son born in the ordinary way persecuted the son born by the power of the Spirit. It is the same now. But what does the Scripture say? Get rid of the slave woman and her son, for the slave woman's son will never share in the inheritance with the free woman's son." Therefore, brothers, we are not children of the slave woman, but of the free woman (Galatians 4:21-31).

After reading this passage of Scripture does it become clear that God sees past and present generations of SDAs as children of the slave woman? I believe so. The fear written across the faces of the children on the magazine covers seen in the dream is because they are holding on to the covenant from Mount Sinai that "bears children who are to be slaves." The dream reveals that we continue to remain in "slavery with our children" because we continue to cling tightly to this "package of Adventism" that has been passed down to us.

God sees past and present generations of SDAs as children of the slave woman, because we continue to nurse at Hagar's breast. That is why He is going to shake this Adventist "movement" to its very core. He wants to release us from our bondage to the unique, erroneous and unbiblical teachings of the church that have their basis in old covenant law instead of the new covenant gospel.

Not only are we seen clinging tightly to our Adventist heritage, but by literally climbing up the "human ladder" that is now many layers thick, we have formed a multi-layered, human organism that is shaped more like a tall pyramid than a mountain. By sheer human effort this multi-layered mountain of slave children, striving to keep from falling into the ocean of God's love, have built a "spiritual kingdom" that has become a towering mountain of offense to God.

Like the people after the flood, we have tried to make a name for ourselves by building our own "Tower of Babel." We have built a spiritual kingdom by our own striving and now this kingdom is about to come crashing down. For God is in the process of shaking this "kingdom" loose from those things that have kept it bound in confusion, because He wants His children in Adventism free from the curse of the law.

Judging from the many layers of slave children's arms and legs that I saw buried beneath the surface, it's obvious that past generations of slave children died climbing this "mountain." If the present generation of Adventist stationed at the closed doors of the church sanctuary opened their packages and saw what they were clinging to, wouldn't they loudly cry out, "Who will rescue us from this "body of death?"

"Thanks be to God—through Jesus Christ our Lord for He has already delivered us from this *body of death* (Romans 7:24-25)." For those who choose to trust in His finished work of grace and let go of their own works, there is no condemnation (Romans 8:1). In Adventism's preoccupation with trying to keep the *"letter of the law,"* we have forgotten that **"the letter kills"** (2 Corinthians 3:6).

As long as we continue to hold on to Adventism's "package" instead of releasing the *entire* contents at the foot of the cross, we are still living under the old covenant from Mount Sinai. As long as we continue to cling to this "body of death" we are children of the slave woman, Hagar.

The Old Covenant

So how are we supposed to relate to old covenant law so that God no longer sees us as slave children? Let's briefly see what the Scriptures have to say.

The Old Testament reveals that the old covenant was an interaction between God and Israel, and included the covenant made between God and Israel at Sinai—the Ten Commandments. Under the old covenant God was the one who dictated the terms of the covenant to Israel, and Israel agreed to obey, by saying, "All that the Lord has said we will do."

The old covenant also included applications and interpretations of the Ten Commandments. The purpose of the old covenant was to provide the basis for fellowship between God and Israel. There were blessings if Israel kept the covenant and cursings if Israel disobeyed. When Israel experienced the "cursings" they had no excuse because the "testimony" was there. The very fact that Israel went into captivity was a witness of God's faithfulness as a covenant partner. Only after Israel had broken the covenant and the nation was headed into captivity do we read about the promise of a new covenant (Jeremiah 31:31).[1]

The old covenant [Ten Commandments] was like a tutor to lead us to Christ, but now that Christ has come we no longer are under a tutor (Galatians 3:24-25). So the old covenant no longer has any authority over the life of a believer in Jesus Christ. For in Christ, "the law of the Spirit of life sets [us] free from the law of sin and death" (Romans 8:2). That's why this command is given by Paul: "Get rid of the slave woman and her son for the slave woman's son will never share in the inheritance with the free woman's son" (Galatians 4:30).

New not like the Old

In Hebrews 8:8 we read, "The new covenant... will not be like the covenant" God made with children of Israel when He led them out of Egypt. No! The new covenant is *not* like the Ten Commandments. The new covenant is between God the Father, and His Son, *not* between God the Father, and the sons of Israel. The new covenant is a "better covenant, which has been enacted on better promises" (Hebrews 8:6).

After the author of Hebrews shares with us the fundamental aspects of the new covenant (Hebrews 8:6-12) he continues, "By calling this covenant "new," he has made the first one obsolete; and what is obsolete and aging will soon disappear" (Hebrews 8:13). With the coming of the new covenant the "first covenant" [called old in other places] grows old and aged and is near disappearing.[2]

Since the New Testament defines the old covenant as the Ten Commandments along with the other laws in the book of Moses, does this mean that the Ten Commandments along with the other laws in the book of Moses are now "old and aged and near disappearing?"

Let's read the next verse and see if this is what the author is really saying. "Now even the first covenant had regulations of divine worship and also an earthly sanctuary" (Hebrews 9:1). Wasn't the Sabbath one of those regulations of divine worship (See Leviticus 23)?

As we continue reading the next few verses we see other aspects of the "first covenant" described. Then in verse 4 the author lists the things that were in the Most Holy Place of the earthly sanctuary, including "the tablets of the covenant" which is a clear reference to the Ten Commandments.

So what do we conclude from reading these clear facts of Scripture in their contextual setting? The "tablets of the covenant" and the "laws for divine worship" are old and ready to disappear.[3]

I believe the symbolic action in the dream of the "mountain" beginning to sink when the earthquake hits, confirms that with the coming of the new covenant, the old covenant is old and ready to disappear.

I know that many Adventist scholars have tried to separate the eternal moral law from the ceremonial aspects of the law at this juncture in order to preserve the Sabbath, but the Bible makes no such distinction. Under the old covenant, law included all the commands God gave. Both moral and ceremonial aspects of the law are intermingled throughout the whole law, and present even in the Ten Commandments.

So what is being said here in Hebrews 8 and 9? The author continues to describe various aspects of old covenant worship, and then says in verse 10 that these "external regulations applying until the time of the new order."

When is the "time of the new order?" The next verse says, "When Christ came as high priest of the good things that are already here..." (Hebrews 9:11). Christ established the new order of things when He sacrificed Himself for our sins. "Therefore, if any man is in Christ, he is a new creation; the old [covenant] has gone, behold, the new [covenant] has come" (2 Corinthians 5:17).

In the new covenant God writes His law of love on our minds and hearts. The very heart of the new covenant is to love one another as Christ loved us. In the new covenant we walk according to the Spirit as the Spirit of God indwells us. Under the new covenant we may experience an intimate fellowship with God that was not possible under the old covenant.

"For all who are being led by the Spirit of God these are the sons of God. For you have *not received a spirit of slavery leading you to fear again*, but you have received a spirit of adoption as sons by which we cry out, 'Abba! [Daddy] Father!" The Spirit Himself bears witness with our spirit that we are children of God, and if children, heirs also, heirs of God and fellow heirs with Christ..." (Romans 8:14-17).

The underlying purpose of the old covenant was to establish a relationship between God and man. This underlying purpose can be fulfilled under the new covenant only in the Christian who walks by the power of the Spirit.[4]

Jesus Christ—God's final Word

The New Testament must always interpret the Old Testament because the Old Testament institutions are shadows of the reality to come—veiled promises of a salvation not yet revealed (Hebrews 10:1). But in the New Testament—the new covenant gospel of Jesus Christ, God's secret is out and His glory unveiled. Jesus Christ is God's final word "beyond which there is no more to be seen or experienced."[5]

Spiritual blindness is the result when we refuse to acknowledge that only *in Christ* is there freedom from old covenant bondage. There is freedom only where the Spirit of the Lord is (2 Corinthians 3:17). Only when we acknowledge that the ministry of the Spirit (the new covenant) is much more glorious than the ministry of death (so vividly portrayed in this mountain of death) is the veil removed (2 Corinthians 3:7-11).

I believe God initially blotted from my memory this "mountain of death" when I woke up from the dream, because He is teaching us that the old covenant law no longer serves as a *guideline* for Christian living and service anymore.[6] Why? Because the Law no longer applies to one who has died with Christ (Romans 7:4-6). Does that mean that the moral principles contained within the old covenant law have been done away with? Absolutely not! We can see evidence all around us of a world suffering from disobedience to God's eternal moral laws.

The point that God is showing us here is that the new covenant offers us a much better guide for holy living than the old in that it operates from basic principles. Besides that, under the new covenant the Holy Spirit has come to take the place that the law used to fill in our lives, and He helps us interpret these principles to our specific life situations.

Notice what Paul says, "But now we have been released from the Law, having died to that by which we were bound, so that we serve in newness of the Spirit and not in oldness of the letter" (Romans 7:6). Isn't the phrase "oldness of the letter" a clear reference to the Ten Commandments that were part of the old covenant law?

The work of Christ in the new covenant is to free us from the law so that we can have a relationship with Him—a relationship of surpassing value in "knowing Him." Although God is telling us that the Ten Commandments are no longer binding upon Christians, the principles upon which they are based are, but not in old covenant form.

I love the Old Testament Scriptures because they are such a gold mine of truth. But we must remember to interpret all old covenant statements in the light of the new covenant gospel. In the old covenant the focus was law, but while the new covenant *has* law (the law of love and liberty), its focus is grace.[7]

Married to the Law or to Christ?

The Scriptures tell us that grace and truth came by Jesus Christ. Now that we have received Jesus Christ as our "new" husband, Paul uses the metaphor of marriage in Romans 7:1-6 to describe our present relationship to the law. Listen carefully to what he says. "Do you not know brothers… that the law has authority over a man only as long as he lives? …So, my brothers, you also died to the law through the body of Christ that you might belong to another, to Him who was raised from the dead, in order that we might bear fruit to God… But now, dying to what once bound us, we have been *released from the law* so that we serve in the *new way of the Spirit*, and not in the *old way* of the written code."

I believe these verses are telling us that before we came to Christ we were married to the law. For example, we all know that we should not covet, but all we can do is covet our neighbor's new Mercedes, his forty-foot yacht, or the key to his executive suite. We know that we should not covet our neighbor's bank account or his possessions, but since the law told us not to, that's all we can do. Old covenant law has absolutely no power to save us from our human dilemma. It only serves to remind us of how sinful we really are. Someone once wrote that the law "critiques our adherence to its standard and provokes our flesh to sin." That's why Paul calls it a "ministry of death" (2 Corinthians 3:7).

So the solution to our problem is to *die to the law* [to this ministry of death] so we can be *married to Christ*. If we choose to be married to Christ, then we will *know* the truth, and the truth will set us free [from this "ministry of death"]. So if the Son sets us free [from the law], we will be free indeed (John 8:32, 36).

Our liberation from the law of sin and death through marriage to Christ entitles us to all the promises and blessings of the new covenant gospel. As a result, the indwelling Holy Spirit's power becomes the unifying factor of our total existence, continually pointing us away from Mount Sinai to our new Husband—Jesus Christ. In Him we experience the inseparable relationship between His promises: "The truth will set you free" and "if the Son sets you free, you will be free indeed." The *truth* that sets us free is Christ Himself. We cannot discover true freedom at any independent distance from Him.[8]

However, if we are dead to the law and married to Christ, and then, out of fear of losing our salvation, choose to go back to focusing again on the letter of the law, aren't we committing spiritual adultery? Doesn't our striving to hold on to our "wrapped packages" mean we have been severed from Christ? Paul unequivocally tells us, "You who are trying to be justified by law have been alienated [separated] from Christ; you have fallen from grace" (Galatians 5:4). We cannot hold on to the old covenant, and at the same time receive the blessings of the new covenant gospel. We cannot serve two masters.

False Intimacy

In essence, the graphic imagery portrayed on the front covers of the magazines reveal that the Adventist people are having an adulterous relationship with the law of sin and death (Romans 8:2). Fear of being lost has caused many to cling to the false savior—the Law—rather than the Groom—Jesus Christ. The futility of trusting in our own obedience instead of Christ's obedience for us is equivalent to spiritual adultery. An equally offensive betrayal of His grace is the belief that He gives us the ability, through the Holy Spirit, to obey the old covenant law. I believe that God is revealing, through the imagery in the dream, a systemic problem of spiritual pornography and adultery within the body of Adventism about which most members are oblivious. Yet, unbeknownst to them, they are most certainly victims of this most subtle form of spiritual impurity.

One of the most alluring attributes of pornography is its promise of intimacy. In fact the entire porn industry is founded upon the premise that everyone needs intimacy. So victims of pornography, having being lured in by loneliness, lust or desire, discover too late that they have become addicted to an empty, false and destructive imitation of their true needs. This false intimacy momentarily gratifies lust but leaves their deeper needs untouched as they slide toward a *black hole* of death. Using the pornographic industry as a metaphor for illegitimate fulfillment of legitimate needs helps to identify some of the ways in which Adventism has appealed to the need for intimacy with God through their man-made solutions.

Adventism's foundational teachings are spiritually destructive in nature precisely because they deceive people into thinking that they will find true intimacy and acceptance with God by striving to obey the Ten Commandments. Consequently, millions have been lured into slavishly striving to obey the Sabbath of the 4th commandment. Instead of finding the true intimacy with God they desired, they strive, out of fear, to obey a poor facsimile (the law of sin and death) of the real thing—Jesus Christ.

Since the truth of the gospel has been perverted by Adventism's unbiblical teachings, I believe most Adventists are unaware of the fact that the brand of "Christianity" being promoted by the SDA church at large is cultic in nature. From the outside, the church looks good as its slick marketing techniques present worthy programs and admirable community endeavors that can fool the casual observer. However, all of the spin in the world is no substitute for the intimacy with our Maker that comes from living in the reality of the gospel by the power of the Spirit.

Pyramid Power Structure

The pyramid-shaped mountain of slave children seen on the front covers of the magazines speaks of a pyramid power structure (imitated by many modern cults) that is held together by fear. From Adventism's very beginnings we have been taught to believe that Ellen G. White is not only a latter-day "prophet" through whom God has revealed His will for the SDA church, but her teachings are a "continuing and authoritative source of truth."

The erroneous teachings of this hierarchical figurehead of the SDA denomination are very difficult to get rid of once they are in the mind. Furthermore, these flawed teachings have been covered up and passed on generationally by the collective leadership of the corporate SDA church whose (derived) authority is still effectively absolute. Any deviation from the SDA "truth" is seen, by those in authority, as heresy that must be squashed to prevent further spread. The church asserts that one cannot challenge Ellen G. White, its teachings or leadership without calling into question the authority of God.

Fear of Falling into the Sea

This truth is vividly portrayed by the actions of the slave children splashing and floundering around in the water at the foot of the "mountain." Some were in the water up to their ankles, others to their knees, still others to their waists and a few were in over their heads. Although all the slave children had been immersed in the "ocean" to some level, they were still very afraid to totally let go of one another and this sinking "mountain".

By holding on to one another these human chains reminded me of how Ellen White's statements have such a deadly grip on the hearts of SDAs. Having been taught that the Adventist message is a "perfect chain of truth" (Review and Herald, 1850, Nov. 1), Adventists are afraid to let go of erroneous teachings even when God's Word proves them wrong.

They represent many in the SDA church who are cautiously "testing the waters" to see if they can continue to hold on to "Adventism's package" while checking out the new covenant gospel and the things of the Spirit. Most are still very fearful of moving in the Spirit, because everything is still being filtered through old covenant understandings of Scripture. There is a profound fear to really "launch out into the deep" for fear that once the "mountain of offense" is left behind it will be impossible to return to the security of Adventism's "package" and the inevitable result will be drowning.

Believing that there is some religious requirement that must be performed before entering into the blessings of the new covenant gospel, many continue to look to Mt. Sinai for guidance instead of looking to Jesus Christ. The confused church has not yet "been released from the Law, and died to that by which we were bound" in order to "serve in the newness of the Spirit…" (Romans 7:6).

This "package" of bondage that most SDAs have unknowingly carried and passed down from one generation to the next is clearly revealed by the symbolic actions of all the fearful slave children in this dream. Rather than fall into the "ocean of God's love" and experience the true freedom of the new covenant gospel, most cling desperately to this "mountain of death"—afraid to let go.

It took a massive earthquake to shake two of these slave children free from the top of the "mountain." The moment they were released from bondage to law, and went somersaulting through the air towards the open sea, their tattered slave clothes were replaced by bright colorful clothing. The incredulous look of surprised joy on their faces stood out in stark contrast to the looks of fear and terror that held the other slave children captive. They broke free from this generational cycle of spiritual abuse when they were separated from this "body of death," and fell into the "ocean of God's love." Now they were no longer children of the slave woman, but of the free.

Exercising Our Spiritual Authority

Through the symbolism in this dream God is teaching that only "those who *trust* in the Lord are like Mount Zion," which *cannot be shaken* but endures forever" (Psalm 125:1). "He who dwells in the shelter of the Most High will *rest* (be free from striving) in the shadow of the Almighty" (Psalm 91:1). Though "the mountains fall into the heart of the sea," we will *not* be moved. For those who trust in the Lord are like a spiritual mountain that cannot be shaken, but endures forever (Psalm 46:1-3).

In some ways, SDA theology is analogous to an onion. Although initially Adventism's "package" may appear to be shiny and attractive on the outside, the inner layers become progressively stronger and more rank until they become intolerable. That is why God wrote these large, bold letters across the base of this mountain: **"SAY TO THIS**

MOUNTAIN, MOVE," because He is shaking us loose from our generational bondage to the false teachings of Adventism. He wants us to embrace the new covenant gospel, exercise our true spiritual authority in Jesus Christ, and speak boldly to this "mountain" of offense, **"MOVE! GO THROW YOURSELF INTO THE SEA!"** [9] And it will be done.

Endnotes: Chapter 5

[1] Dale Ratzlaff, *Sabbath in Crisis* (Life Assurance Ministries, 1990) 45. Title later changed to *Sabbath in Christ*.
[2] Ibid., 192.
[3] Ibid., 193.
[4] Ibid., 204.
[5] Robert D. Brinsmead, *Verdict* (Fallbrook: Verdict Publications, June 1981) Ch. 1.
[6] Ibid., 204.
[7] Ibid., 191.
[8] John Lloyd Ogilvie, *Silent Strength for my Life* (Harvest House Publishers, August 1990) 69.
[9] Matthew 21:21; See also: Mark 11:22.

I began to understand more fully not only the laughter
I experienced then, but also the laughter I have experienced
in the Spirit many times since that first time.

Chapter 6
THE "REST" THAT REMAINS

*"...anyone who enters God's rest also rests from his own
work, just as God did from His."*
Hebrews 4:10

Our history as a denomination reveals that generations of Seventh-day Adventists (SDAs) have been involved, to some degree, in striving to obey the Ten Commandments, especially the fourth. The idea we inherited from our forbearers was that in order to please God we must obey His law. In the dream our striving to obey the law was represented as our holding on to endless columns of indecipherable fine print inside the magazines that were impossible to read without the aid of a magnifying glass.

The man-made rules and teachings of Adventism that have been added to the old covenant lists of requirements for proper Sabbath observance have replaced the list that the Pharisees added, but both have caused a heaviness on the people. However, those who were carrying the packages in the dream did not realize this heaviness. As long as the content of Adventism's package remained tightly sealed it didn't appear to be a heavy burden to those carrying it. It was only *after* the content of my package was ripped open and exposed to the light of the cross that the growing "weight" of Adventism's package became unbearable.

I remember well my *striving* in the dream to hold on to Adventism's package *after* the brown paper covering was ripped and the "package" contents exposed, because I supposed it was a "gift." Since Archie was the giver of that "gift", and was watching me from where he was seated next to the "center pillar," I didn't want to offend him by dropping it on the floor.

Unfortunately such striving to please God has *self* at the center, instead of Jesus. My striving caused me to focus on my behavior—what *I must do* in order to please my friend. Ultimately this kind of striving to please others around us leads us even more importantly to focus on what we must do in order to please God. We forget about everyone and everything else except the object of our striving. Ultimately striving is spiritual bondage. It is the opposite of *resting* in the Lord.

A Writhing Snake

But with every forward move that I made in the direction of the cross, the outer covering of Adventism's "package" continued to tear. The stack of twenty-some magazines continued to increase in weight, squirming and wriggling around in my arms like a writhing snake. I believe the Lord is saying through this imagery that when our foundational beliefs are exposed to the light of the cross—teachings that do not line up with the gospel will be exposed as falsehood so that we can be released from deception and no longer remain in slavery.

Remember how Satan disguised himself as a beautiful serpent in the Garden of Eden in order to deceive our first parents into distrusting God's love for them? In a similar way, Satan is being revealed (in the dream) for the writhing snake that he is. Through perpetuating the generational cycle of spiritual incest, the enemy has skillfully used the unbiblical teachings of Adventism to enslave generations of Adventists to old covenant law. The closer I moved towards the cross, the more uncomfortable the "father of lies" became, because the strongholds that were attached to the erroneous teachings suddenly became exposed by the light of the cross.

After the outer wrapping of the "package" finally fell to the ground, the magazines became like a twisted and distorted mountain of lead in my arms, forcing me to bend over double. When I could no longer bear the weight, I was forced to let go. Just as soon as I released my death-like grip on the *entire* "package" of twenty-some magazines, I watched them quickly slide across the floor, finally coming to rest at the foot of the cross. Although I was bent over double as if I had a millstone around my neck, the same unseen hand that had thrown me forwards on to the desk, now threw me backwards on to the floor, away from this supposed "gift" that had now become a "curse"—an unbearable burden.

Didn't Jesus talk about "things that cause people to sin are bound to come, but woe to that person through whom they come?" Didn't he say "it would be better for (that person) to be thrown into the sea with a millstone tied around his neck than for him to cause one of these little ones to sin" (Luke 17:1-2)? In other words, Jesus is saying that it would be better for that person to drown than for them to cause others to be led astray by their sin.

Hope in the Shadows

Sometime after receiving this dream I began an in-depth study of the old and new covenants of the Bible in order to learn how I was supposed to relate to them in regard to the Sabbath-rest of the fourth Commandment. Somewhere deep down inside of me I knew there was something I had been missing out on all these years in my Sabbath observance.

When I read in the book of Hebrews that "the law is only a shadow of the good things that are coming—not the realities themselves" (10:1), it was a familiar passage to me, but up until now the significance of it had never caught my attention before. Since the Sabbath is at the very center of the Ten Commandments, and the Ten Commandments are a part of the old covenant law, could the Sabbath also be a "shadow" pointing us to something even better (See Matthew 5:17-19), I reasoned?

Although I knew I had received a taste of that "something even better" as I lay resting in God's presence on the floor of the church, I thought initially it was an isolated experience. I didn't know that it was possible to experience this "rest" in His presence continually.

As I read and studied God's word for myself, I came across Dale Ratzlaff's book, "Sabbath in Christ."[1] For the first time in my life troubling questions regarding Sabbath observance and the old covenant biblical mandate to "remember" to keep it holy began to be answered one by one from the Scriptures.

Since the root meaning of Sabbath is *rest* and the primary purpose of the Sabbath is to provide rest, I decided to take a brief look at the religious celebrations of the old covenant. There were weekly Sabbaths (Leviticus 23:1-3), seasonal Sabbaths (Leviticus 23), and sabbatical years where even the land was to have a "Sabbath to the Lord" (Leviticus 25:1-7). In *all* of these "Sabbaths" work was prohibited and they were called "holy" or said to be a "Sabbath to the Lord."

As I took a further look at this sabbatical cycle I saw that the seventh day Sabbath was a weekly reminder of the coming seasonal Sabbaths. The seasonal Sabbaths were reminders of the coming sabbatical year. The sabbatical year was a reminder of the coming year of Jubilee—a high point in the sabbatical cycle time when the people of the covenant community were to experience a whole year of Sabbaths that was ushered in on the Day of Atonement.[2]

The year of Jubilee was supposed to be a joyous time of celebration and fellowship where records of debt were to be wiped clean and freedom was proclaimed to the captives! Among other things, they were to rest from sowing and reaping in the fields because God promised that the crop they planted in the sixth year would produce a crop for three years!

The Year of the Lord's Favor

Unfortunately, from reading the Scriptures it appears that this Jubilee was something that was written about but never experienced! Perhaps the people were too afraid of the economic monetary loss they imagined they would sustain should they not sow or reap (Leviticus 25:8-12, 20, 21). So the three-year's worth of blessings that they continually forfeited because of unbelief were not realized until Jesus walked into the temple in the power of the Spirit and picked up the scroll of the prophet Isaiah and began to read:

"The Spirit of the Lord is on me, because He has anointed me to preach good news to the poor. He has sent me to proclaim freedom for the captives and recovery of sight to the blind, to release the oppressed, to proclaim the year of the Lord's favor" (Luke 4:18-19).

Jesus announced that *He* was the fulfillment of the Jubilee that had been foretold by the prophet Isaiah (Isaiah 61:1-3). The Lord's favor rested upon *Him* when He walked into the temple on that day. For *three years* the Spirit of the Lord anointed *Him* to fulfill His Jubilee mission by freeing captives and releasing God's children into the joyous Good News of the gospel.

Now I understood more fully the exuberant joy I had experienced in the dream and that continued into the vision I was given when I awoke. I began to understand more fully not only the laughter I experienced then, but also the laughter I have experienced in the Spirit many times since that first time. The "laughter" meant freedom, deliverance, and release from bondage. I could laugh in the enemy's face knowing that Jesus has won—knowing that I have won because I choose to trust in what He has done for me on the cross. I choose to believe that it is Christ's righteousness alone that God is pleased with and accepts as if it were mine. What an awesome transaction!

Jesus is our Jubilee—He is our reason for living—He is our Everything! He is Jehovah Jireh—the Lord who provides—not just material provisions as He promised the children of Israel who were part of the old covenant community. No, far more than that. Clearly, by his life and death he has made provision for us to "rest"—to enter into the Sabbath, because He has done all the work that is necessary for our salvation. All of our needs are met in Him.

Working from a position of "rest"

During this time of studying the old and new covenants, God began impressing me in the spring of 2001 to make a Prayer Garden in my backyard. It was to be a place of sanctuary—to reflect what He had been teaching me about His "rest" as I waited on Him…

As I "toiled" tirelessly in my garden to make the vision God gave me a reality, I found I was "working" from a position of "rest." Although the work tested my physical endurance at times, it was always a joy to be part of what God was doing to bless others. I never felt I was performing or that the work I was doing needed His approval, because I was in His presence continually. Daily I was energized by the Spirit to continue the "work." Constantly the Spirit led me and showed me what to do next.

Through this experience of working in my garden to make it a place of sanctuary I learned how to enter into *His Garden* where the "work" has already been done. As I entered by faith into the "rest" of His grace

I found that it is a place where **no "work" is allowed.** For in *His Garden* the **"work" is already finished!** The only thing left for us to do is to enjoy sweet fellowship with Him as we hear Him calling us upon the gentle wind of His Spirit to enter more fully into the **"rest" that he has already provided**.

Then from this place of "rest" He shows us the "work" He has prepared in advance for us to do. From this place of "rest" where we abide in His presence continually, we "work". But it is not like the "work" we are use to performing under the old covenant—it is not heavy or burdensome. For His yoke it easy and His burden is light (Matthew 11:28-30).

As I would hear the soft cooing of turtledoves in the early morning or late afternoon hours, I would be reminded of how the Holy Spirit is drawing us to come into *His Garden* and find true intimacy as we enter into the "rest" of His grace. Can you hear the Lord calling you to come into His Garden and find rest? He is waiting for you with outstretched arms. He has placed you like a seal over His heart because His desire is always for you (Song of Solomon 8:6; 7:10).

"Arise, my darling, my beautiful one, and come with me. See! The winter is past; the rains are over and gone. Flowers appear on the earth; the season of singing has come, the cooing of doves is heard in our land... Arise, come my darling; my beautiful one, come with me" (Song of Solomon 2:10-13).

God is calling us to **"come" into His Garden and rest**. As we linger in His presence and enjoy close fellowship and intimacy with Him, He will heal our brokenness and restore our soul.

Rest for those who "believe"

For many years the presence of the Holy Spirit in my life had been healing my soul and restoring my brokenness as He drew me away from Sinai towards the cross. Suddenly, I began to see that the many old covenant teachings, including the Sabbath, must be understood from a new covenant perspective. The new covenant must always take precedence over the old because it is a "better" revelation. In these last days God has spoken to us by His Son who is the radiance of God's glory and the exact representation of God's nature (Hebrews 1:1-2).

As I continued to study the Scriptures I discovered that I had been trying to live in both worlds. I had been trying to hold on to some of the old covenant teachings regarding Sabbath observance while at the same time endeavoring to embrace the blessings of the new covenant gospel. I began to see that the two covenants were in direct conflict. I could not be a disciple of Moses and Jesus at the same time (John 9:28).

Under the old covenant, "rest" was mandated for the children of Israel on the seventh day of the week. But under the new covenant can't we enter into God's rest every day? "Therefore, God again set a certain day, calling it, Today... 'Today if you hear His voice, do not harden your hearts'" (Hebrews 4:7). The writer of Hebrews goes on to say, "For if Joshua could have given them rest, God would not have spoken later about another day. There remains, then, a Sabbath-rest for the people of God; for anyone who enters God's rest also rests from his own work, just as God did from His" (Hebrews 4:8-10).

A "Damascus Road" Experience

Suddenly I began to see why God slew me in the Spirit, not just once but twice in the dream. The Spirit knocked me over because I was trying to enter God's rest while frantically holding on to the ripped package of "magazines." I was clinging to my Adventist heritage—striving to please Him by my obedience.

Remembering how uncomfortable I had felt in the dream, it occurred to me that God had removed the chair from the desk I was draped over because He wants to teach us that before we can sit down and experience the "rest" of His grace we must first let go of what we have in our hands. As long as we strive to hold onto any lists of "good works," we have fallen from grace. Our acceptance with God is based upon Christ's obedience, not ours.

Even after I was slain the first time in this dream, I still refused to let go of Archie's "gift," preferring instead to hold on to it so as not to offend his feelings. How many of us in the church have held on to erroneous teachings for fear of upsetting friends, family or those in authority in the church? It was only after Adventism's package became unbearably heavy, and I was forced to let go of it that the Lord slew me again, separating me from the terrible weight I had been carrying.

In the dream I remember trying to count the number of magazines that fell out of my hands, but I couldn't get an accurate number because of the way they overlapped each other as they slid across the floor towards the cross. Perhaps the reason God did not give me a specific number of magazines (but left it at "twenty-something") was that the number has been changing over the years, and indeed He knew it would change again by the time this book came to print.

Every Adventist knows what I am talking about. This package of twenty-something magazines represents the twenty-eight Fundamental Beliefs[3] of the SDA church that initially appears to be a "gift" that we have been given. While some of the 28 Fundamental Beliefs of the church have some truth in them, the Adventist system that issues out lists of rules, and dictates 28 beliefs is not one that is based on the simple belief of what Christ has done for us. In other words, how we treat and practice these fundamental beliefs is not done from a position of resting in Christ's finished work.

This *packaging* of "truth" (mixture of truth and error) identifies who we are in such a way as to keep us separate from the rest of the body of Christ. That is why Adventism's *whole* package must be released at the foot of the cross, for God is calling the *whole* body of Christ to become unified in Him. What we are holding on to as SDAs prevents us from coming into unity with the body so that Christ's prayer for us in John 17 can be answered.

I believe these encounters I experienced were something like Saul of Tarsus experienced when he was "slain by the Spirit" on his way to Damascus. God had abruptly stopped his plans to continue persecuting believers who belonged to the Way. Like Saul, I was also unknowingly "persecuting" Him by wanting to take Adventism's package and pass on its errors to the next generation.

Like a bolt of lightening the cycle of spiritual incest in the SDA church became crystal clear! God had abruptly stopped me [an incest survivor] from passing on this package of unbiblical teachings that had been passed down to me from Archie, [another incest survivor]. Why? So that I, a third generation SDA, wouldn't continue the cycle of spiritual incest by passing on unbiblical teachings that pervert and undermine the gospel to the next generation of "handicapped students", and cause them to become victims of spiritual incest, too.

The Spirit of the Lord stopped me dead in my tracks because the SDA church, like Saul, has been persecuting Jesus Christ! Generations of SDA's have become "handicapped" by unbelief because they failed to recognize the truth of Christ's finished work on the cross. Only the liberating power of the gospel of Jesus Christ can break open this terrible cycle of abuse that has robbed so many of the joy of their salvation.

Isn't the Holy Spirit teaching us that as soon as we release our death-like grip on Adventism's package, and let it fall at the foot of the cross, we will be instantly catapulted into the "rest" of His grace? As soon as the heavy burden was removed from me in the dream I suddenly understood the laughter and exuberant joy of the two children who were thrown off the mountain and flew somersaulting through the air towards the open sea. I had finally become one of them—free from the heavy weight of bondage I had unknowingly been striving to hold on to.

As I lay on the floor "resting" in this new freedom and joy in God's presence, I began to identify with the woman in the Bible who had been healed from a long-term infirmity that had caused her to be bent over double (Luke 13:10-17). I understood the thankfulness in her heart and why she began glorifying God the moment she was healed, because it mirrored my own thankfulness the moment I was released from the bondage of Adventism I had been carrying for many years. How appropriate that Jesus should overthrow the power of Satan on the Sabbath, and restore both of us "daughters of Abraham" to the "rest" that is available for "those who believe."[4] The prophet Isaiah tells us that Jesus came to "untie the cords of the yoke [of bondage], to set the oppressed free and break every yoke" (Isaiah 58:6). That's what Jesus did for me.

This "rest" I experienced as I lay on the floor of the church laughing was an abiding assurance, an exhilarating knowing that my sins—everyone's sins were forgiven *in* Christ. I knew that God had already taken care of the sin problem—forever. I was "resting" in the knowledge that God's Son had already defeated the enemy. The wonder and expectant joy that filled my soul as I worshipped Him and experienced His awesome presence cannot be adequately described in human words. I entered into a secret and most glorious place of "rest" that I had not known before—a "rest" that my soul had always longed for, The Sabbath.

No Biblical mandate to Rest

As I thought about the old covenant "reminders" to rest that God had ordained for His covenant people, Israel, they were like mini rest stops along the way designed to keep hope alive in their hearts—hope in the coming Messiah.[5] But now that the Messiah has come, do these mini rest stops along the way continue to serve the purpose for which they were originally intended? Now that the Messiah has come is there still a biblical mandate to "remember" to observe and celebrate these old covenant weekly, monthly and seasonal reminders to "rest"? Particularly, are we still to "remember" the Sabbath day of the fourth commandment by keeping it holy? Is this old covenant command still binding upon new covenant Christians today?

The conflict I began to experience in my study of the Sabbath was that the things I had been taught about the Sabbath in growing up in the SDA church didn't line up with the Scriptures. The rules I had been taught to observe to "keep" the Sabbath day holy I learned would have either meant nothing to Adam and Eve in the Garden of Eden, or they were something that would have been natural for them to do without being told.[6]

God placed them in the Garden to work it and take care of it, but the "work" they were called to do was not "work" as we know it (Genesis 2:15). They didn't need to "rest" from "toiling" by the sweat of their brow for the ground produced no thorns or thistles that would make their "work" painful. They didn't need to make fires to keep themselves warm or even to cook. What's more, they were in perfect communion and fellowship with their Creator every day. In the Garden, Adam and Eve lived in His presence and so "worked" from a position of "resting" in all that God had lovingly provided for all of their needs.

All these Sabbath rules that I had been taught to observe regarding the seventh-day Sabbath didn't apply to Adam and Eve at all, but rather to the children of Israel after God had delivered them from Egyptian bondage. In fact it seemed that the Sabbath laws God gave Israel were designed to encourage the children of Israel to "rest" very much like Adam and Eve "rested" in Eden *before* they sinned. The mini rest stops along the way that God provided for them were designed, not only to point them back to Edenic rest, but also point them forward to the fulfillment of the Edenic rest that would be found in Christ alone.

Furthermore, since the Genesis account of creation does not mention an end to God's seventh-day rest (See Genesis 2:1-3), could it mean that the conditions that existed on that seventh day were intended to last forever? When sin interrupted that "rest" Adam and Eve were excluded from God's presence, and so God began the "work" of restoring man back to Himself. This "work" began when God clothed them with garments of skin from a lamb (Genesis 3:21), and this "work" continued throughout the centuries until its significance would be fully realized in the death of Jesus Christ—when the True Lamb of God would clothe all His children with the eternal and perfect Lamb Skin.

That "work" was accomplished—finished through the death of His Son. God has graciously provided *everything* that is necessary for our salvation, just as He graciously provided *everything* for Adam and Eve in the Garden. There is *nothing left for us to do* but to enjoy His gracious provision.

No longer banned from His presence because of our sin, we can now enter boldly into His presence—into His "rest"—by the blood of Jesus Christ. I believe that God's actions toward me in the dream reveal the longing in His heart to be in constant fellowship with His redeemed new creation by His Spirit.

Apparently, merely the "remembering" or the "keeping" of a certain day does not guarantee us that we will experience the "rest" the writer of Hebrews is talking about. The children of Israel did that but they never entered His "rest." I had done that for most of my life, but I never entered His "rest." Although there are obvious benefits to a corporate day of worship, such as bodily renewal, fellowship with our Creator and one another through worship and praise, but this spiritual exercise in itself is not "rest."

"Rest" of the New Covenant Gospel

So what is the "rest" that the writer of Hebrews is talking about? It is the "rest" that has been available in Christ ever since the creation of this world. It is the "rest" that Adam and Eve experienced in Eden before they sinned as they fellowshipped in unbroken communion with God. It is the "rest" I experienced as I lay on the floor near the foot of the cross "resting" from my "work" of striving to hold on to Adventism's "gift." It is the "rest" of the new covenant gospel.

When Jesus Christ came, very few recognized Him or received Him for who He was. Not until after His death did the words He had spoken regarding the "rest" make sense. Not until the promised Holy Spirit was released on the day of Pentecost did these familiar words begin to find a true resting-place in the hearts of those who had ears to hear. Let us read them again now with new insight.

"Come to Me, all you who are weary and burdened, and *I will give you rest.* Take My yoke upon you and learn from Me, for I am gentle and humble in heart, and *you will find rest for your souls.* For My yoke is easy and My burden is light" (Matthew 11:28-30).

As Jesus looked upon the multitudes of people surrounding Him on a daily basis, it must have been obvious to Him that the people were still striving to earn God's favor, as their forefathers had done, by carrying heavy burdens. As we look in the Scriptures for the context in which Jesus spoke these familiar words we see that He had been denouncing the cities in which most of His miracles had been performed because they did not repent. We discover that He contrasts the "wise and learned" that are unrepentant with the innocence of "little children" to whom He reveals His secrets (Matthew 11:20-25).

Then He goes on to explain to the Pharisees, who are accusing His disciples of breaking the Sabbath that One greater than Moses or the Temple is here speaking to them (Matthew 12:1-8). If they had only known the Lord of the Sabbath desired mercy and not sacrifice. If they had only known the Holy One of Israel would rather they acknowledge Him than offer any more burnt offerings (Hosea 6:6; Matthew 12: 6-8).

Seven hundred years earlier the One who was speaking these words to them had spoken through the prophet Isaiah saying, "In repentance and rest is your salvation, in quietness and trust is your strength, but you would have none of it" (Isaiah 30:15). Like their forefathers, the Pharisees continued to reject Christ's offer of "rest" for their souls. Instead, they preferred to carry heavy burdens and require others to do the same.

Notice what they asked Jesus: "What must we do to do the works God requires?" His reply was direct and simple, "The work of God is this: to *believe* in the One He has sent" (John 6:28-29).

Like our spiritual forbearers the dream reveals that many SDAs in the church today are in a similar predicament. They are also seeking to earn God's favor by striving to hold on to Adventism's "package". So "what must we do to do the works God requires?" God's reply to us today is the same as He gave the people in Christ's day: "Believe in the One I have sent!" "Whoever believes in [Me] will not be disappointed" (Romans 10:11).

Striving is the Opposite of "Rest"

Paul dealt with this burden of "striving" to obey old covenant law in the Council at Jerusalem by confronting some Jewish believers who belonged to the party of the Pharisees. These Jewish believers came down to Antioch insisting that gentile Christians couldn't be saved unless they were circumcised. For the Jew, submitting to circumcision meant they were in subjection to the whole law. These Jews wanted gentile Christians to be in accordance with the "custom taught by Moses," because "circumcision has value if you observe the law" (Acts 15:1-5; Romans 2:25). When a proselyte was circumcised he accepted the yoke of Jewish law, and was "obligated to obey the **whole** law" (Galatians 5:3).[7]

But Peter got up and addressed these Jews that came down from Antioch saying, "Now then, why do you try to test God by putting on the necks of the [gentile] disciples a yoke that neither we nor our fathers have been able to *bear?* No! We believe it is through the grace of our Lord Jesus that we are saved, just as they are" (Acts 15:10-11).

The "yoke" mentioned in this verse refers to the old covenant. The context of this passage also implies that this yoke is a heavy yoke that makes us weary and heavy-laden. It is a yoke that neither the Jews of New Testament times, nor their forefathers were able to bear. It is a yoke that neither you nor I is able to bear. The symbolic action in the dream of my trying to hold on to the "yoke of Adventism" confirms this.

What will it take for this present generation of SDAs to admit that they are weary and heavy burdened and need to come to God to receive His "rest"? Only those who choose to "*believe* in the One He has sent" will enter into that rest, *not* by the things that they do, *not* by their works, but *by faith* in the righteousness that He has already provided. We enter that "rest" by the simple act of *believing* that **Jesus is greater than Moses**—by believing what God has already done for us in Jesus Christ.

Under the new covenant we no longer have to wait until the end of the week before we can "believe in the One He has sent" and enter into God's rest. In fact, the writer of the book of Hebrews encourages us as new covenant believers to rejoice in God's rest *continually*. To be *in* Christ means we are resting *in* Him daily. "Through Him then let us continually offer up a sacrifice of praise to God, that is, the fruit of lips that give thanks to His name" (Hebrews 13:15).

The Better Sabbath-Rest

The better "Sabbath rest" that God is revealing in this dream is the "rest" of trusting in Christ's *finished* work of redemption. Just as God ceased from His work of creation, so we are to cease from our works of striving to fulfill old covenant law (See Exodus 31:17; Hebrews 4:3-4). He alone can bring us the "rest" of His grace. "To Him who loves us and has freed us from our sins by His blood… to Him be glory and power forever and ever! Amen" (Revelation 1:5-6).

Those who "enter" by faith alone into His salvation find rest for their souls and receive "the seal of God". Hebrews 4:6-9 assures us that "some will enter that rest." The prophet Isaiah looks forward to this day and proclaims, "His place of rest will be glorious" (Isaiah 11:10).

Since the blood of Christ's sacrifice has canceled the debt of our sins, He is calling us, both individually and as a community of believers, into a gracious and intimate fellowship with Himself. This close fellowship of resting in Him remains for the one who believes in Him. "Therefore, since the promise of entering His rest still stands, let us be careful that none of [us] be found to have fallen short of it" (Hebrews 4:1).

Let us not be like the children of Israel who rebelled against the Lord in the desert. Although they had the gospel preached to them, they did not share in the faith of those who obeyed. As a result, "the message they heard was of no value to them, because those who heard it did not combine it with faith" (Hebrews 4:2). The generation of Israelites that left Egypt never entered into the Promised Land. Their sinful, unbelieving hearts turned away from the living God, and eventually they all died in the wilderness—all except faithful Caleb and Joshua (Hebrews 3:12-14).

Although they followed the command to keep the Sabbath and punished those who disobeyed, they did *not* enter "His rest" (Numbers 15:32-36; Hebrews 3:16-19). They failed to look beyond the "shadow" that was pointing them to something better. They failed to put their faith in the coming Reality—Jesus Christ.

The Testing Truth

As I continued to carefully study the New Testament Scriptures from my newfound place of "rest," I found that the Scriptures allow no room for Sabbath-keeping to be a testing truth for new covenant believers. The testing truth for all new covenant believers is NOT the Sabbath of the fourth commandment as I had been taught in Adventism, but faith in Jesus Christ's righteousness alone. Even though Ellen White wrote that Sabbath observance is the seal that separates those who are saved from those who are lost,[8] this teaching cannot be supported from Scripture. Only in the old covenant was the Sabbath a sign or seal between God and the sons of Israel—not in the new covenant (Exodus 31:13, 17; Ezekiel 20: 12, 20)

The following Scriptures confirm that in the new covenant the Holy Spirit is the seal of God, which the Christian receives when he believes.

- "Now it is God who makes both us and you stand firm in Christ. He anointed us, set His seal of ownership on us, and put His Spirit in our hearts as a deposit, guaranteeing what is to come" (1 Corinthians 1:21-22).
- "And you also were included in Christ when you heard the word of truth, the gospel of your salvation. Having believed, you were marked in him with a seal, the promised Holy Spirit, who is a deposit guaranteeing our inheritance until the redemption of those who are God's possession—to the praise of His glory" (Ephesians 1: 13, 14).
- "And do not grieve the Holy Spirit of God, by whom you were sealed for the day of redemption" (Ephesians 4:30).
- "God... has given us the Spirit as a deposit, guaranteeing what is to come." (2 Corinthians 5:5).

Clearly, our good behavior does *not* determine our eternal destiny or our acceptance with God. Therefore, Sabbath-keeping does *not* entitle us to favor with God, because "He saved us, not on the basis of deeds that we have done in righteousness, but according to His mercy, by the washing of regeneration and renewing of the Holy Spirit" (Titus 3:5). "For we maintain that a man is justified by faith apart from works of law" (Romans 3:28). "You have been severed from Christ, you who are seeking to be justified by law; you have fallen from grace" (Galatians 5:4).

New wine and old wineskins

In a parable that Jesus told He reveals how prone we are to believe that the "old order" of things is better. "No one tears a patch from a new garment and sews it on to an old one. If he does, he will have torn the new garment, and the patch from the new will not match the old. And no one pours new wine into old wineskins. If he does, the new wine will burst the skins, the wine will run out and the wineskins will be ruined. No, new wine must be poured into new wineskins. And no one after drinking old wine wants the new, for he says, 'The old is better.'" Luke 5:36-38).

Through this parable we can see that Jesus knew the hearts of His children. He knew that so many of us would try to hold on to the old wineskin of old covenant law believing it to be better than the new wineskin of the new covenant gospel. He knew that in the natural realm old wine tastes better than new wine. That was why the people at the wedding in Cana where Jesus performed His first miracle were so surprised when they tasted the new wine. The old wine—the good wine was always served first, but at this wedding the best wine *was served last!* Do you see the prophetic picture? Jesus was declaring Himself to be the New Wine—the Best Wine. The Son of God was declaring Himself to be God's final Word.

Jesus is saying through this parable that although we have been accustomed to drinking "old wine," believing the "old" is better, He has come to show us that the "new wine" of the new covenant gospel is far better than the old wine of old covenant law. He is defying our expectations just like He surprised the guests at the wedding feast by showing us that the new wine—what came later is better. Indeed, the host of the wedding banquet did serve his best wine at the beginning. But like the glory of the new covenant (2 Corinthians 3), the New Wine surpasses the old! We thought we had great wine through Moses, but it doesn't begin to compare with the New Wine of the Spirit.

Drunk on Old Wine

The host at a wedding usually serves the best wine (the old) and then as the night wears on, serves cheaper wine. The host hopes that the people will be so drunk they won't notice the wine has gotten less glorious. Isn't that drunkenness like Moses putting the veil over his face so that the Israelites couldn't see the fading glory?

In a similar vein is it possible that leaders in Adventism have been veiling people's minds—making the old covenant *seem* glorious when it isn't? Have we been intoxicating ourselves by drinking this old wine, afraid of facing the truth that deep inside (under the veil) we know the glory of the old covenant is dead and fading? For the only way we can possibly imagine that the old wine (old covenant) is better is for our judgment to remain clouded—veiled!

Releasing Old Wineskins

Since the Scriptures tell us that God cannot pour His new wine into an old wineskin because if He does it will burst, we must let go of our old wineskins and receive the new. We cannot mix the old with the new. SDAs must stop trying to make their old covenant understanding of the Sabbath fit into the new wineskin of the new covenant gospel. It can't. Trying to do this only brings chaos and confusion as we have already seen from Adventism's history.

Scripture makes it very clear that it was the work of Jesus to provide the righteousness we needed. It was the work of Jesus to receive the curse of the broken law. But it is our work to *believe* in Him—to let the New Wine fill our new wineskin. "Before this faith came, we were held prisoners by the law, locked up until faith should be revealed" (Galatians 3:23). But now that Christ has come we are no longer held prisoners by the law—we are no longer locked up because He has supernaturally opened that locked door! He is now the Door we must enter by faith into the blessings of the new covenant gospel—without works.[9]

"The flickering candle of truth which lighted the shadowy pathways of Old Testament history must give way to the unveiled glory of the risen Son!"[10] All the "shadows" of the old covenant pointed towards the coming Reality. In Christ alone we now find true freedom and spiritual "rest" for our souls.

New Covenant Remembrance

Although under the old covenant people were to "remember the Sabbath," under the new covenant Jesus reminds us to celebrate the

Lord's Supper in *remembrance* of Him who is our Sabbath rest (Luke 22:19; 1 Corinthians 11:23-26). We are to remember His body that was broken for us. He says of Himself: "I am the living bread that came down from heaven. If anyone eats of this bread, he will live forever. This bread is my flesh, which I will give for the life of the world… I tell you the truth, unless you eat the flesh of the Son of Man and drink His blood, you have no life in you… Just as the living Father sent me and I live because of the Father, so the one who feeds on me will live because of me… The words I have spoken to you are spirit and they are life. Yet there are some of you who do not believe" (John 6:51-57, 63-64).

Having the Sabbath be our focus of attention instead of our Redeemer, Jesus Christ, takes away from fellowship with the One to whom the law pointed. We undermine our standing in Christ when we continue to worship weak and worthless shadows. Intimate fellowship with God is available to us now through the Spirit because of the new covenant of grace.

We can spend time daily *with* our heavenly bridegroom in honest, intimate fellowship with Him instead of just looking at His picture one day a week. The new "rest" allows us to enter by faith daily into God's Sabbath-rest. Our "work" is to *believe in Him*, and in so doing we enter into the blessings of the new covenant and find Sabbath-rest for our souls.

Spiritual Blindness

In John's gospel a story is told that illustrates for us the true nature of the Sabbath-rest of the new covenant into which Jesus is calling SDAs to enter. In this story Jesus healed a man who was born blind. Have many SDAs been born blind because of spiritual incest issues that have been passed on from one generation to the next? The Scriptures tell us the reason this man was born blind was so that "the works of God might be displayed in him" (John 9:3). Has God allowed this generational spiritual abuse to go on in the SDA church so that the works of God might be displayed in the lives of those who become free from their spiritual blindness? I believe so.

We are all familiar with the paradoxical nature of this story. It clearly illustrates for us the contrast between the striving of the Pharisees, and the lack of striving on the part of the blind beggar. The

Pharisees' meticulous observance of the Sabbath laws was like a strangling yoke around their necks, binding them to their religious traditions and practices. In striving hard to obtain acceptance from God, they failed miserably. Their striving in fact caused them to reject their Messiah.

On the other hand, this blind beggar did not strive. His healing and acceptance with God was the result of God's sovereign grace. Jesus gave this new believer a revelation of truth that met his deepest needs. He revealed Himself. Immediately this healed beggar fell down and worshipped Him. This previously blind man confessed himself on the side of Jesus even though he *knew* he would be put out of the synagogue.

Since he had found rest and intimacy in face-to-face fellowship with Jesus, nothing else mattered. Jesus' healing presence had met the deepest need of his heart and brought the restoration for which his soul longed. He instantly became a new creation *in* Christ Jesus. Old things passed away because the new had come (2 Corinthians 5:17). It will be the same with us. Worshiping Him will become our highest priority and greatest joy.

It appears from this story that Jesus intentionally healed this blind beggar in such a way that His actions would be seen to be in direct violation of Sabbath law, as the Jews understood it. Doesn't it appear from what we have discovered from God's Word that the new wine of the gospel will NOT fit within the present day structure of Adventism any better than it would fit within the rigid framework of Judaism? Through the healing of this blind man, Jesus desperately sought to reach the hearts of His hearers with the truth of who He was.[11] He is still doing the same today. He is still continuing to do the "work" that His Father called Him to do—***releasing captives!***

Paul reminds us that whenever Moses is read through old covenant understanding, a veil lies over our eyes; but whenever we turn to the Lord, the veil is taken away (2 Corinthians 3:15-16). In other words, Paul is saying that unless the old covenant is interpreted by the new covenant, the reader will not understand it correctly. The verses in the following passage provide us with a deeper insight into the true nature of the Sabbath rest that God is calling all His children to enter into.

After Jesus had healed the blind man he said, "For judgment I have come into this world, so that the blind will see and those who see will become blind." Some Pharisees who were with Him heard Him say this and asked, "What? Are we blind too?" Jesus said, "If you were blind, you would not be guilty of sin, but now that you claim you can see, your guilt remains" (John 9:39-41).

These tragic words of Jesus serve as a solemn warning to this present generation of SDAs standing at the "shut door" of the church, clinging to Mt. Sinai for their reference point of life and judgment. For Adventists who continue to worship God according to the "old order of things", these are very sad and fearful words.

If you identify with the spiritually blind Pharisees who failed to enter into God's true "rest," I pray that you will let go of the shadow to embrace the Real, and become like the humble blind beggar who was healed by the "work" of Jesus on that Sabbath day. Release your "package" of bondage at the foot of the cross, and enter into the true Sabbath-rest of God *without works*. Enter by faith into the "rest" that "remains" for the one who believes. Enter into Jesus Christ—the true "rest" of God!

Endnotes: Chapter 6

[1] Former edition was titled, "Sabbath in Crisis."
[2] Dale Ratzlaff, *Sabbath in Christ* (Life Assurance Ministries, January 2003) 66.
[3] Twenty-seven "fundamental beliefs" were recently expanded to 28.
[4] Ratzlaff 130.
[5] Ibid., 77.
[6] Ibid., 71-77. See also http://sabbath-rest.blogspot.com/2006/04/work-in-garden-of-his-rest.html.
[7] Ellen G. White, *The Great Controversy Between Christ and Satan* (Mountain View, California: Pacific Press Publishing Association, 1950) 605. Revised edition first published 1911.
[8] Ratzlaff 416.
[9] Ibid., 163-173.

There's nothing left for me to do but enjoy His "good work," and enter by faith into the rest" that He has provided for the one who believes.

Chapter 7: The Vision
ENTERING THE SCHOOL OF THE SPIRIT

But when He, the Spirit of truth, comes, He will guide you into all truth."
John 16:13

My exuberant laughter finally woke me up from this remarkable dream I received on April 11, 1996 (the focus of the past six chapters). I was filled with such unspeakable joy after releasing my brown paper "package" at the foot of the cross that I could not stop laughing. For the first time in my life I *knew* what it meant to "rest" in God's presence. After all, He has done all the work. There's nothing left for me to do but enjoy His "good work," and enter by faith into the "rest" that He has provided for the one who believes. As I continued to bask in His presence the Lord suddenly appeared to me in a vision—a series of vivid images appearing while I was awake and very aware. I believe God is calling us in our "sleep" to wake up and put on Jesus Christ. Then we will *see* clearly who He is and what He has already done for us.

First Scene: Our High Priest

Jesus appeared before me standing in a beautiful white cloud. I had to shield my eyes at first because the light and glory that emanated from His very being was so intense, like the brightness of the sun. As I continued to fix my gaze upon Him, I could see nothing else but Jesus. He was *smiling* at me! He was *laughing*, too!

I was filled with awe and wonder as I looked into His kind and compassionate eyes. His brown shoulder-length wavy hair framed a strong yet tender, kingly yet humble, smiling face. The radiance of His being penetrated my very soul. I felt the love of His heart being poured out for me, His child.

I noticed that He was dressed in the royal garments of a high priest. The colors in His blue robe were magnificent, and the jewels in the breastplate dazzled my eyes. On his head He wore a tall, shining, gold crown instead of the high priest's miter.

Then He purposefully raised His hands and began to slowly remove His blue outer garment. Underneath this outer garment [ephod] was a pure white linen robe. Although the breastplate was worn on top of the ephod, it was *not* removed. It somehow continued to remain in the same position over His heart. As He *continued to smile* intently upon me, I heard the familiar words, "...let him who is holy be holy still" (Revelation 22:11). Then the scene gradually faded.

Second Scene: An Adventist Keepsake

In this second scene of the vision I saw a large, gold picture frame. Inside the ornate, metal frame was an empty gold canvass. At the left bottom corner of the canvass was a sculpture the size of a playing card. The sculpture was of a little baby with only a swaddling cloth wrapped around his loins. Immediately I thought of the humble beginnings of Christ's birth. As I looked at this antique sculpture, I was reminded of the bronzing process that is done to preserve a baby's first pair of shoes. This baby sculpture, as well as the background, looked like it had been bronzed with a high lustrous gold finish, sealing the baby's pose to preserve it for years to come.

While I contemplated what God might be saying through this bronzed sculpture, suddenly the baby began to move. As I watched, countless sculptured scenes from Christ's life began to pass before me as if someone was dealing a deck of cards. Every sculpture within every scene was the size of a playing card and appeared to be bronzed with many layers of a high lustrous gold finish like the first sculpture of the little Baby.

As I watched, the Baby sculpture quickly grew up. Immediately a new scene of Jesus laughing and playing with other children covered up the earlier scene of the Baby sculpture. Instantly this second scene was followed by a third scene of Jesus working in the carpenter shop that quickly covered up the previous childhood scene, and so on. I noticed that the movement of the sculptures within each scene appeared to be labored as if they were having difficulty moving freely.

Then quite suddenly, after I saw Jesus in several scenes ministering to the multitudes of people, it was impossible to see the sculptured scenes that were lain down in front of me anymore. They were coming so rapidly that each consecutive scene of Christ's life overlapped the previous one so I could no longer see the full scene.

This rapid succession of sculptured scenes continued to be lain down in a long row that stretched off at some distance to the right of me until the last two scenes appeared. They came down in slow motion—the cross and the grave. A hazy film appeared to cover them, preventing me from clearly seeing the images. As I watched this unfold, I eagerly waited for the final scene to be shown—the resurrection. But it never appeared and I was left disappointed.

As the vision began to slowly fade, I was left with the impression that these countless sculptured scenes of Christ's life were originally intended to be mounted inside the ornate, gold frame that I had seen around the first baby sculpture. They had been sealed and preserved against tarnish so they would maintain their brilliant gold luster when passed on to the next generation of SDAs as a beautiful *keepsake*.

But that was no longer possible after the sculptured scenes "came to life." The growing pile of overlapped scenes that was stacking up outside of the gold picture frame was never going to fit inside the intended area. Whoever had gone to all this trouble to preserve these lifeless sculptures decided to quickly "cover them up" the moment they "came to life".

Third Scene: A Fisher of Men

After this second scene faded, I saw the simple outline of fish being drawn one after another by an unseen hand. The image suddenly appeared in mid-air, as if it was being slowly drawn on a child's magic slate. As I watched, the child-like drawings of fish continued to multiply. I heard the familiar words; "Follow Me and I will make you a fisher of men!" Again this scene too gradually faded.

Fourth Scene: Hiding Your Head in the Sand

Thinking the vision was over I sat up in bed and grabbed a pad of paper, eager to write down what I had just been shown. I didn't want to forget the details of the scenes I had just witnessed. Since I was having difficulty controlling my hand because there was still some shaking, I asked the Lord if there was anything else that He wanted to show me. There was!

Immediately the Lord showed me a very large ostrich, hurriedly trying to hide its head in the sand. Then quite unexpectedly it stood up, turned its head to the left and looked right at me. For a fleeting moment I felt great fear as the very large bird stared at me with an icy cold yet penetrating look. As the final scene of the vision began to fade I heard these words from the Lord in my mind: *"Don't hide your face because you think you appear foolish to others. Stand erect and tall in Me!"*

Only **after** we have released the "old order of things" at the foot of the cross will we be able to enter by faith into the "new order of things".

Chapter 8
I SAW HIS GLORY

*"... by one sacrifice He has made perfect forever those
who are being made holy."*
Hebrews 10:14

For seven years I found myself standing before a "shut door" in my mind, not able to fully grasp the significance of this vision that immediately followed the dream of April 11, 1996. Like Adventism's spiritual forbearers, I was also stuck and unable to move forward because a veil had to be lifted from my own mind before I recognized that this vision was an outline of what God wants to teach the body of Adventism *after* we release Adventism's bondage at the foot of the cross. God desires to transform the church into a classroom as we choose to become students in the School of the Spirit.

Understanding the meaning of this first scene of the vision was the *key* that opened the "locked door" of my mind so that I could understand the meaning of the dream—a portrayal of past and present generations of SDAs stuck in erroneous teachings and old covenant interpretations of Scripture with a "shut door" mentality. Just as Old Testament Scriptures must be interpreted from a new covenant perspective, I saw that the bondage revealed in the dream must be released at the foot of the cross as God's Spirit opens people's hearts to see that the new covenant is a better covenant built on better promises.

The Good News of what Jesus Christ has done for us demands a response. We will no longer be able to remain neutral in our devotion to God once we understand the call of the Spirit that God is bringing through this revelation of Jesus Christ as our High Priest. Only *after* we have released the "old order of things" at the foot of the cross will we be able to enter by faith into the "new order of things"—the new covenant gospel of Jesus Christ and His finished work of grace that brings the fullness of the Spirit.

Jesus only

In the first scene of this vision I saw Jesus Christ "transfigured" before me in His royal priestly robes. As I fixed my gaze upon Him, I could see nothing else in the room, but Him. He was *smiling* at me! He was *laughing*, too!

I believe the Holy Spirit wants us to understand that as we fix our gaze upon the Risen Son who is our High Priest, the Author and Finisher of a *new* and *better* covenant, everything else will fade away. The glory of His manifest presence changes everything. The cares of this life will be put into proper perspective when seen through the blood. The ordinary tasks of life must not cause us to stay away from His presence lest our eyes adjust and we go back to what we had previously considered "normal" [the bondage of the dream]. Nothing will be "normal" again after being in His presence. Once we see the vision of His glory nothing in this world will ever satisfy us again.

This scene reminded me of the disciples' response after Jesus was transfigured before them. When they heard a voice from out of the cloud say, "This is My Son… Listen to Him!" they fell to the ground terrified. Then when Jesus came and touched them and they looked up, they saw no one but Jesus. It will be the same with us when His Spirit touches us. Everything that has held us captive before will disappear when it comes into the light of His manifest presence.

In this scene of the vision Jesus was pictured both as our High Priest, and also as our King. He is our Royal High Priest, after the order of Melchizedek, not after the order of Aaron. His priesthood is not based on human lineage, but on His holy and righteous character. Melchizedek was the only example of royal priesthood in the Old Testament in which royalty and priesthood were blended successfully. All other attempts failed. Although Melchizedek was without a Levitical father and mother, he was called by God to be His representative in a pagan city, and was considered to be a type of Christ (Hebrews 7:3).

Hebrews 7:1 tells us that Melchizedek's name means "king of righteousness" and also "king of peace". Jesus Christ, our Great High Priest is also "King of Righteousness" and "King of Peace", "not on the basis of a regulation as to His ancestry (tribe of Judah) but on the basis of the power of an indestructible life. For it is declared: 'You are a Priest forever, in the order of Melchizedek.' Therefore He [Jesus Christ] is able to save completely those who come to God through Him because He always lives to intercede for them" (Hebrews 7:15-16, 25).

In a similar way, all those who come to Jesus are called to be His "royal priesthood" of believers, who walk not after the flesh, but after the Spirit. They walk not after the order of Aaron, not after the "old order of things," but after the order of Melchizedek, after the "new order of things"—Jesus Christ" (1 Peter 2:9).

Garments of Salvation

As I considered the high priestly garments that I saw Jesus Christ wearing in this scene, I realized He was wearing the garments of salvation. The white linen tunic that was beneath the elaborate outer blue garments represents His righteousness. "For He has clothed me in garments of salvation and arrayed me in a robe of righteousness…" (Isaiah 61:10). God no longer sees us as slave children, but sons and daughters dressed in the fine robe of Christ's righteousness. John alludes to this in Revelation as he witnesses the wedding of the Lamb about to take place: "Fine linen, bright and clean, was given [the bride] to wear" (Revelation 19:8).

The white sash around His waist and the sash of blue, purple, scarlet and gold that bound the ephod to his chest will be His belt and faithfulness the sash around His waist" (Isaiah 11:5). "Stand firm then with the belt of truth buckled around your waist" (Ephesians 6:14). The Spirit wants us to know who we are in Jesus Christ. He is the belt of Truth that keeps us focused on Him instead of ourselves.

Trophies of His Grace

As I looked at the outer garments that I had seen Jesus wearing, my eyes were drawn to the embroidered shoulder pieces of the ephod, because of the reflected light that appeared to come from them. As I looked in the Scriptures in order to understand what I had seen and what it represented, I discovered that two onyx stones mounted in gold settings were attached to the shoulder pieces of the ephod. Engraved in these stones were the names of the sons of Israel (Exodus 28:9-12).

Doesn't the parallel become stunningly clear? Shoulders are meant for carrying. So Jesus Christ, our High Priest carries His people upon His shoulders. "Let the beloved of the Lord *rest secure in Him*... and the one whom the Lord loves *rests* between His shoulders" (Deuteronomy 33:12). Just as the names of the twelve tribes of Israel were inscribed upon the two onyx stones worn upon the high priest's shoulders, so are the names of God's children who make up spiritual Israel, the church, carried upon Christ's shoulders.

Jesus illustrated this parallel for us in His parable of the lost sheep, when He told His audience that the lost sheep is joyfully placed upon the shepherd's shoulders and carried home (Luke 15:5). The psalmist, David, echoes this same theme when he exclaims, "Save your people and bless your inheritance; be their shepherd and carry them forever" (Psalm 28:9). The lost sheep is an example of a trophy of His grace. We are all trophies of His grace—trophies of the new covenant gospel.

"For to us...a Son is given, and the government will be on *His shoulders*. And He will be called Wonderful Counselor, Mighty God, Everlasting Father, Prince of Peace" (Isaiah 9:6). For "I will place on *His shoulder* the key to the house of David; what He opens no one can shut, and what he shuts no one can open" (Isaiah 22:22). Jesus is the Key.

Our Names upon His Heart

The final outer garment of Christ's High Priestly clothing that caught my attention was the breastplate that He wore above the ephod and over His heart. It caught my attention because of the brilliant light that appeared to be coming from the twelve gemstones that were lined up in four rows, across the face of it. In Scripture we are told that each gemstone represented one of the twelve tribes of Israel. For God told Moses: "Whenever Aaron enters the Holy Place, he will bear the names of the sons of Israel over his heart on the breastpiece of decision as a continuing memorial before the Lord" (Exodus 28:29).

What a beautiful picture of our God! Just as Aaron bore the names of the children of Israel upon His heart, so our High Priest, Jesus Christ, has our names engraved upon His heart forever. Nothing will be able to separate us from the love of God that is in Christ Jesus our Lord (Romans 8:39).

We are His spiritual sons and daughters. "Therefore, since we have a great high priest who has gone through the heavens, Jesus the Son of God, let us hold firmly to the faith we profess. For we do not have a high priest who is unable to sympathize with our weaknesses, but we have One who has been tempted in every way, just as we are, yet without sin" (Hebrews 4:14-15). He feels our pain, He sympathizes with our sorrows, and He understands our needs. Jesus Christ, our High Priest carries the names of His repentant children upon His shoulders and upon His heart into the very presence of the Shekinah glory (God's presence).

Significance of Each Gemstone

As I gazed at Christ's high priestly attire the brilliant, reflected light that sparkled and danced off the beautiful gemstones dazzled me. I believe that each gemstone on the breastplate and its position on the breastplate had a special significance. I believe God told Moses where to place each gemstone so that each would enhance the beauty of the others. As the Shekinah glory would fall upon each gemstone, each stone would reflect its own unique light and reveal its own true colors that would compliment and add beauty to the stones around it.

Is it possible that the color and beauty of each precious stone represented the characteristics of each tribe—perhaps their strengths and weaknesses? A similar application can be made today for us in the church—God's spiritual sons and daughters who are called to be the "living stones." Peter says, "You also, like living stones, are being built into a spiritual house to be a holy priesthood, offering spiritual sacrifices acceptable to God through Jesus Christ" (1 Peter 2:5). Peter goes on to tell us that to those of us who *believe*, this Stone [Jesus Christ] is precious... but to those who do *not believe*... this Stone causes many to stumble. It becomes a Rock that makes them fall (1 Peter 2:6-8).

In His presence we are to shine and reflect His glory so that the world will be drawn to the Living Stone—the Chief Cornerstone—Jesus Christ. Individually and corporately we are called to bear witness to the "true Light who gives light to every man" (John 1:9). "Those who are wise will shine like the brightness of the heavens, and those who lead many to righteousness, like the stars for ever and ever" (Daniel 12:3). "They will be mine," says the Lord Almighty, 'in the day when I make up my *treasured possession*'" (Malachi 3:17). They will be Mine when I come to make up My jewels. I am reminded of the old hymn that that expresses these thoughts…"All His jewels, precious jewels, His loved and His own. Like the stars of the morning, His bright crown adorning. They shall shine in their beauty, bright gems for His crown."[1]

Notice that there are many different gemstones, but they are all attached to only *one* breastplate. In the church there are many different members, but only *one* body. "Now you are the body of Christ, and each one of you is a part of it" (1 Corinthians 12:27). Paul reminds us as members of God's household: "In Him you are being built together to become a dwelling in which God lives by His Spirit… in Him the whole building is joined together and rises to become a holy temple in the Lord" (Ephesians 2:22, 21). Don't lose "connection with the Head [Jesus Christ], from whom the whole body, supported and held together by its ligaments and sinews, grows as God causes it to grow" (Colossians 2:19).

I believe that the square breastplate containing the twelve gemstones has as its counterpart the New Jerusalem that is also laid out in a square, and has foundations of twelve precious stones. Engraved on the foundation stones of the New Jerusalem are the names of the twelve apostles that appear to be the counterpart of the twelve tribes of Israel (Revelation 21:14). The names of the twelve apostles, each inscribed on a different stone, will be a lasting testimony of the transforming power of God's grace, the Living Stone.

To the right and to the left of the gemstones on the breastplate were the Urim and the Thummim, gemstones that shone more brilliantly than the other twelve. I learned from the Scriptures that Urim starts with alpha, the first letter of the Greek alphabet, and Thummim starts with omega, the last letter of the Greek alphabet. Isn't God telling us through this symbolic picture that Jesus Christ is the "Alpha and the Omega, the First and the Last, the Beginning and the End" (Revelation 1:8, 17; 22:13)? Isn't Jesus Christ the vehicle through which God the Father expresses His thoughts to us? Isn't our High Priest, Jesus Christ, God's final Word made audible?

God's temple

Instead of God's presence and glory dwelling in an earthly temple He now chooses in this "new order of things" to dwell in us by His Spirit. "Now to Him who is able to do immeasurably more than all we ask or imagine, according to His power that is at work within us, to him be glory *in the church and in Christ Jesus* throughout all generations, forever and ever! Amen" (Ephesians 3:20-21).

God's presence and glory have now been transferred to the church—the body of Christ. No longer is God's presence limited to physical buildings. God plainly tells us in His Word that His presence and glory no longer reside in temples made with human hands. "The Most High does not live in houses made by men. As the prophet says, 'Heaven is my throne and earth is my footstool. What kind of house will you build for Me? says the Lord. Or where will my resting place be?'" (Acts 7:48-49).

God is seeking to make His dwelling place in our hearts. In Paul's prayer for the Ephesians he says, "I pray that out of His glorious riches He may strengthen you with power through His Spirit in your inner being so that Christ may *dwell in your hearts through faith*" (Ephesians 3:16-17). Our hearts have become His temple (I Corinthians 3:6). God has chosen to reside in His people by His Spirit through faith (I Corinthians 6:9). He wants His name sealed in our foreheads and in our hearts forever (Revelation 7:3; 9:4).

The prophet Haggai, speaking of Solomon's time, and prophetically, our time, tells us "The glory of this present house will be greater than the glory of the former house" (Haggai 2:9). What is this glory that the prophet is speaking about? Does he mean that the temple the returned exiles were rebuilding would be greater than the magnificent temple that King Solomon built? No! In fact, the latter house was by far inferior to the former house. When the glory of the Lord filled the temple back then, it was not the temple that was greater but the glory of God's presence *in* the temple. The presence of the Lord was greater!

In a similar way today the presence of the Lord will be greater in our hearts as we allow Him to cleanse us and fill us with His Spirit. He wants to pour out His latter rain Holy Spirit upon us to empower us to share the Good News of His finished work with the rest of His children. But we must first relinquish our hold on Adventism's package at the foot of the cross, because it perverts the gospel.

In these last days, as God's presence and glory fill our earthly temples our one desire as a "royal priesthood" of believers will be to please and honor the One who has "called [us] out of darkness into His wonderful light" (1Peter 2:9). Having received God's mercy and forgiveness ourselves we will long to freely give it to others. As God releases the latter rain power of His Spirit upon us, His presence in us will be greater than we have experienced before.

All self-centered worship will cease as we bow humbly in awe at His feet. As He is exalted to His rightful place, *He alone* will become the focus of our attention. *He alone* will be magnified as King of Kings and Lord of Lords. *He alone* will receive the honor and glory due His name. Our own accomplishments will fade into obscurity as the consuming fire of His presence overwhelms us. We will desire nothing else but to sit at His feet and worship Him as beholding His glory in the face of Jesus Christ changes us from glory to glory.

Change in the Role of Ministry

Having obtained eternal redemption for us, the Scriptures portray our High Priest, Jesus Christ as seated at the right hand of the Father, waiting for His enemies to be made His footstool (Hebrews 10:12-13). However, in this scene of the vision He is shown standing, wearing a tall gold crown instead of a miter. Is a change soon to take place in His role as our High Priest and is He preparing us for this good news?

He is shown wearing a tall gold crown on His head because He is not like any earthly high priest who wears a miter. The gold crown is a symbol of His kingly authority. This Faithful and True Witness will soon lead the armies of heaven riding on a white horse. On His robe and on His thigh will be written, "King of Kings and Lord of Lords" (Revelation 19:11-16). He is telling us that the time is drawing near when He will appear in the clouds of heaven to come and claim His chosen bride. There was not the slightest trace of condemnation or hint of disapproval on His lovely face, but only a "joyful-ready-to-burst-smile" full of expectant joy.

As the Lord stands before me, His feet resting upon a white cloud, He is shown removing the outer blue garment from His shoulders while the breastplate (ephod) continues to remain in place over His heart. Through this symbolic act the Spirit is revealing two important points He wants us to consider.

First, the outer blue priestly garment being removed indicates that Christ is soon going to put on His royal robes as He prepares to come and claim us—His chosen bride. Secondly, He is telling us that as the climax of Christ's ministry of intercession draws to a close, He continues to carry the names of His repentant children upon His heart as He prepares to come and claim them as His chosen bride. Just as Aaron bore the names of the children of Israel upon His heart, so our High Priest has our names engraved upon His heart forever. What a beautiful picture of our forgiving God!

"By one sacrifice *He has made perfect forever* those who are being made holy" (Hebrews 10:14). For it is "God who makes both us and you stand firm in Christ. He anointed us, set His seal of ownership on us, and put His Spirit in our hearts as a deposit, *guaranteeing* what is to come" (2 Corinthians 1:22).

May our response to such love be: "I belong to my lover, and His desire is for me. Place me like a seal over your heart, like a seal on your arm; for love is as strong as death, its jealousy unyielding as the grave. It burns like blazing fire, like a mighty flame. Many waters cannot quench love; rivers cannot wash it away" (Song of Solomon 7:10; 8:6-7).

Promise of the Spirit

Jesus already knows those who are His. Listen to the Scriptures that remind us of this truth. "The Lord knows those who are His" (2Timothy 2:19). "For He chose us in Him before the creation of this world to be holy and blameless in His sight... And you also were included in Christ when you heard the word of truth, the gospel of your salvation. Having believed you were marked in Him with a seal, the promised Holy Spirit, who is a deposit guaranteeing our inheritance until the redemption of those who are God's possession—to the praise of His glory" (Ephesians 1:4, 13-14). But He also knows those who are not His—"the inhabitants of the earth whose names have not been written in the book of life from the creation of the world..." (Revelation 17:8).

As Christ's work of intercession draws to a close and He prepares to come for His children, let us rejoice in the fact that we have the promised Holy Spirit to be with us forever. Just as this promised Spirit was poured out at Pentecost, so it is being poured out again now. Many of us have heard the sound of the approaching rain. Many of us are beginning to experience the refreshing that is coming from the presence of the Lord.

"And I will ask the Father, and He will give you another Counselor to be with you forever—the Spirit of Truth. The world cannot accept Him, because it neither sees Him nor knows Him. But you know Him, for He lives with you and will be in you… But the Counselor, the Holy Spirit, whom the Father will send in My name, will teach you all things and will remind you of everything I have said to you. …But when He, the Spirit of Truth, comes, He will guide you into all truth… and He will tell you what is yet to come" (John 14:16-17, 26; 16:13).

Continue to be Holy Still

He has given us His Spirit as a guarantee of our inheritance in Him. He has already placed His seal of approval upon us. Therefore, as we hear these words, spoken with such love and unmistakable clarity by Jesus, "Let him who is holy continue to be holy still," we may know that the verdict in the courts of heaven has *already* been decided. Those who have chosen to be found *in* Christ have already been judged and found *not guilty*. Praise God! Our righteous Judge has already taken the penalty for our sin.

In the very last chapter of the book of Revelation John reminds us of the words of the angel who had shown him all these things. "Worship God!" said the angel. "Do not seal up the words of the prophecy of this book, because the time is near. Let him who does wrong continue to do wrong; let him who is vile continue to be vile; let him who does right continue to do right; and let him who is holy continue to be holy" (Revelation 22:9b-11).

"Behold, I am coming soon! I am the Alpha and the Omega, the First and the Last, the Beginning and the End" (Revelation 22:12-13). "I, Jesus, have sent my angel to give you this testimony for the churches. I am the Root and the Offspring of David, and the bright Morning Star" (Revelation 22:16).

No Fear in Love

These words, spoken by the angel to John, were never designed to bring terror to our hearts as believers. In fact, just the opposite is true. John's prophetic visions were designed to bring hope and encouragement to the early Christians who were suffering severe persecution for their faith. Not only was the book of Revelation given for their day but also its message is relevant to every generation. It is especially applicable to our day because the end of all things is at hand.

In the same way, this scene in the vision that I received was not given in order to create fear in our hearts, but to bring peace. For as Jesus Christ stood there smiling at me, I was filled with reverent awe and unspeakable joy. There was no fear intended in His pronouncement: "… Let him who is holy be holy still", because His perfect love casts out all fear. There was no fear in me, because I knew that I was in Him. "There is no fear in love. But perfect love drives out fear, because fear has to do with punishment. The one who fears is not made perfect in love" (I John 4:18). How can I fear the One who has already taken all my sins upon Himself? Such love defies human reasoning.

This scene of the vision of Jesus stands out in stark contrast to the picture of "Jesus" painted by Ellen White—a Jesus who smiles or frowns in response to our keeping or breaking the law. Jesus is smiling at us and laughing with us because He is telling us that we have been freed from carrying that burden of old covenant law. The verdict of "righteous" and "holy" has already been decided in Heaven because our High Priest of the new covenant has interceded for us.

Instead of being filled with fear over this pronouncement that I heard, we should be filled with exuberant joy. For the One who chose us to be holy and blameless in His sight is able to make us holy in His sight. The apostle Paul reminds us:"…He has reconciled you by Christ's physical body through death to present you holy in *His sight,* without blemish and free from accusation—if you continue in your faith, established and firm, not moved from the hope held out in the gospel" (Colossians 1:22-23). The hope held out in the gospel is a glorious hope. It is our *only* hope!

Listen to the words of encouragement that Paul writes in his letter to the church in Thessalonica. He urges them to be brave and not give up their faith in Jesus Christ as a result of the persecution they were receiving. "May God Himself, the God of peace sanctify you through and through. May your whole spirit, soul and body be *kept blameless* at the coming of our Lord Jesus Christ. The One who calls you is faithful and He will do it" (1 Thessalonians 5:23-24)!

He will do it. He is faithful to keep His word. What was spoken to the church at Thessalonica is being spoken again to the body of Christ today, particularly the Adventist body. He will purify and sanctify us, "For we are God's workmanship, created in Christ Jesus to do good works, which God has prepared in advance for us to do" (Ephesians 2:10). The good works that He has prepared for us are not works of the law, but works of faith. For the just (those who have been justified) shall live by faith. "Whatever is not of faith is sin" (Hebrews 11:6). "For in the gospel a righteousness from God is revealed, a righteousness that is by faith from first to last, just as it is written: "the righteous will live by faith" (Romans 1:17). Clearly, from first to last our righteousness is found in Jesus Christ alone.

"By one sacrifice," God has already made us perfect forever in Jesus Christ. By faith in His finished work we are justified. At the same time that we are justified, we are being made holy—sanctified (Hebrews 10:14). By faith in Him we are complete.

Purified and Made Spotless

Another Scripture that confirms what has already been discussed is found in Daniel. Speaking of the end times, the man clothed in linen, who was above the waters of the river, told the prophet Daniel: "Many will be purified, made spotless and refined, but the wicked will continue to be wicked. None of the wicked will understand, but those who are wise will understand" (Daniel 12:10).

So the righteous remnant will not be taken by surprise when all these things begin to happen, because they will receive prophetic understanding of the Scriptures through the ministry of the Holy Spirit. As a result, God will prepare them for what is ahead.

Through the prophet Isaiah, God urgently calls the church to wake up. "Awake, awake, O Zion, clothe yourself with strength. Put on your garments of splendor, [Christ's robe of righteousness]… The uncircumcised and defiled will not enter you again. Shake off your dust; rise up… Free yourself from the chains on your neck, O captive Daughter of Zion" (Isaiah 52:1-2).

God is urgently calling us to free ourselves from Adventism's bondage that has become like a millstone around our necks. As we repent of trusting in false teachings, we will discard our garments of guilt and shame in exchange for Christ's robe of righteousness, and walk by faith in His finished work of grace. Then it will be said of us, "Instead of their shame, my people will receive a double portion, and instead of disgrace they will rejoice in their inheritance…" (Isaiah 61:7). He has already given us His righteousness in exchange for our rags! He has already sealed us by His Spirit! Let us rejoice in our inheritance—Jesus Christ!

Endnotes: Chapter 8

[1] Words by William O. Cushing, Music by George F. Root, "When He Cometh".

The "first steps" of Adventism were not something a "parent" should be proud of because they were not the steps of a precious baby, but rather the steps of a slave child.

Chapter 9
EXPOSING A SACRED COW

"I am astonished that you are so quickly deserting the one who called you by the grace of Christ, and are turning to a different gospel—which is really no gospel at all…"
Galatians 1:6-7

After seeing a glorious revelation of Jesus Christ as our High Priest in the first scene of the vision, I initially thought that in the second scene God was portraying scenes in gold from the life of Jesus Christ to emphasize the priceless value of the character of His Son. I believed God was using the gold baby sculpture that reminded me of the bronzing process done to seal and preserve a baby's first pair of shoes, to let us know that the life of God's Son has been preserved for all time and eternity. I reasoned that God was telling us through this symbolism that if we choose to place our trust in Christ's righteousness alone, we are sealed for eternity too.

Although a number of things disturbed me about this scene, such as it not making sense, or lining up with Scripture, I finally decided that God would bring further interpretation in His time. I didn't understand why countless numbers of sculptured scenes from Christ's life were quickly covered up. I wondered what the purpose was of flipping through scenes as quickly as someone dealing out a deck of cards.

In the few scenes that I did see, the many layers of gold bronzing made everything look alike and hard to distinguish until the traditional and very antiquated pieces of art "came to life". Then it became apparent which figure in each sculpted scene represented Jesus Christ. He was the One trying to move beneath the layers of gold paint that appeared to become flexible and stretch as if it were a covering of skin. I wanted to peel off the "skin" so that Christ could move freely.

As the last two scenes of the cross and grave were laid down in slow motion I didn't understand why a veil seemed to cover them. What's more, I became very troubled when what should have been the final scene—the resurrection—never appeared. I felt compelled to "fill in" the missing scene by adding my own thoughts and words to make the vision line up with the truth of Scripture. For without the resurrection of Jesus Christ we have no hope.

Baby's First Steps

As the veil that had covered my own eyes for seven years began to lift, I began to understand the meaning of the gold baby sculpture. God was using the gold baby sculpture (that reminded me of the bronzing process done to seal and preserve a baby's first pair of shoes) to show how the corporate Seventh-day Adventist (SDA) church has bronzed Adventist history in order to try to preserve it. In the same way a baby's first steps are like a memorial you never want to forget, so Adventism's "first baby steps" have been bronzed so that SDAs will never forget their Adventist heritage.

Since Adventism's first steps have been mentioned in earlier chapters, I will briefly summarize them here. When Jesus didn't come in 1844 as early Adventists expected, they still insisted that their message had been right **(Great Disappointment of 1844).** They still hoped Christ would come and expected Him any day. They stopped trying to convert sinners and ceased praying for them because they believed that the door of probation was shut to the rest of the world **(Shut Door Theory).**

Instead of dealing with the bitterness of the Great Disappointment by confessing their mistakes and repenting of their errors, they came up with a reinterpretation of the 1844 Disappointment to apply to a change in the ministration of Jesus Christ in the heavenly sanctuary **(Sanctuary Doctrine).**

Instead of returning to Earth on October 22, 1844, they believed Jesus passed from the Holy Place into the Most Holy Place of the heavenly sanctuary at that time in order to begin a work of judgment. Since only

Adventists knew about this work of judgment, the rest of the Christian world must be warned *(Investigative Judgment Doctrine)*.

Ellen G. White (EGW), claiming to be an inspired prophet of God, placed her stamp of approval upon these changes in Adventist doctrines by receiving confirmation through prophetic dreams and visions. The "miracles" and "signs" that accompanied EGW's early ministry served to make this period of time (SDAs first steps) more attractive, more miraculous, and thus more correct. I believe this is the reason the SDA denomination is always pushing to get back to the passion and energy that accompanied the early days of Adventism.

In reality, Adventism's first steps were not grounded in the gospel. When early Adventists began following William Miller, they were walking by works instead of by faith. This is clearly illustrated by Ellen White's "first vision," where she saw early Adventists climbing up a steep path to Heaven. They were already striving to get to heaven by their works before the Sabbath truth arrived. They were already walking in the steps of slavery, in the steps of the law. So when they accepted the "Sabbath truth," it became the missing good work they needed in order to be endorsed by God!

Unfortunately the SDA church refuses to admit that the "first steps" of Adventism were truly wrong. They were not something a "parent" should be proud of. They were not the steps of a precious baby, but rather the steps of a slave child.

I believe it is evident from this scene of the vision that our Adventist forbearers had a vested interest in protecting and exalting the old covenant (Ten Commandments), because EGW consistently used erroneous "proof texts" from the old covenant to support Adventism's "unique" contribution to the SDA worldwide message.

Meaning of Sacred Cow

Suddenly I was reminded of the scene I had witnessed on TV several years ago as millions of Hindus descended upon the Ganges River in order to be spiritually cleansed. Immediately I had seen the word "sacred cow," and was hit with weeping as the Spirit of intercession came upon me to stand in the gap for these dear people.

Those of us in the west may have a hard time understanding how Hindus could consider the cow to be sacred. We wonder how many people in India worship cows, but would not think of eating them. What God provided for food holds them in bondage.

But lest we miss the point, we certainly have our own "sacred cows." In fact it is clear from Adventism's "first steps" that Adventists have a number of "sacred cow" Scriptures that hold them in bondage to a false system of truth. Certain preconceived ideas about what the Bible teaches become a curse when we don't rightly divide the Word of God for ourselves. When Adventists worship certain Scriptures, but won't dare eat the Bread of Life, then those Scriptures hold them in bondage.

The Lens of the Law

As I read the following passage of Scripture in 2 Corinthians 3:7-18, I realized that the gold bronzing that covered every sculpted scene of Christ represents the law that the corporate SDA church continues to protect and exalt. The sculpted scenes of Christ's life that passed quickly before me were bronzed in gold because in Adventism the glory of the new covenant gospel is seen through the lens of the law (Ten Commandments).

"Now if the ministry that brought death, which was engraved in letters on stone, came with glory… will not the ministry of the Spirit be even more glorious? If the ministry that condemns men is glorious, how much more glorious is the ministry that brings righteousness! For what was glorious has no glory now in comparison with the surpassing glory. And if what was fading away came with glory, how much greater is the glory of that which lasts!

"Therefore, since we have such a hope, we are very bold. We are not like Moses, who would put a veil over his face to keep the Israelites from gazing at it while the radiance was fading away. But **their minds were made dull, for to this day the same veil remains when the old covenant is read. It has not been removed, because only in Christ is it taken away.** *Even to this day when Moses is read, a veil covers their hearts. But whenever anyone turns to the Lord, the veil is taken away. Now the Lord is the Spirit, and where the Spirit of the Lord is, there is freedom. And we, who with unveiled faces all reflect the Lord's glory, are being transformed into his likeness with ever-increasing glory, which comes from the Lord, who is the Spirit."*

Suddenly it all became clear. Adventism has taken the ministry that brought death (Ten Commandments engraved in letters on stone) and that came with glory, and made it *even more glorious* that the ministry of the Spirit (2 Corinthians 3:7-8).

In Galatians 3:23, Paul talks about the law being our schoolmaster. He says, "...we were held prisoners by the law, locked up until faith should be revealed." In other words Paul is saying that while we were under law, we were children and were no different from slaves. The bronzing may look glorious, but it keeps us in childhood—slavery actually.

What's more, because EGW is considered to be an authoritative source of truth that the corporate SDA church continues to promote, many Adventists remain in slavery to the law because of Ellen White's insistence on glorifying the old covenant. Because of this tragic error many Adventists have not been "changed from glory to glory." Many Adventists have not experienced the freedom of the Spirit. Many Adventists cannot behold Christ because the veil of the law still blinds them (See 2 Corinthians 3:12-18).

As a result of this veil, many Adventists cannot see the full meaning of Christ's death and especially the meaning of His resurrection. They are left in darkness—never being brought into the glory of the new covenant gospel—never truly experiencing "resurrection."

Drunk with the old wine (old covenant) that gets more and more intoxicating, SDAs cannot see the fullness of what Christ did for them through His death. They cannot see what ended at the cross. They cannot see the glory of His resurrection. That is the reason why the last two scenes of the vision appeared to be veiled. Could that be the reason why many SDAs can't understand the joy many non-SDAs experience when they jump up and down and shout about the glory of Jesus' resurrection?

Seen through the veil of the law, the Adventist message is one that ends in death, because as Paul said, the old covenant law is a ministry of death—a ministry that brings condemnation. For the past 150 years the Adventist message has been, in essence, that Christ came to show us we could keep the old covenant law—that we could become good enough to become righteous—of course with His help. That is a vision of death—with no resurrection! That is why the scene of the vision ended with the grave.

No wonder the scene of the cross and grave was blurry! The Adventist church has used the old covenant to interpret the new covenant instead of the other way around. Adventism has had it backwards. By looking at Christ through the lens of the law the corporate church hasn't allowed Him to be *greater than the law*. We encased Him in the law—in the many layers of gold bronzing, instead of realizing that Christ came and fulfilled the law. A study of the Greek in Matthew 5:17 reveals that Christ not only fulfilled the law, but more than fulfilled it to overflowing! When Jesus said He was "Lord of the Sabbath," He literally meant "Lord over the Sabbath!"

Unreliable Source of Truth

I believe my lack of understanding the meaning of this scene of the vision for seven years had to do with the meaning the SDA church has given to Christ's life based on EGW's interpretation of Scripture. Instead of encouraging its members to test everything by God's Word for themselves, the corporate institution of the SDA church has used the prophetic 'gift' of Ellen White to preserve the historic teachings of Adventism, promote old covenant law, and confine the work of the Holy Spirit.

The covering up of the outdated sculpted scenes of Christ's life and the many layers of high lustrous gold finish given to each one, speaks of the "glossing over" done in order to preserve the errors and perpetuate the deceptions regarding the identity and ministry of Jesus Christ, and the work of the Holy Spirit. For instance, the non-scriptural details of Christ's early life that were shown in this scene of the vision, namely Jesus laughing and playing with other children and Jesus working in the carpenter shop with Joseph, reminded me of the many non-scriptural details of Christ's life found in the book, "The Desire of Ages" (DA) by Ellen G. White.

When I read that book years ago I found the descriptions of Christ's life an inspirational blessing. Believing at that time that Ellen White was a reliable source of truth caused me to accept everything that she had written as given her by God to the point that sometimes I couldn't tell the difference between what God was supposed to have said through her and what the Scriptures actually taught.

However, that was before allegations of plagiarism began circulating regarding her literary borrowing from the works of other authors without giving them credit. In order to investigate these disturbing questions Dr. Fred Veltman was asked by the SDA church in 1982 to analyze the charges of plagiarism brought by Walter Rea and others against Ellen White. In his research Veltman spent eight years studying the Desire of Ages. His findings were printed in the December 1990, issue of Ministry (p. 11-14)—the SDA church's official magazine for clergy.

His five conclusions concerned me and will no doubt disturb any honest seeker after truth. Evidently Adventists have used this book more than any other to authenticate EGW's prophetic "gift." Although there is no way to actually know how many sources she used in writing it, Veltman found she used a minimum of 23 sources, including fiction, without giving the authors any credit. In essence he found that the content of DA is, for the most part, derived from other authors rather than original.[1]

But most SDA lay people are unaware of this fact. They are attracted to her book because of the many non-scriptural "fill ins" of Christ's life that they believe God revealed to EGW. Because of the fact that Ellen White copied other author's ideas so profusely in the writing, not only of DA, but also the rest of her books, we can no longer afford to claim what she wrote as being inspired by God, especially when many of her ideas are not revealed in Scripture.

Although I remember the typical Adventist response in learning that Ellen White "borrowed" from other authors in making DA ("So God led her to those other sources. What's wrong with that?"), I think there is a bigger problem than the obvious copying from other sources without giving them credit. I think the bigger problem is in the *message* of DA rather than in the *making* of it. Let me explain.

Desire of Ages' extra "fill-ins"

"The Desire of Ages" is attractive and authoritative to Adventists largely because of the extra "fill-ins." They show what's missing in Scripture by giving a fuller picture. The "fill-ins" are distracting in that sense. Because they're considered prophetic revelations, they're exciting.

Because they tell the story more fully, it's better than reading Scripture. DA paints a picture that is more detailed and more emotionally moving. Lots of Adventists cling to DA because of the emotions they felt while reading it. The glory is then shifted away from Jesus to the book and its author and her prophetic revelations.

Remember the reaction of many SDAs to the recent Mel Gibson film, "The Passion of the Christ"? They said that it was good, but they liked the account in "The Desire of Ages" better. They found EGW's version more moving. Others who recoiled at the Catholicism in the movie immediately began to use DA as an evangelistic tool—an account of Christ's life that they felt was better than the film and more Biblical. In fact one Adventist website even proudly displayed the great number of "Biblical references" in DA.

One example of DA's distracting fill-ins was about the parable of the Good Samaritan. Ellen White said it was a true story, not just a parable, and that the people in that recent event were standing among the listeners when Jesus was speaking. When He finished speaking, EGW said that the Samaritan knew he was vindicated and the priest and Levite were convicted of their wrongdoing.

The problem with the Ellen White's "fill-ins" is that they distract us from the main point of the parable by adding peripheral information that the Bible is silent about. The point of Jesus' parable was that God values love and compassion more than He values ceremonial righteousness. God saw the Samaritan who was theologically very incorrect as being more righteous than the priest and Levite who had "more truth". In essence, this parable shows that righteousness does not come through the Law!

Unfortunately because of the EGW "fill-ins" in DA, the "wow" shifted away from Jesus' message to the extra knowledge she supplied. Readers of Scripture focus on and are in awe of Jesus, His love and His grace. But readers of "The Desire of Ages" often feel that they already know those things (Jesus, His love and grace) and that those things are somewhat elementary. Many of us in Adventism have been more impressed by EGW's further "revelations" and proud of our "bigger" picture. But the deeper insight is not deeper at all—it's just distracting.

When we choose to be a Protestant Christian it means we choose to rest in the revelation of the Bible as God's complete message to us. God knew what He said, and while He could have told more of the story, He didn't. He believed what He had delivered to us in Scripture was sufficient. But whether EGW and the Adventist denomination realized it or not, I believe these extra "fill-ins" served another purpose.

The New Testament is largely silent about Sabbath observance, but the Desire of Ages is not. Whether they realized it or not, it appears that the authors of DA were trying to reconcile the New Testament with the Sabbath. They were trying to harmonize Christ with the Law. They were trying to show that Christ upheld the Law and that He intends for us to be obedient to the Ten Commandments, especially the Sabbath.

Thus the prophetic "fill-ins" serve to give divine credibility to this Ten Commandment-based account of the gospel. They showed through their further revelations that this re-reading of Scripture was the correct view. Because it was also more emotionally moving, the belief in Sabbath/Ten Commandments became more emotionally fixed and entrenched inside of us. How could it be wrong if it was so moving? We thought DA made us appreciate Jesus and Scripture more.

Adventism's other Jesus

The many scenes in gold that I was shown are of *Adventism's Other Jesus*, as seen through the glory of the Law and through SDAs "first steps." However, they pale in comparison to the greater glory of the living Christ described in Chapter 8.

In remembering the scenes of gold, I was reminded of something I had read several years ago regarding the "gold plates" that Joseph Smith, the founder of Mormonism, was supposed to have received from the angel, Moroni.

"The Golden Plates" is the name most frequently used to refer to the "gold plates" that Joseph Smith, Jr. said he received from the angel Moroni and used as the ancient source for the English translation of The Book of Mormon. In reference to the plates, the Book of Mormon was commonly known as the "Golden Bible" during the 1830s. Smith later became the founder of the Latter Day Saint Movement."[2]

Isn't God perhaps showing us His view of "Adventism's Jesus" (as seen through the lens of the Law and Adventism's "first steps") and saying that it is like the Mormon's other Jesus? Isn't He saying that the same kind of "gold bronzing process" was used in making both Jesus'?

I believe Jesus viewed through the "lens of the law" is just as different a "Jesus" as the Mormon's other Jesus!

The Brass children

As one of my editors was reading the following paragraph that began the description of the scene in this vision, he was reminded of an incident that happened eight years ago that suddenly made this scene become larger than life for him.

At the left bottom corner of the canvass was a sculpture the size of a playing card. The sculpture was of a little baby with only a swaddling cloth wrapped around his loins. Immediately I thought of the humble beginnings of Christ's birth. As I looked at this antique sculpture, I was reminded of the bronzing process that is done to preserve a baby's first pair of shoes. This baby sculpture, as well as the background, looked like it had been bronzed with a high lustrous gold finish, sealing the baby's pose to preserve it for years to come.

He told me that several years ago when he first came to California in 1998, he and his friends took a trip one evening down to Laguna Beach, an artsy town that is filled with lots of art galleries. At one of them there were these sculptures they dubbed, "The Brass Children".

The nearly life-size children were in classic everyday poses not unlike those familiar Saturday Evening Post pictures by Norman Rockwell. One child was reaching for an apple, another was fishing, and another was eating ice cream. The statues were kind of eerie because they looked so real, but yet were in brass. So he and his friends joked that there were real children inside.

They joked that someday when they became parents and their children were acting bad they would take them to this art gallery and tell them that these sculptures were real children who had been pestering their parents. In an ominous voice they pretended they would tell their kids, "You want that ice cream? Okay, you can have it... FOREVER!" It became a running joke with them. "You want to go fishing? You can go fishing... FOREVER!"

He said that was really funny to them then, but of course the thought of real children being encased in brass is horrible, and now he realizes that the idea of threatening a kid with that kind of fear is a terrible abuse, too.

Perhaps the words used to describe the scene in the vision reminded him of this experience in a Laguna Beach art gallery because this is another way of God telling us that, "Whatever you have done to the least of these [children!], you have done to Me"? Just as many SDAs have been killing themselves and their children with this "ministry of death" (the gold bronzing process), many have also unknowingly been doing the same thing to Jesus.

A Different Jesus—another Gospel

After studying Ellen White's views of Jesus Christ, and the SDA Church's understanding of those views, I am shocked to discover that Adventism's faith is based on an entirely different Jesus and a totally different ministry. (See Appendix A, p. 123, "Aberrant views of Jesus"). I am reminded of the warning Paul gives in 2 Corinthians 11:3-4 where he says, *"But I am afraid that just as Eve was deceived by the serpent's cunning, your minds may somehow be led astray from your sincere and pure devotion to Christ.* **For if someone comes to you and preaches a Jesus other than the Jesus we preached, or if you receive a different spirit from the one you received, or a different gospel from the one you accepted,** *you put up with it easily enough."*

The Scriptures reveal that there is only one true gospel—the gospel of Jesus Christ—the God-Man who liberates the sinner by granting him eternal life, whereas the false gospel of Adventism places the sinner in even greater bondage. Read the following statements from Ellen White's writings and honestly consider whether these quotations more fully liberate one to understand freedom in Christ, or if they lead, instead, to greater spiritual bondage.

- "After Jesus opened the door of the Most Holy the light of the Sabbath was seen, and the people of God were to be **tested and proved, as God proved the children of Israel anciently, to see if they would keep His law.**"[3]
- "Christ died for a ruined world, and through the merit of Christ, God elected that **man should have a second trial, a second probation, a second test as to whether he will keep the commandments of God** or walk in the path of transgression, as did Adam… The conditions of eternal life have been plainly stated… here are the conditions upon which every

soul may be elected to eternal life. Your obedience to God's commandments will prove that you are predestinated to a glorious inheritance."[4]
- "It is Satan's studied effort to divert the minds of men from the one way of salvation,—faith in Christ, **and obedience to the law of God.**"[5]
- **"If we live a life of perfect obedience**, His promises will be fulfilled toward us."[6]
- "Christ gave His life as a sacrifice, not to destroy God's law, not to create a lower standard, but to maintain justice, **and to give man a second probation**. No one can keep God's commandments except in Christ's power."[7]
- "If they [His people] will live according to every word He has spoken, every good word and promise will be fulfilled unto them. **But if they come short of perfect obedience, the great and precious promises are afar off, and they cannot reach the fulfillment.**"[8]

From the references given above we see that the hope SDAs have is in receiving a second probation, a second chance because of the cross to see if they will keep God's law. Evidence that they are keeping the commandments is believed to be in keeping the Sabbath.

But wait a minute! The New Covenant gospel knows nothing of a second probation. It's Christ obedience that saves us, not ours. Only He could fulfill the Law. The Law brought death to us because we couldn't fulfill it. Christ didn't die for our sins only to hand us back to the ministry of condemnation and death—back to the schoolmaster—back to the position of slavery!

We are not being tested to see if we will obey God's law (conditional). Rather, because we have been forgiven through the blood of Jesus Christ, we have been freed from the law of sin and death and now choose to live in obedience to the law of the Spirit. Ours is the obedience of faith—not obedience to Old Covenant law. We have received an unconditional pardon that offers us eternal life. Adventism's "gospel" speaks of continual bondage, whereas the New Covenant gospel speaks of instant liberty for those who place their faith in Christ's finished work (See John 8:31-36; Romans 8:2; Galatians 4:22- 31; 5:1)!

After reading the previous quotations on second probation, it becomes clear that for many SDAs what is done *in* them is as integral to salvation as what is done for them. However, in the new covenant gospel *what is done **for** us is salvation. What is done **in** us is the lifetime work of the Holy Spirit.* What is done *in* us is the benefit of being completely saved by the blood of Jesus Christ.

Listen to the words of Paul as he addresses the Galatians on their desertion of Christ for a different gospel. "I am astonished that you are so quickly deserting the One who called you by the grace of Christ, and are turning to a ***different gospel***—which is really no gospel at all. Evidently some people are throwing you into confusion and are trying to pervert the gospel of Christ. But even if we or an angel from heaven should preach a gospel other than the one we preached to you, let him be eternally condemned! As we have already said, so now I say again: If anybody is preaching to you a gospel other than the one what you accepted, let him be eternally condemned" (Galatians 1:6-9)!

The Greek word for "desert" in this passage does not mean "absent" but it means to "defect." Paul is saying that those who are "throwing you into confusion" are urging you to defect—to commit treason and go over to the enemy's side. In essence Paul is saying, "How could you defect from the One who called you by His grace for a life of imposed works?

The message of the true gospel is based on the truth of who Jesus Christ is. Because He is the Truth, if we preach a message of "another Jesus," there is no truth or hope in that false Jesus. By trying to incorporate their forbearer's erroneous views of Jesus Christ's into their present theology, Adventists have been forced to create "another Jesus" whose inherent qualities do not line up with the real nature of the biblical Jesus. No amount of "repainting" by skilful artists can bring life into the lifeless images of the Jesus that the SDA church has created—none but the Holy Spirit can bring life to the dry bones of Adventism.

The "bronzing" used to gloss over unscriptural teachings about Christ's identity and nature is nothing but a cheap imitation. No amount of gold lacquer can prevent scriptural inconsistencies and gross biblical errors from tarnishing over time. Although Adventist leaders have managed by deception (using layers of gold paint) to preserve the group's heritage for over 150 years, the time has come to admit that the Adventist "keepsake" so diligently preserved is not genuine gold, but base metal.

Playing a Game of Poker

As I remembered the gold scenes from Christ's life pass before me it looked like someone was dealing out a deck of cards. I was reminded of how the corporate SDA church has used Ellen White's words to frown upon those who would engage in the vice of gambling. Traditional Adventism considered poker cards to be an abomination and practice that Christians should never engage in.

Yet in a very real sense this scene of the vision reveals that the SDA institution has become "hooked" on the very thing that she condemned. It is as if they have been playing a game of Poker with a deck of fancy playing cards. Having Jesus' picture engraved in gold on them makes gambling *kosher* as they play this game of deception using Ellen White's "gift".

I believe God is telling us through this creative imagery that we did the same thing to His Son's life and witness by treating it like a game of cards. The corporate SDA church has managed to skillfully control the story of Jesus' life by adding to it, subtracting from it, and bronzing it in gold in order to make it look good. It has managed to cover up Adventism's errors with layers of doubletalk (gold paint) in order to keep the SDA laity, at large, in the dark about the true nature of "the spirit of prophecy". By dishonest means and at whatever cost, they are determined to preserve Adventism's unique historical doctrines even when they are not based on the truth of Scripture and the irrefutable facts about the nature of Jesus Christ. With unwavering resolve they continue to defend the identity of the corporate SDA church by using Ellen White's words as the voice of final authority in all doctrinal matters instead of listening to the voice of the Spirit.

In the same way that Adventism considered poker cards to be an abomination, God sees all of this as an abomination in His sight. Clearly, there's too much at stake for the corporate SDA church to lose their bet on this Adventist "keepsake" that they plan to pass on to the next generation.

The Resurrection

But there's one thing the corporate SDA Church hasn't counted on that this scene reveals. No amount of touching up by skilful artists and theological doubletalk can prevent the real Jesus from coming forth from the grave where Adventism has tried to keep Him entombed for the past 150 years.

Yes, the "resurrection" was there all the time as Jesus Christ labored to come forth from under the layers of gold paint that the corporate SDA church has used to secure their "unique" gospel message. Although the SDA denomination has *encased Jesus Christ in the law* for over 150 years, He is greater than the law and He will come forth!

Through this creative imagery the Holy Spirit is revealing that the corporate SDA church has lost their bet on this glorious Adventist "keepsake" that they planned to pass on to the next unsuspecting generation of spiritual incest victims. This scene of the vision reveals that victims of spiritual incest have repeatedly chosen the Law as their "Guardian" instead of the Spirit. Of course the Law will always exercise "parental" control over them because the Law always knows what it right and wrong and what is best for the "child." But because the "child" can never measure up to the requirements and demands of the Law feelings of worthlessness and shame set in, forcing the "child" to deny his or her own reality. Since the victim of spiritual incest has been taught to admire and trust and respect the Law as their "Guardian," the incest victim becomes a collaborator in the cycle of spiritual abuse. The conflicting emotions of love and hate, trust and distrust towards the offending "Guardian" only intensify the fear, shame and feelings of betrayal and worthlessness in the "child". This vicious cycle of spiritual incest will end when the spiritual incest victim becomes a survivor and recognizes that the "club of the Law" has abused them and they choose to get rid of their "Guardian". Only in Christ is the Law/Guardian taken away. For where the Spirit of the Lord is there is freedom (2 Corinthians 3:14, 17)!

The light of Truth has exposed the "sacred cow" of Adventism. Once the glory of the new covenant gospel is seen everything else quickly falls by the wayside. The law will never fit within the intended gold frame that Seventh-day Adventism has prepared for it, because the Holy Spirit cannot be confined or boxed in by limited understandings of the nature and character of the triune God. It is way past time for this "Central Pillar" to be removed and given a decent burial once and for all so that there's no hope of its' ever being resurrected again.

To those of you who have found yourselves buried beneath the layers of deception that have characterized the cover-up of Adventism's "sacred cow," the Holy Spirit would speak to your heart right now. **"Peel off the grave clothes that have tightly bound you, for I am releasing captives this very hour. LAZARUS, COME FORTH!"**

Endnotes: Chaper 9

[1] http://www.adventistarchives.org/docs/MIN/MIN1990-12/index.djvu.
[2] "Wikipedia" encyclopedia online: http://en.wikipedia.org/wiki/Golden_plates
[3] White, *Spiritual Gifts,* Vol. 1, p. 164.
[4] *Adventist Review and Sabbath Herald* (Review & Herald Publishing Association, September 28, 1897) par 4 Article, Title: Preach the Word, 5.
[5] White, *Sketches from the Life of Paul*, p. 192.
[6] White, *Testimonies for the Church,* Vol. 2 (Mountain View, California: Pacific Press Publishing Association, 1882) 122. Nine volumes published from 1885-1909.
[7] *Adventist Review and Sabbath Herald* (Review & Herald Publishing Association, May 7, 1901) par. 1 Chapter Title: The Great Standard of Righteousness.
[8] White, *Testimonies for the Church,* Vol. 2, 148.

Will we leave our Adventist nets at once at the foot of the cross and follow Him?

Chapter 10
RECEIVING THE FATHER'S HEART

"Come, follow Me," Jesus said, "and I will make you fishers of men."
Mark 1:17

As I pondered the significance of this third scene of the vision where fish after fish was being drawn in outline, it was reminiscent of how early Christians used this symbol to declare the simplicity of their faith in Jesus Christ. Isn't God drawing us back to the simple gospel "that was once for all entrusted to the saints" (Jude 3)?

I believe the previous scenes of gold have been the "gospel net" that many members in the SDA church have used, and now God is calling us to leave this "net" and follow Him. He's calling us to leave our gold and our "first baby steps," and to follow Him to places that we do not know. Just as Jesus called the disciples of His day one by one to follow Him to places they did not know, the same Holy Spirit is still drawing men and women, boys and girls, to Him today, one by one. For it's not by might, nor by power, but by the Spirit that God calls us and makes us "fishers of men" (Zechariah 4:6).

He's calling us to become disciples of His alone, but like Andrew and Simon Peter who were already fishermen, many Adventists feel like they *already* know this. Because many feel that they *already* know Christ's love, and they *already* know about His grace, they are experts in "fishing". Adventism's pride has been in believing that they knew *more* and understood *more* so they could offer *more* than other churches. Other denominations only had Christ, but SDAs had more—the missing commandment, health insights, prophetic understanding of the end times, and the "big picture" of the final controversy between Christ and Satan which Adventism believes is about God's law.

But now Christ is beckoning us to leave the "net" we have trusted in and follow Him instead. Many of us need to be taught all over again how to become like little children, and sit at the feet of the Master for His first lesson. God is fishing for children so that He can bring them back into childlike joy and freedom—back into the simple Good News that was once for all entrusted to the saints. With each fish God draws, He is saying, "Christ! Christ! CHRIST!" The cry of the Father's heart is for us to know that when we accept the sacrifice of His Son we have *everything!*

Will we respond to His urgent call upon our hearts as the disciples did? Will we leave our Adventist nets at once at the foot of the cross and follow Him? Will we leave our comfort zones that we have been holding on to and become teachable in the School of the Spirit? Will we choose to follow wherever *He* is leading us?

Leaving My Net

When God first began calling me to leave the comfort and security of my public school teaching position I was shaken to the core. It didn't make sense. Didn't He know that I was single and had no large savings account? Then when the Spirit began to move on me in unusual ways in the classroom during my teaching day I began having difficulty focusing on my teaching responsibilities.

As the Lord brought my public school teaching career to a jolting halt in January 1998, my only consolation during this difficult time was that God had shown me in a dream a year in advance that this was going to happen, but I had been reluctant to admit that He was sovereignly in charge, and had fought Him on it all the way.

I was afraid to face the areas of my weakness—fear of man and a lack of trust in God's ability to provide for my financial needs. So God began refining and testing me in this area of my life in order to prepare me for the arduous and difficult task of writing the prophetic message contained within the pages of this book. Throughout the last twelve years since I resigned from public school teaching God has miraculously provided for my every need. And He will do the same for you as you choose to leave your "net" and follow where He leads.

Toiled all Night and Caught Nothing

When God first led me to the story of the miraculous catch of fish described in John 21:1-6, I was reminded of how the disciples had toiled all night in their own wisdom and strength and caught no fish. Hasn't Adventism also toiled all night in its own wisdom and strength and caught nothing? Hasn't Adventism sought the fruits of the Spirit, and all of the Bible's promises as if they would be given to them because they kept the Sabbath or because they had the "truth" and did the right works? Hasn't Adventism failed to acknowledge that God has been with many of the "Gentiles" (non-SDA churches) and they have been righteous in His sight because they have put their faith in His Son—not in their right-ness?

The following passage of Scripture suggests that Adventism has failed to bring in the desired catch of fish because they sought it by works instead of by faith.

"What then shall we say? That the Gentiles who did not pursue righteousness, have obtained it, a righteousness that is by faith; but Israel, who pursued a law of righteousness, has not attained it. Why not? Because they pursued it not by faith but as if it were by works. They stumbled over the 'stumbling stone.' As it is written, 'See, I lay in Zion a stone that causes men to stumble and a rock that makes them fall, and the one who trusts in Him will never be put to shame'" (Romans 9:30-33).

In clinging to their "right-ness" many SDAs have tripped over Christ, the Stumbling Stone. But now the Spirit is calling us to go back to that Stone—to go back to the One Foundation and fall upon Him. He's calling those of us who have been clinging to our good works to fall upon Him and be broken—to accept brokenness—to accept that we have not been right and we have been desperately hurting.

So much of SDAs history has been covered up in order to make it look good, because the church has been ashamed of being totally forthcoming about its past. Even those of us who haven't been leaders in the church, and have heard rumors of Adventism's cover-ups and theological problems have sometimes been afraid of searching them out—afraid of even considering that our "gold" might really be dross. We've been afraid of being caught naked—afraid of being ashamed.

But as we accept our brokenness and fall on the One Stone—on the One and Only Jesus Christ and *His* righteousness instead of our own, we will find freedom from our shame. We will find freedom from our fears. Clothed with His righteousness instead of our right-ness, we will no longer be ashamed of being naked, because after all, the Good News will no longer be about us, but about Him.

Haven't we suffered long enough under the pressure of making the Good News be about us? Hasn't it been a burden and a yoke too heavy for us to carry (Acts 15:10)? Haven't we been totally insufficient for that task? Of course! God didn't create us to be sufficient as ministers of the old covenant. He created us to be clothed with Christ's righteousness—not with our own. We are created to be ministers of the new covenant, a sufficiency that comes from God, not from keeping the Law (2 Corinthians 3:5-6).

Ministers of Reconciliation

As SDA believers become willing to release Adventism's package at the foot of the cross and choose to become child-like students in the School of the Spirit, we will learn how to catch men and women for God. Certainly we have toiled all night in our own wisdom and strength and caught nothing. But as we choose to release our own Adventist "net" at the foot of the cross and follow the Spirit's leading He will use us to help bring in the final harvest of souls for His kingdom—this miraculous end time catch of fish described in John's gospel.

The great commission given to the disciples of Christ's day has been given to us. As a result of Christ's sacrifice, God has "made us competent ministers of a new covenant" written by the Spirit on the tables of our hearts (2 Corinthians 3:6). This ministry of the Spirit is more glorious than the old covenant because it is a ministry that brings righteousness. By beholding the glory of Christ's righteousness that will never fade, we are being transformed into His likeness with ever increasing glory, which comes from the Lord who is the Spirit" (2 Corinthians 3:18).

Christ's love compels us to action. Christ's love compels us to urge those who have not yet accepted the Good News of Christ's sacrifice to hesitate no longer. God's grace is for *all* people. Therefore, as Christ's ambassadors, "we implore you on Christ's behalf: Be reconciled to God. God made Him who had no sin to be sin for us, so that we might become the righteousness of God" (2 Corinthians 5:21).

God is calling us to go forth under the anointing of His Spirit as ministers of reconciliation—to "go and make disciples of *all* nations..." (Matthew 28:18-20). The nations need to know that God has already reconciled them to Himself *in* Jesus Christ. The people in our city streets need to know they are unconditionally loved and already forgiven *in* Jesus Christ. The people we pass every day on our way to work need to know that "everyone who calls on the name of the Lord *will* be saved..." (Joel 2:32). Will we let the Holy Spirit teach us how to catch men and women for God's kingdom?

Just as Christ opened the minds of His disciples to see that everything was fulfilled that had been written about Him (in the Law of Moses, the Prophets and the Psalms), so He will open our minds to *see* the same truth. They were to take the message of His grace, the message of the finished work of the cross, the message of repentance and the forgiveness of sins, and preach it in His name to all nations, beginning in Jerusalem. But before they set out on the task He had assigned to them, He told them to wait for the blessing "My Father has promised." They were to stay in the city of Jerusalem until they had been "clothed with power from on high" (Luke 24:44-49).

Only as the early church came together in repentance, praying for one another as they considered one another better than themselves, could the Holy Spirit be poured out upon them in power. The love and unity that was lacking before became the glue that held them together. They left that upper room, men and women changed by the power of the Spirit. Burning with a passionate desire to share the Good News with the world, they turned their world upside down. It will be the same with us today. But first we must choose to wait on the Spirit, and be taught by the Spirit in order to receive the heart of the Father, and be clothed with power from on high. Only whom God appoints and anoints, will He empower.

Knowing the Heart of God

I am reminded of the story of Abraham—a man whom God called. Just as God called him to leave the security and safety of his comfort zone in Ur of the Chaldeans, so God is calling many SDA believers to leave the security and safety of their comfort zone within the walls of Adventism and go to the "land" He will show them.

I have often wondered what gave Abram the courage to leave his home, his old style of worship, his country and go to a place he hadn't seen. Was it because Abraham heard something different in *this* Voice that spoke to him? The Lord had told him that He was not just going to bless him, but He was going to *make him a blessing* to all the nations of the earth. For through his seed the Promised Seed would come. Did this promise capture the heart of Abram? Did he want to *know* the One behind *this* voice? Did he want to *know* the heart of *this* God? Is that why He chose to *follow* Him?

I believe the Holy Spirit is moving upon the hearts of many SDA believers because He wants us to *know* the One behind *this* Voice. God's calling us just like He called Abram. God's calling us just like Jesus, called Andrew, Peter, James and John to leave their nets and follow Him.

He's calling us away from our sufficiency in order to follow Him into a land we do not know. Is it possible that God has sovereignly allowed us to persist in our works in order to bring us to a place where we will admit our brokenness, choose to find our sufficiency in Christ alone, and let go of our Adventist "nets" and follow Him instead?

Receiving the Father's Heart

In order to get a better grasp of why God is calling SDAs to leave the comfort zone of Adventism, let's take a further look at Abraham's life. Did stepping out by faith and leaving the stability and security of his former life change Abraham's heart? I don't believe so. Did seeing the fulfillment of God's covenant through his son Isaac give him sufficient evidence that God had called him to be the father of many nations? I don't think so.

So how did God change Abraham's heart? I believe it began when He asked Abraham to offer up his son that he dearly loved as a burnt offering. Even though Abraham didn't understand why God was requesting the sacrifice of his beloved son of promise, he trusted Him and obeyed.

We all know the rest of the story. God stopped Abraham from offering his son because God didn't want Abraham's son. He wanted Abraham's *heart*. Through this experience God put into Abraham the heart of a Father who had lost *His* Son! As a result, I feel certain that

Abraham began to find the deepest and most precious things in the heart of God. He began to lay aside his own problems and share God's problems. What were the problems on God's heart? God wanted the nations to return to Him.

In the same way that God wanted Abraham's heart, God wants your heart. Abraham had every right to be afraid of sacrificing his son, because God had told him that all the nations of the earth would be blessed through Isaac. All God's promises to Abraham depended on Isaac.

Similarly, I think many of us in the SDA church are afraid of sacrificing our Adventist "baby" because we're afraid that everything we've believed and trusted in will be lost if we give up our "heritage". Our hearts have been torn between God and our identity and all the promises that we felt we had from Him as Adventists. Abraham had only one heir, and similarly we perhaps worry about the future of the SDA church if we acknowledge the truth of things that were covered up in Adventism. We fear that God can't use us if we break or lose our connection with our Adventist heritage.

But isn't God calling us to sacrifice these things so that we can receive His heart? If we aren't willing to sacrifice them, then God's desires and purposes for us might not be realized. Haven't we been running away from this test for as long as we have been a church because deep down we knew that the SDA church has been hiding something? Haven't we avoided facing these things because we're afraid that sacrificing them will destroy everything we have built?

Abraham was called to offer God his heir, and we are being called to offer God our heritage in Adventism. He's calling us to let go of our pride in our Adventist heritage and humbly embrace His inheritance alone. He's looking for heirs of the righteousness of Abraham, the righteousness that comes by faith and not by works. He's calling us to leave the heritage of works and all its bondages, and instead embrace the inheritance of His Son—His righteousness in place of our own. He's asking us to let go of our special identity in our Adventist heritage, and to find our specialness and identity in the heritage of His Son alone, for He is the special and unique One!

Remember the promise that God gave through Paul to the ship that he was on when it was going to be destroyed? Aren't we on a ship (our

SDA heritage and institution built on it) that God is breaking apart? Isn't He calling us to face the "breaking" ahead that He has for us? And isn't He telling us that we will survive the breaking, and that not one hair of our heads will perish if we choose to find our identity in Him and in His inheritance alone?

The Nations are Our Inheritance

So what is on God's heart that He shared with Abraham and that He wants to share with us? "The nations," you answer, and that is correct. "Ask of Me" the Father said to the Son, "and I will make the nations your inheritance, the ends of the earth Your possession" (Psalm 2:8). Since every one of the Father's promises that were made to the Son will be fulfilled, we can be sure that this promise given to Him will be fulfilled, too. For every one of God's promises are "Yes!" in Christ. But we need to *ask* Him for the nations. They are our inheritance, too.

I was born in England, but has England been born in my heart? I lived in Ireland for several years as a child, but has Ireland been born in my heart? I'm sure there are many of you reading these words right now who have been born in America, but has America been born in your heart? On the other hand you might have been born in Korea, the Philippines, China, Africa, Japan or some other country, but have these nations been born in your heart? But America is your inheritance. Ireland is your inheritance. Korea is your inheritance. The Philippines are your inheritance. China is your inheritance. Africa is your inheritance. Japan is your inheritance. The nations of the world are our inheritance. In Christ, we are the possessors of many nations.

Let's bring it closer to home. These nations that are *our* inheritance are made up of diverse people of many races and different ethnic and cultural groups. They belong to different faiths, and worship God in a variety of different ways. Some are believers in the body of Christ, and others profess faith in other forms of religion or no religion at all.

So let's get to the difficult questions. Even though I am no longer an Adventist, I was born and raised in the SDA church. But have the almost 16 million people who make up the membership of this church been born in my heart? Aren't the members of the SDA church that are found in nations all over the world, also my inheritance in Christ?

Receiving The Father's Heart

This particular SDA church that is the setting of this dream became my spiritual family 20 years ago when I left traditional Adventism. But have my spiritual brothers and sisters who make up this church family been born in my heart? Within this SDA church many nations of the world are represented. So I am the possessor of many nations in Christ. So are you.

But has the Adventist church really been born in our hearts? Yes, we say. But when we hear of problems such as denominational cover-ups, legalism, theological inconsistencies, rationalizations, and grievous errors from Ellen White's writings, why do we pretend there are no problems? Why do we hush it up instead of going to the Doctor?

I think many turn a deaf ear to the problems because our pride in who we are as Adventists is bigger than our love for the people of the SDA church. We have loved our "church" (institution and heritage) more than we have loved our "church" (the people). But isn't God calling us to receive His heart for His children in Adventism? Isn't He calling us to have Adventists born in our hearts more than Adventism? Isn't He begging us to receive His heart and take our brothers and sisters in Adventism to the Doctor for healing?

History reveals that many of us as believers often try to leave our respective countries or homelands or churches when persecution or war breaks out. Fear of losing our lives motivates many of us to protect ourselves by leaving when trouble comes. Is this because the people of our country, or homeland, or church have never been born in our hearts?

I believe the Spirit of God is saying to us as believers, "Now is the time for you to rise up and become a "nation of priests" and stand in the gap so that nations who don't know Me can be born in your hearts—*particularly* the nations that are represented within the walls of Adventism!" As He places our brothers and sisters of Adventism in our hearts we will begin to feel the birth pangs as the time draws near for delivery.

Not everyone can come into the presence of the Lord as we can. There are many countries and places and churches where freedom and expression of worship is forbidden. So when we enter into His presence in worship we must remember that we should not come just to *get* blessed ourselves. We have been called to enter into the presence of the Lord on behalf of others. Since we have been called out of darkness into His wonderful light, we have been called to become a kingdom of priests. We have been called to *be a blessing to the nations*. So when we come into the presence of the Lord we must not just come for ourselves, we must bring a nation, a people group, our churches of origin before Him, and ask the Father to reveal *His* heart of love to them.

I heard a Chinese man say one time that the Chinese consider *only themselves* to be people. The rest of the nations are devils. That's how the Jews regarded the Gentiles at the time of Christ. They had no mercy or compassion for the other nations around them. Unfortunately that same sectarian spirit exists even within the church.

I remember growing up believing that the SDA church was the "remnant church" while believers in the other churches were poor, lost souls in need of receiving "the truth" that we alone possessed. I know that many of you grew up believing similar lies. Unknowingly, many of us fell into the same pharisaical trap—the same proud attitude that God hates. I pray that we as believers "who have been called out of darkness into His wonderful light" will not repeat these same mistakes by neglecting our responsibility to share the insights we have gained along our journey.

Isaac is called to Bless Ishmael

As we remember the life of Abraham we see that both sons of Abraham were blessed—Ishmael, the son of Hagar the slave girl as well as Isaac, the son of promise (Genesis 17:20). So what's the difference between the promise God made to Ishmael and the promise He made to Isaac?

The difference is that Isaac, the son born by the power of the Spirit, was to *become a blessing* to Ishmael, the son born in the ordinary way. In a similar way the church—the body of Christ that is born of the Spirit is called to *be a blessing* to the nations [born in the flesh] who don't know the Spirit of the Lord.

Speaking of the church, listen to the prophetic words of the prophet Isaiah: "Before she goes into labor she gives birth; before the pains come upon her, she delivers a son. Who has ever heard of such a thing? Who has ever seen such things? Can a country be born in a day or a nation brought forth in a moment? Yet no sooner is Zion in labor than she gives birth to her children. Do I bring to the moment of birth and not give delivery?" (Isaiah 66:7-9).

I believe this passage of Scripture is prophetically speaking of the rapid work the Lord is going to do by His Spirit as believers are called into travailing intercession to call forth the rest of God's children. Since God has promised to give us the nations for our inheritance, will we offer our hearts as a womb for Him to give spiritual birth to the rest of His children? Will we cry out in crisis intercession as the Spirit falls on us and pray for the lost so that multitudes of people will be born into the family of God in a day?

Entering into the Father's Heart

Before I had a child I didn't fully understand how a parent's heart could be pierced through to the quick at the thought of their child suffering for any hurt. Three months after my son, Rob, was born, my whole insides were turned upside down as I agonized over the suffering and shock that my baby endured one morning.

He was lying in his bassinet on the kitchen counter while I was working at the counter beside him. On this particular morning I had somehow neglected to strap him in. Suddenly he did something he had never done before. He sat up. In a flash I watched him lean forward, flip over, and fall headfirst onto the cement kitchen floor before I could catch him. Providentially the foam pad underneath him traveled with him.

Although I was only three feet away, I couldn't reach him in time. Crying out in agony, I scooped him up in my arms as my tears bathed his little ashen face. I was afraid he was dead. Suddenly his whimpering voice consoled me that God had heard my loud cries for help. He was alive. Quickly I grabbed my bag, ran out the door of my apartment, and a passing neighbor rushed me to the nearest doctor. "Oh God, don't let him die!" I prayed repeatedly all the way to the doctor's office.

Although the X-rays showed no obvious damage, I was bruised and damaged and suffered intensely in my emotions long after this incident. He recovered quickly, but it took me far longer. Because I loved him, I identified with his suffering. I would have done anything to take his place. I would have given my own life for my son if need be.

Through this frightening experience, on some minor level, I entered into the pain that ripped open the heart of the Father as He watched His Son suffer on the cross. We know that the Father and Son were both willing to bear everything on the cross for us. For each nail that was driven into the Son's hands and feet, thousands ripped into the heart of the Father. Why was He willing to suffer like that? Why was He willing to bear such awful pain? Because the eternal loss of one child hurts a lot more than the crack of a whip or the severing of crushed nerves.

The Cry in the Heart of the Father

Do you know why the angels rejoice when one son or daughter repents and turns to God? Do you know why the Father rejoices over one sinner who comes back to Him (Luke 15:7)? The costly sacrifice of giving up His Son for us so that we can be reconciled to Him is worth all the pain and agony that it took. He would have given up His Son for any one of us. Such is the great love in the heart of the Father.

But the Father wants to share His heart for the lost with you and me as He continues to call down through the ages, "Adam, where are you? Eve where are you?" We desperately need to receive the heart of the Father so that His love compels us to bring lost sons and daughters back to Him. Only then will we see the nets bulging with the fish of the harvest.

Why have some of us never felt the burden to intercede for a hurting neighbor, or weep for a suffering nation, let alone intercede for our enemies? Is it because we have been worshiping a "system of truth" instead of the Truth Giver? Do our self-sufficient attitudes identify us as the Pharisees of our generation? Or is it because we have been going through the motions of worship, but we have never entered into the *heart* of worship? Are we only singing words when we sing "Change our hearts. Renew us"? Could it be that we have not yet received the heart of the Father? We may know Psalm 23 by heart, but do we know the heart of the Shepherd?

Giving Birth to Nations

Many things are born through travailing intercession. "The work of Christ in reuniting God and man is intercession in its fullest sense.

Receiving The Father's Heart

There is no other mediator between God and man but Jesus. All of *our* intercession must be an extension of *His*. Through His [Jesus'] union with us, we represent Him and fulfill His will and purposes, the same way He represented and fulfilled the Father's. Our intercession goes through Christ and, as far as God is concerned, is really *His* [Christ's] intercession. This *only* makes it effective."[1]

Jesus told us that He could do nothing of Himself, but it was the Father who dwelt in Him that did the works" (John 5:30; 14:10). We must also come to this same realization if we desire to be used by God in these end times. Jesus was sent by the Father to this earth to reveal the Father's love to us. Now Jesus intervenes in the affairs of this world through the Church. Jesus sends us out in the same way that He was sent by the Father. We are His ambassadors representing Him here on earth. We are to be filled with the Spirit, led by the Spirit, empowered by the Spirit, and anointed by the Spirit to fulfill what the Head, Jesus Christ, wills. "The Father has no other plan but Jesus. Jesus has no other plan but the church"[2]

Will we as believers release our own burdens at the foot of the cross and take up the burden of intercession that is on God's heart? God wants to share with us His heart for the nations. But first we are called to minister to the nations that are at our back door—the *nations that are represented within the SDA church*—our family of origin that God's heart is waiting to embrace.

Only a revelation of the Father's love will make us willing to release Adventism's barren history that is riddled with deceptive practices, and unbiblical teachings at the foot of the cross. Once we release our SDA baggage to God, will we choose to become pregnant with His living Word for others?

Are we willing to *become a blessing to others* and offer our hearts as wombs where many spiritual births can take place? Are we willing to let the Lord seed the wombs of our hearts with His burden for the nations represented in Adventism?

"Father, I ask that you begin to pour out the fire of Your Spirit and place Your seed of Truth in the spiritual wombs of your children. Let travailing intercession give birth to the outbreak of Holy Spirit repentance. Let the pregnant seed of the living Word of God not return to You void (Isaiah 55:11).

Father, we choose to embrace the travail of Your heart, and receive the birth pangs that the Holy Spirit wants to bring forth within us (Isaiah 42:14;

Romans 8:22-27). Fill our hearts with the tears of the Father so that we might feel the pain of the Father's heart for the lost and deceived. Break our hearts now with the things that break Your heart.

Oh God, we repent for our hardness of heart—for our lack of love for others. Give us Your heart of intercession so that Your power will be released within us to share Christ's work of victory with the rest of Your children so they can be freed to enter into the joy of Your rest. Father, make us deliverers so that Your lost sons and daughters will return to the Father's heart.

Endnotes: Chapter 10

[1] Dutch Sheets, *Intercessory Prayer: The Lightning of God, Course Syllabus* (Published by Dutch Sheets, 1986) 20.

[2] Ibid., 14.

Only when we choose to repent and release our "good" works at the foot of the cross will we be free to enter into the joy of His "good" work.

Chapter 11
SOUNDING A CLEAR CALL

"If the trumpet does not sound a clear call, who will get ready for battle?"
1 Corinthians 14:8

Although the symbolism of an ostrich hiding its head in the sand seemed clear in this fourth scene of the vision, I was mystified by the icy cold stare in the ostrich's eyes that momentarily brought fear to my heart. Since I am prone to hide my face and withdraw from people when I think I appear foolish to them, because of the unusual way the Lord manifests His presence on me, I was encouraged by the words of the Lord, *"Don't hide your face because you think you appear foolish to others. Stand erect and tall in Me."*

However it was well over a year before the Lord began to show me from the book of Lamentations the connection between this scene of the vision and the hidden bondage of Adventism that people were seen holding on to in the dream. "How the gold has lost its luster, the fine gold has become dull! The sacred gems are scattered at the head of every street. How the precious sons of Zion, once worth their weight in gold, are now considered as pots of clay, the work of a potter's hands! Even jackals offer their breasts to nurse their young, but **my people have become heartless like ostriches in the desert.** Because of thirst the infant's tongue sticks to the roof of its mouth; the children beg for bread, but no one gives it to them" (Lamentations 4:1-4).

Jerusalem's Sins

As I looked at the historical setting of these verses my heart became strangely moved by God's heart of love and sorrow for His rebellious people Israel whom He was chastening because of the hardness of their hearts. History records for us that the inhabitants of Jerusalem died a long and lingering death by famine because they refused to *hear* the word of the Lord spoken to them through the prophet Jeremiah.

This "famine from hearing the word of the Lord" caused them to stubbornly refuse to surrender to the Babylonian army as the prophet Jeremiah had told them to do. They chose to be tortured in their minds and bodies as they slowly died for lack of food and water rather than submit to God's way of disciplining them—by surrendering to this gentile army.

A sorrow wrought by the Holy Spirit began to well up in me, and I began to weep over the past sins of God's people that had grieved and broken the Father's heart. Jeremiah saw God's rod of affliction fall on His people as He brought Jerusalem grief because of her many sins (Lamentations 1:5). He says, "The kings of the earth did not believe, nor did any of the world's people, that enemies and foes could enter the gates of Jerusalem. But it happened because of the sins of the prophets and the iniquities of her priests, who shed within her the blood of the righteous" (Lamentations 4:13).

It appears that nothing ripens a people more for destruction and ruin than the unconfessed sins and crooked practices of corrupt priests and false prophets. Nothing fills up the measure of God's cup of wrath faster than false prophets and corrupt priests joining their power and political interests to shed the blood of God's true prophets and of those righteous people who believed in them. Clearly it was the spiritual leaders of the nation of Israel who were the ringleaders in persecution. They condemned and killed the just.

Jeremiah acknowledges that it was because of the sins of Israel's leaders that God punished Jerusalem (Lamentations 4:13–16). However, this did not mean that the people who were led astray by them were innocent. Scripture reveals that the people loved to have the prophets prophesy lies and the priest's rule by their own authority. Their worship practices had become so corrupt that they shed the blood of their innocent children by sacrificing them to Molech.

So it was to please the people that the false prophets and corrupt priests did as they did (Jeremiah 5:31). But the fault is still chiefly laid upon the leaders who should have taught them better. They should have reproved and admonished the people and reminded them of the terrible consequences of disobedience and unbelief. Instead they *compromised the truth and corrupted the word of the Lord*. These false teachers tickled the people's ears and told them what they wanted to hear, thus blinding their minds and hearts. They preached, "Peace! Peace!" and refused to "see" the Sword of the Lord coming against them because of their rebellion.

The only reason enemies could have entered the gates of Jerusalem was that there were no watchmen posted on the walls of the City. There were no watchmen ready to blow the trumpet and sound the alarm to alert the people to take action against a sudden attack. Jerusalem fell because no one was "seeing" the approaching enemy—no one save the prophet Jeremiah. Although God used his voice as a trumpet to sound a clear call, no one believed his message and so no one was prepared for battle (1 Corinthians 14:8). What's more his voice had been silenced because King Zedekiah of Judah had thrown him into a dungeon for daring to speak the truth about the coming Babylonian attack.

History clearly records for us that during the siege of Jerusalem the Jews had become so wicked that they appeared to have lost all natural feelings of affection for their own flesh and blood—even to the point of eating their own children. They were concerned primarily with their own survival in the awful famine and not the welfare of their own offspring. From what the prophet Jeremiah witnessed in the siege of Jerusalem he compares the cruel actions of his people to women who forsake their children like an ostrich does its eggs (Job 39:17). In other words, the "heartlessness" of the ostrich that forsakes her offspring is being compared to the heartlessness of professed believers who will betray their own flesh and blood in the hope of saving their own lives.

The Ostrich

As I read about the sins of Israel's leaders—the crooked practices of corrupt priests and false prophets, I saw that these spiritual leaders were perpetrators in the cycle of spiritual incest that affected the

Jewish nation. The abuse of their power and spiritual authority was wielded against the common people who became pawns in their hands—victims of spiritual incest in that generation. These spiritual leaders set themselves up as gate keepers using religious performance rather than faith in the coming Messiah as the criterion for accepting or rejecting their spiritual children.

By using this *forgotten book* of Lamentations, God is arresting our attention in order to remind us of the *forgotten cry of the Father's heart* towards His rebellious people, Israel. He's reminding us again of the generational cycle of spiritual incest that continues to be passed down from one generation to the next, particularly within Adventism.

As I remembered the confusion and fear I experienced the moment the large ostrich turned and looked at me with an icy cold stare, I saw in that soul-less look, a cold heart of rebellion. Just as the spiritual pride and the coldness of unbelief of God's people in Jeremiah's day caused them to be taken into captivity, so this present generation of believers within Adventism has also allowed spiritual pride and cold unbelief to cause them to be taken captive by the lies of the enemy.

The icy coldness of people in Jeremiah's day caused them to be taken into captivity—in the natural, because spiritually they were already in captivity. Indeed, God's judgment may have come upon them because they continued to keep each other in spiritual bondage. So God used the captivity in the natural (judgment) to break them, and set them free from further spiritual bondage.

Through this symbol of an ostrich God is warning of judgment coming upon the SDA church, because of icy-cold spiritually abusive captivity. He's reminding us of "Lamentations" because He doesn't want to bring harsh judgment upon the church. He's reminding us of the weeping and anguish and cruel torment that came upon the inhabitants of Jerusalem as a result of their rebellion and sin, because He wants "to turn the hearts of spiritual fathers towards their spiritual children, and the hearts of spiritual children towards their spiritual fathers in Adventism so that He doesn't have to come and strike the land with a curse" (my paraphrase of Malachi 4:6).

Even though many of us claim to have left traditional Adventism behind us by becoming a part of a non-traditional SDA church, the dream revealed that our Adventist roots run very deep. Even though we claim to be free God sees us as slave children who are unaware of the weight of deception we unwittingly continue to carry. Rather than face our fear that Adventism's package deal may not be such a good deal after all, many of us have chosen to bury our heads in the sand and ignore the twisted ways Adventism has used Ellen White's writings as a filter through which to interpret Scripture and support error.

Students in "school"

As I remembered the ending of the dream where every seat in this SDA church became a desk, I realized that God's heart for this body of believers is that every member will choose not to bury his or her head in the sand, but instead, choose to become a student in the School of the Spirit.

The symbol of "desks" and "studying" that God is bringing before us here becomes clearer as we humbly admit that we have felt like we understood more about grace, and more about the cross than other churches. But God is throwing a desk into our denominational "guts" and saying, "No, you need to learn all over again!"

We need to be re-educated, to learn all over again beginning at the Cross! It's a humble step to take. We thought we were advanced, but He is putting desks in front of us and asking us to become students of the Cross all over again. God wants to teach us by His Spirit how to discern truth from error through the pages of Scripture. He wants to reclaim the true meaning of verses that have been perverted by false interpretations. He wants us to no longer act like sons and daughters of the slave woman, but of the free.

So in order to become teachable to the things of the Spirit we must first release any lingering remains of a rule-based and shame-based theology at the foot of the cross. Our preconceived ideas and opinions must also be left there as we come with open minds to see what the Spirit will teach us through the Scriptures.

I discovered that when something was out of order in the early church, Paul almost never defined right and wrong behavior with a written law. Instead, when he saw something out of order, as he did with Peter at Antioch, he told Peter and his brethren "they were not acting in line with the truth of the gospel" (Galatians 2:14).

In a similar way God wants to teach us by His Spirit how to discern truth from error by making sure that every teaching from His Word lines up with the truth of the gospel. What has already been given to us in the new covenant gospel of Jesus Christ, and His finished work on the cross must become the plumb line that puts everything else in its rightful place.

Calling forth a Gideon-like Army

As I pondered the possibility of every desk in the church being filled with a seeker after Truth I was excited. God's heart for us is that everyone who has been a victim of spiritual incest will choose to become a survivor by acknowledging their pain, and choosing to forgive their abusers instead of burying their heads in the sand. Although battle-scarred and broken, looking more like a motley crew of rejects than an army dressed for battle, our Commander-in-Chief is calling forth a Gideon-like army from this group of spiritual incest survivors who will go forth into battle to contend for the freedom of those still held in captivity.

Just as Gideon's army of three hundred men was used by God to defeat the Midianites who had become their oppressors, so God will use a Gideon-like band of spiritual incest survivors to defeat the enemy's plans of taking yet another generation of God's SDA children captive. As the agape love of the Father flows through this army of broken clay pitchers, they will become a beacon of light and hope to the rest of God's captive children. Just as Gideon gave every man who went into battle with him a trumpet to blow at the given signal, so God is going to be "blowing the trumpet" through each of us who choose to release Adventism's bondage at the foot of the cross.

As released captives corporately blow the trumpet and sound the alarm it will arrest the attention of the larger Adventist circle. Their corporate prophetic voice will rock Adventism's shaky foundation as it is gripped by the naked truth of the gospel.

Fear of Losing Control

A number of years ago God called some of us who were open to the move of the Spirit to be prophetic intercessors and watchmen on the walls of this SDA church that was the setting for this dream. Whenever we would see the enemy approaching we were called to abort his plans by blowing the trumpet, and sounding a clear call in order to awaken the rest of the body to action against his advances.

Unfortunately some of our voices were never heard, because those in leadership at that time ignored the word we received from the Lord. Consequently, human trumpets that were meant to awaken this sleeping church into action were silenced by leadership's fear of losing control.

As times changed and new leadership came, God began raising up more prophetic intercessors and watchmen so that more human trumpets could sound a clear call. Will we choose to be counted as watchmen and sound the corporate trumpet so that our fellow brothers and sisters, not only within this particular church body, but also within the Adventist church at large, can be freed from the cycle of spiritual incest that keeps them in bondage to a false belief system? Will we choose to stand up for truth and allow the Spirit of Truth to use us to expose the lies that hold millions of spiritual incest survivors in bondage to unscriptural teachings and deception?

We must refuse to be manipulated by fear-induced loyalty to a religious group that still wants to define our Christian duties by a system that carefully outlines what is permissible and what is not. We must choose *not* to hide our heads in the sand like the proverbial ostrich, and allow our voices to be silenced by those who fear the reprisals that will most certainly come if we choose to obey the voice of the Lord? Because we can no longer stay within the safety of our familiar comfort zones, we must *choose* to stand tall in Christ and release Adventism's errors at the foot of the cross. Clearly we are being called as a church to forsake the heartlessness of the ostrich and receive the heart of the Father for our own flesh and blood.

Aborting the Enemy's Plans

Could the "heartlessness" I saw in the eyes of the ostrich represent many perpetrators and victims of spiritual incest within Adventism who are in danger of turning against their own flesh and blood and "falling away" because they refuse to acknowledge their participation in this cycle of spiritual abuse? They want to continue to cover up the mistakes of their forbearers rather than admit they have been deceived? Judging by the size of this very large bird it appeared, not only to be pregnant and ready to give birth to more of its own kind, but pregnant with the same fear-induced loyalty that pressures incest victims into silence while trying to perform well enough so they will be accepted by those in spiritual authority over them.

The only way this spiritual pregnancy can be aborted and the cycle of spiritual incest within Adventism stopped is for this present generation of spiritual incest survivors to sound forth the trumpet with a clear call of warning regarding the contents of Adventism's package as they release it to the foot of the cross. For Adventism's "righteousness" can never be dressed up to look like anything but filthy rags, and is a more formidable enemy of the gospel than most of us realize.

Even after SDAs find the Spirit and come to accept the whole body of Christ, they often still feel there is something unique about Adventism they must share with the rest of the body of Christ. Most often they feel it is their special understanding of the Sabbath or end time events.

I believe God does have a unique purpose for "released captives" from Adventism in the end-times Body. But our importance in the Body is *not* because we will add a unique teaching, for our uniqueness is in Christ. He is our Chosen One. He is all we need, because we no longer need affirmation from "getting something right" where the rest of the Body didn't.

Admitting our Addiction

I believe our role as "released captives" in the end-times body of Christ will NOT come from what we got "right," but from where we were wrong! The things we were wrong about are strongholds covering the weaknesses that God wants to use to glorify Himself by removing blinders of similar strongholds from the rest of the body of Christ. So Christ will be magnified through our weaknesses by our choosing to surrender our addictions to Him.

Adventism's primary weakness has been its addiction to the "old wine" of the old covenant by which it has been intoxicated. The old wine has literally been the life-blood of its theology. Adventism has sought after it and run after it with a vehemence rarely matched by other zealots in Christian denominations. In Adventism we pursued character change and strove to live righteous lives. Character change was our anchor and the measure of our spirituality.

But as "released captives" from Adventism our spiritual anchor will be replaced with reliance on the steadfastness of Jesus Christ who doesn't change, no matter how often our faith waivers with the ups and downs of life. Released captives from Adventism will "trumpet" dependence on Jesus' character, Jesus' purity and Jesus' righteousness alone. The same zeal with which we pursued error, calling it "truth" will now forbid us from settling for anything less than the righteousness of Jesus Christ Himself found in the new covenant gospel.

Because the old covenant has been so strongly built into the Adventist DNA, God will use freed captives to release those who are still bound, not only within the SDA church, but also in other churches where old covenant bondage is subtler and not so obvious. Having been indoctrinated and intoxicated by old covenant theology to the extreme, we will recognize the symptoms of addiction in others because we have been immersed so deeply in it ourselves.

For instance, a man who has been delivered from his addiction of sleeping with prostitutes can aid another brother who is addicted to pornography. For the same foul spirit is behind each addiction. But the man who was further in bed with the spirit will recognize the characteristics and the subtleties of its attack and be able to warn and help his brother.

It was very difficult for me, and I'm sure for most other believers who have been released from Adventism's bondage, to initially recognize and admit the theological mistakes and serious errors found in Adventism's belief system. Where once we were afraid of being on the wrong path in our pursuit of truth we now have no fear of being wrong. As liberated captives who now know the heart of the Father we are learning how to "rest" in Christ with a new humility because we have been **very** wrong.

Admitting our errors will eventually bring a much-needed *rest*, and its effects will spread not only into other SDA churches, but also to other non Adventist churches that have covered up error as well. We will no longer fear being mistaken, for Christ is "right" and He is our rightness. Our reliance will move from trusting in our rightness to His.

For a moment imagine the corporate body of Christ, with all of its divided churches choosing to become one giant support group. Now imagine Adventism as a whole — historical master at covering up error, and putting off dealing with rejection, choosing to step up to the plate and confessing what has been hidden in the archives for over 150 years.

Imagine the response of members of the body of Christ as they see the SDA church become naked before God and before them. Imagine how they would no longer fear to repent. For we have *nothing* to fear and nothing to lose in Christ who loves us and gave Himself for us. If Adventism would choose to take off its filthy rags in public and help other churches to do the same, it would find its true identity and the measure of its worth and acceptance in Jesus Christ Himself.

If only Adventism would choose to expose its nakedness, Jesus would most certainly cover it with His banner of love. If only the SDA church would choose to admit its errors and weaknesses it would help other churches that have been similarly addicted to the old wine of the old covenant escape from their bondage as well. If only Adventists would taste and see that the Lord is good, they would no longer crave the "old wine" for the new wine of the Spirit is so much better (Luke 5:36-39).

A Hardened Heart

I believe the warning is clear in this scene of the vision. If we insist on holding on to Adventism's package after its contents have been exposed to the light of truth, we will be in danger of having our hearts become hardened like an ostrich that deserts its young. Eventually the darkness of deception will overcome our own hearts because we have taken our eyes off Jesus Christ. Our only guarantee of *not* becoming like a heartless ostrich is to receive the heart of the Father. Only as we receive His heart will we choose to love our own as Christ loves the church. For "a darkened heart is a far country, for it is *not* by our feet but by our affections that we leave Thee or return to Thee" (St. Augustine).

Through the imagery of the ostrich the Lord is telling us that unless we choose to become willing to repent of the offenses that we are harboring in our hearts towards one another, we will eventually become hardened and calloused and unable to respond to the Spirit of God. After a period of time, hardened hearts become "turncoats". In order to save our own lives we will be willing to secretly join forces with the enemy and become traitors, abandoning and betraying our own flesh and blood.

Set Free from Judgment

Doesn't the imagery of the heartless ostrich reveal that many of us who are spiritual incest survivors need to cry out to God to place His mercy in our hearts so that we may forgive those who have wronged us? Many of us carry deep scars that have appeared to lie dormant for years, festering silently, under scabs of bitterness. As a result of this spiritual wounding, we need to be set free from the bondage of judgment.

Whether it is those in leadership who have sinned against us, or our brother or sister beside us, we need to forgive them. Not only must we choose to forgive those who have wronged us, but also we need to repent of our own sin of judging their motives. Our bitter and judgmental reaction to those who have hurt us is also sinful. And the enemy, being the legalist that he is, will use our judgment against us in order to bring more judgment upon us in the areas where we have been wounded and hurt. It is called the law of sowing and reaping.

Could it be that one of the reasons the cycle of spiritual incest in Adventism has continued for so many generations is that up until now we have *not* chosen to confront and forgive those who have spiritually abused us? Is it also possible that many of us who are still victims have not repented of our sin of judging the perpetrator's motives? Consequently the enemy has gained the legal right to bring the law of sowing and reaping into our lives in the very areas where we have been repeatedly hurt.

Power of Unconditional Forgiveness

Wasn't this law of sowing and reaping manifested in the lives of the hypocritical Jewish leaders of Christ's day who represented the religious institution with its cherished traditions and forms of religion? Remember how some of them used the woman caught in adultery to try to entrap Jesus? Even though some of them set her up in order to humiliate Jesus and bring Him down, Jesus never publicly exposed their individual sins of adultery. Jesus showed those unrepentant leaders mercy. "He that is without sin" chose not to cast a stone at her or them. Mercy was shown towards both the perpetrator and victim alike.

I believe the Lord is saying to each one of us who are survivors of spiritual incest that unless we offer restoration and forgiveness to our spiritual abusers, we cannot hope to preach the message of Christ's unconditional love to the world. Since He has already reconciled the world to Himself by His sacrifice, God wants to bring down the wall of bitterness and offense that separates us from our brothers and sisters *within* the church. For God wants to bring new life to both the perpetrators and victims alike

Recognizing abuse

Unfortunately, sometimes people who are abused by their natural parents aren't always able to recognize their abuse until much later in life, sometimes never at all. I believe this is because we love our natural parents, even if they abuse us. Similarly, in the SDA church, we have loved our history, our heritage, our pioneer fathers and mother (Ellen White). We've grown up in a peculiar community and grown close to one another. We've grown to enjoy the traditions we've been raised in. When bad things happened, we would rather hold onto the good and forget about the bad.

Through confronting the members of this SDA church with the bondage they are holding on to perhaps God is in the process of helping us get back in touch with our inner child. He's addressing that part of us that initially cried and recoiled when we first experienced spiritual abuse, but later denied it because it hurt too much, or it hurt too much to think of our spiritual parents badly.

Anyone who has been abused by a parent knows that healing in this area doesn't come overnight. It takes time. I think in the same way, God is bringing the members of this church through a long process of being able to face the spiritual abuses we've suffered from our spiritual parents and from our own hands. This process will be frustrating for many because we are used to a works-mentality: "Tell me what to do and I'll do it." We're used to looking for the missing part, that complete truth that we need to know and obey in order to be accepted by God.

But we don't have to think of our spiritual parents badly. I love my natural father and mother even though they abused me because God helped me forgive them. Forgiveness is essential for us as believers. Not cover-up and denial, but forgiveness. We are no better or worse than our spiritual parents who abused us with the law. We are both called by God's grace in His Son. Jesus died for all of us because we have all been guilty. We've all been broken. Now it's time to bring everything into the light and lay our wounds down at the foot of the cross and be healed.

Power of the cross

I am reminded of a devotional written by Lloyd John Ogilvie in which he describes how Paul used two vivid metaphors to communicate the power of the cross for our forgiveness. Both metaphors have to do with the judicial custom in Paul's day of writing a charge list against a person. The charge list of wrongs committed or debts owed was then displayed where everyone could see it—in a city square or near a town hall. Imagine how the offended person was thoroughly shamed.

Ogilvie goes on to share that God had a charge list against us. But there was no way we could pay our debt of sin. Paul illustrated grace by telling the Colossian believers that redemption through Christ was like wiping the charge list clean, and then nailing it to the cross (Colossians 2:13-17).

Since there was no indelible ink in Paul's day, and parchment was often smooth, writing could be wiped off with a damp sponge. The analogy becomes clear. In Christ's death all our sins were wiped from our charge list.

But not only is our charge list wiped clean, it is also nailed to the cross. In Paul's day, when a nail was driven through a displayed charge list, it was proof that the charges that had been levied against the offending person had been paid or cancelled. Do we see the point that Paul is trying to make? He is proclaiming that when the nails were driven through Christ's hands and feet, our debts were cancelled—paid in full. So whenever the enemy reminds us of our sins, we need to claim that our failure has been nailed—paid in full by Jesus Christ.

Forgiveness is a Choice

Jesus clearly demonstrated for us that our forgiving others is as important as the air we breathe. When we refuse to forgive one another, we harden our own hearts so that they eventually become callused and cold like the heartlessness of an ostrich that forsakes her young. Then it becomes impossible for us to receive God's forgiveness for ourselves.

Our decision to forgive someone who has wronged us has got nothing to do with who's right or who's wrong or even how we feel. To choose to forgive does not mean we condone what others have done, but it *does* mean that we won't let their sin destroy us. It means that we let go of the painful memories of past hurts and abuses. It means that we will let go of the lies that have been told, and even the gossip that has been shared that has hindered the cause of Christ. It means that we choose to obey the biblical principle of forgiveness and forfeit our personal rights to hold on to a grudge. It means that we choose to let go of our pride and walk in humility as we let go of our grievances and any lingering resentment, no matter how justified. Ultimately, our willingness to forgive others means that we choose to let go of the charge lists that we carry against those who have hurt or abused us and we nail them to the cross.

Warning against falling away

As we choose *not* to hold on to any bitterness or anger in our hearts toward our brothers and sisters, our forgiveness prevents their actions from producing a root of bitterness or offense in us (Hebrews 12:15). For bitter roots grow up to cause trouble and defile many in the church. The Scriptures remind us "anyone who claims to be in the light but hates his brother is still in darkness" (1 John 2:9). "Anyone who hates his brother is a murderer, and you know that no murderer has eternal life in him" (1 John 3:15).

Rather, since "Jesus Christ laid down His life for us… we ought to lay down our lives for our brothers [and sisters]. If anyone has material possessions and sees his brother in need but has no pity on him, how can the love of God be in him? Dear children, let us not love with words or tongue but with actions and in truth" (1 John 3:16-18).

The author of the book of Hebrews wrote a solemn warning to Jewish Christians who were ready to give up their faith and return to the Jewish faith because of persecution. He says, "It is impossible for those who have once been enlightened, who have tasted the heavenly gift, who have tasted the goodness of the word of God and the powers of the coming age, if they fall away, to be brought back to repentance..." (Hebrews 6:4-6).

Peter goes on to tell us that "it would have been better for them not to have known the way of righteousness, than to have known it and then to turn their backs on the sacred command that was passed on to them. Of them the proverb is true: 'A dog returns to his vomit,' and 'A sow that is washed goes back to her wallowing in the mud.'" (2 Peter 2:21-22). Unless we let God change our hard hearts and receive *His* heart, we will go back to wallowing in our long lists of rules that continue to hold us in captivity.

We can choose to not be found among those who fall away and cannot be brought back to repentance because bitterness and unforgiveness in our hearts has made them callous and impenetrable to the voice of the Spirit of God. Instead, our eyes must be fixed upon Jesus Christ whose life is the only Life that pleases the Father. The priceless value of His life becomes ours by faith as we choose to depend upon His righteousness alone.

May the Spirit help us all see that man's righteousness continues to be the most formidable enemy of the new covenant gospel. Throughout history it has been the religious people who stumbled over the Rock—Jesus Christ. Those who profess a form of godliness, but deny the Spirit's power will continue to bring the greatest persecution against true believers in the body of Christ who are born by the power of the Spirit.

Sounding the trumpet

Over the last three years I have come to better understand the purpose of God in causing someone to become drunk in the Spirit as I am reminded that the early church was born with the sign of intoxication. When the Holy Spirit fell at Pentecost believers drank Him in to such a degree they were accused of being full of new wine because they looked drunk to the natural eye.

One of the benefits of being intoxicated with the new wine of the Spirit was that they were given boldness to fearlessly proclaim the Good News. They were freed from old religious mind-sets and paradigms to such a degree that they became totally abandoned to God and His purposes. Even though to the natural eye they appeared drunk on new wine to their listeners they were, in fact, very sensitive to the Holy Spirit and could hear His voice and obey freely.

What was God's purpose in causing them to become drunk in the Spirit? Clearly it must have been similar to the intoxication Jeremiah experienced as he was called to prophesy to a people in bondage under the Babylonian system. He said, "I am like a drunken man whom wine has overcome because of the Lord and His holy words" (Jeremiah 23:9).

As the Holy Spirit intoxicated Jeremiah he was enabled to prophesy to God's rebellious people in order to break through religious mindsets and the judgmental spirit created by the false prophets of his day. Because the church today (especially the SDA church) has become a "wilderness" of confusion, the Holy Spirit is moving through various prophetic voices at this time in order to draw people's attention away from the old wine of institutionalized religion so that they will become thirsty for the New Wine—Jesus Christ.

We must choose not to frustrate the purposes of God in the way He chooses to awaken the church out of her sleepy condition. For He sometimes uses what appears to be foolishness in order to address modern-day pharisaic spirits and disable the self-righteous mindset of many in the body of Christ today.

The prophetic sign of 'ho!'[1] that has both blessed and frustrated the body of Christ is given as a trumpet call to startle us and awaken us out of our spiritual slumber. God wants us to desire Him… to become thirsty for the Living Water. His desire is to unlock our hearts and minds so that we can be set free from sectarianism, particularly Adventism. He is overturning the "tables of the money changers" so that His house is no longer "a den of thieves". He's bringing up the perversion of truth that Adventism has so diligently tried to ignore and cover up.

Yes, even at this SDA church that is the setting for this dream many have tried to make it look petty and divisive to uncover the truth, and have sometimes even judged it to be a religious spirit. But in response to Pilate's question, "What is truth?" Jesus replied, "In fact, for this reason I was born, and for this I came into the world, to testify to the truth. Everyone on the side of truth listens to me" (John 18:37-38, NIV).

People in the world and even some in the church don't know that they can find truth, because they don't rely on the Holy Spirit who has said He will lead us into ALL truth. But Jesus said that everyone on the side of truth listens to Him! Can we hear Him calling us by His Spirit?

God is "releasing captives" from spiritual incest at this very hour so they can respond **by faith** to the **truth** of the Good News of Jesus Christ and His finished work for all people.

This Good News is not about you or me—it's about Him! Only when we choose to repent and release our "good" works at the foot of the cross will we be free to enter into the joy of *His* "good" work. The Good News is an announcement, a shout, a cry and a proclamation of what God has *already* done for us in Jesus Christ for *all* the inhabitants of planet Earth.

As repentant believers who have been freed by the power of His unconditional love we are being called to share Christ's work of victory *for us* with the rest of His children. It's time to celebrate *His* victory and enter into *His* rest. In the words of a popular worship song, "Shout to the North," it's time to shout about this Good News! Will you join me in a shout of victory as we blow the trumpet together and wake up the sleeping Church?

Endnotes: Chapter 11

[1] In the fall of 1997, the Lord began manifesting the Hebrew word "Ho!" through the author. The Hebrew word "Ho" is found around fifty times in the Old Testament, usually translated as "woe, ho, alas, come, pay attention, listen up, etc." and sometimes retained in Old King James English. Most times in Scripture it appears to be used as a warning to alert people to pay attention to what God is saying through His prophets. I believe that today God is using men and women as "human shofars", as trumpets to wake up those who are spiritually asleep (see Joel 2:1). The "Ho!" is a call to forsake our empty cisterns (Jer. 2:13) and come drink the living water of intimacy with Christ: "Ho, everyone that thirsteth, come ye to the waters and drink, and he that hath no money; come ye, buy, and eat; yeah, come, buy wine and milk without money and without price." (Isa. 55:1, KJV)

The mythical heritage of Adventism glorifies Adventist pioneers and their teachings while glossing over the deception, error, and spiritual abuse that existed from the beginning.

Chapter 12: Epilogue
ADVENTISM'S ANCEINT STRONGHOLD

It finally became obvious after three years that the present leadership of this new church "experiment" within Adventism was *not* going to heed the call to stand on the truth of the Scriptures, and let go of historical Adventist doctrines that are contradictory to God's Word. As the Holy Spirit began to further expose the "naked truth" behind Adventism's cover-up, the leadership, along with many of its members, dug in their heels, and adamantly refused to heed the warning to lift the veils and throw off the yoke of bondage.

Knowing that I could no longer be a part of a church that refused to walk in the light of truth that God was bringing to us through His Word, I sorrowfully began to prepare my heart to leave my church family for the second time around. As I was coming to terms with the fact that our prayers for this church to become a catalyst for change within the SDA denomination were not about to be realized any time soon, God spoke to me quite unexpectedly Saturday morning, January 13, 2007.

I was in the bathroom getting ready for church when I clearly heard the words, "The Last Samurai" spoken into my mind. I was surprised to hear the title of a movie about a Japanese warrior that I had no interest in seeing when it came out. As I mused about this word, wondering what was on God's heart, I received another word two days later on Monday morning, January 15, 2007. God spoke the words, "Custer's Last Stand" into my mind the same way. Again I received a witness in my spirit that God was drawing another important parallel between "The Last Samurai", "Custer's Last Stand", and the reluctance of SDA leadership to let go of historical Adventist doctrines that are contradictory to God's Word.

Not having seen "The Last Samurai", and knowing very little about Japanese history, I emailed my friend, Ramone, in Japan (see Foreword) hoping to find the needed historical context for the movie that might shed some light on this puzzle. Ramone not only gave me the historical background of "The Last Samurai", but also of "Custer's Last Stand." He was also given an understanding of the bearing these two phrases had on the messages God had been downloading into my spirit.

As you prayerfully read the background summaries of these two events, along with the interpretation Ramone received from the Lord, I pray that the eyes of your heart may be opened to see how God is pouring forth His heart of concern and love toward His children who remain stuck in the malaise of Adventism. This word is given to forcefully remind us that history has a way of repeating itself. Men in positions of leadership and power who are blinded by pride often make tragic errors in judgment. Unfortunately, they are often exonerated by their followers who also believe the lie, and perpetuate the deception by passing it on to the next generation.

Background of "The Last Samurai"

The "Last Samurai" is a fictional character who rebels against the government because of its immorality as it modernizes. The movie portrays noble motives for the samurai's rebellion based on honor, honesty, better ethics and a better way of life.

However, in the real life historical samurai rebellion, the primary motive was self-preservation of their unique and privileged social class. The true-life samurai rebellion was a last desperate attempt to hold onto a traditional social caste and position of power that crippled the country by marginalizing and denigrating a great many of its people. Modernization was resisted because it would put an end to the old system. The movie ignores the historical truth and adopts the myth of the superiority of the old *bushido* system. It is filmed through rose-tinted glasses, portraying a noble fight to preserve a fictional ideal that never quite was.

What is God saying?

Like old "bushido", the Law also "keeps people in their place." This "Ancient Stronghold," that is called a "ministry of condemnation and death", keeps people from rising above sin and death in their lives, because a veil covers their eyes. The abolition of the Samurai class and feudal Japanese society spelled freedom for many people. Of course it took many years for attitudes to change (and some things are still being changed), but in general, it was this crumbling of an ancient stronghold ("bushido") that liberated many classes of people in society.

I believe God is saying that "The Last Samurai" applies to many Adventist leaders who are unwilling to let the "old" go. They are looking through rose-tinted glasses at Adventism's heritage and insist on holding onto a delusion. They may feel like they are fighting to the death to preserve a noble code of honor, a noble Adventist history. But, in truth, it is a fictional ideal, because the history never really existed as they want to believe. The mythical heritage of Adventism they invoke is a creation of imagined self-importance. It glorifies Adventist pioneers and their teachings while glossing over the deception, error, condemnation and spiritual abuse that existed from the beginning.

Additionally, Adventism has always felt it was more correct and more "moral" because it re-instituted the Old Covenant Law. It returned to the old written code and pointed the finger of accusation at Christians who did not do the same. It sang the virtues of the old system and claimed that without the Law, we are deficient and morally lost. In truth, however, the Bible states that we are no longer under the old code (the Law), because the purpose of the Law was to reveal sin and death so that we might cling to Jesus instead! The Law was "the ministry of condemnation" and "the ministry of death". In the presence of Life Himself how could the ministry of death hold greater appeal? How could the Adventist pioneers have been induced to prefer condemnation?

The old samurai looked upon suicide as noble and as an honorable way out of a situation. In a sense, it was often seen as the consummation of an honorable life, deed or heroic effort. It fulfilled the *bushido* code of honor and was, in a way, the perfection of honor. After the "last samurai" lost the battle and stabbed himself, his dying words were "It's perfect".

Just as the *bushido* code climaxed in the act of suicide, the Law's purpose was to "administer death". It was meant only as a tutor to lead us to faith, but now that faith has come we are no longer under the Law. If we have come alive with Christ in faith then return to serve the Law, we have chosen spiritual death! In trying to heroically hold onto the Law Adventism is committing spiritual suicide. Adventism honors the Law of death as the way to perfection, just as the samurai viewed suicide as the summit of perfection and honor?

In the movie and in history, the "last samurai" *rebelled* against the established governmental authority of the day. Adventism—by returning to the Law—has rebelled against God's authority to govern under the New, rather than the Old, Covenant. Adventism's willful rejection of God's "new" order as *insufficient* declares their superior wisdom that "the old way" is better.

Interestingly, a lot of the pressure to change "closed" parts of Japanese society came from outside Japan, particularly the West. This, of course, hurt Japanese pride. For 400 years, Japan sealed itself off, refusing trade or contact with the West until the mid-1800s. When Japan finally became "open" to the outside world, conflicts of pride arose as Western influences began to infiltrate their insular society.

This parallels Adventism's history, which, for 40 years, was without the gospel until the Minneapolis General Conference in 1888 in which the truth of salvation by faith alone began to break through the heterodox doctrines. For the vast bulk of Adventism's history it has isolated itself from mainstream Christianity both socially and theologically. In more modern times there has been a move to associate with other churches while holding tenaciously to the distinctives that set Adventism apart from the rest of Christianity. As doctrinal flaws have been more and more difficult for the theologians to defend, the focus has changed from theology to community. Members are called to loyalty toward their history and identity.

Similarly, Japan has struggled with the more unsavory details of Japanese history as the people attempt to venerate their unique heritage. Many resort to denial of the abusive acts of aggression exacted on their neighboring Asian nations during war times in order to avoid taking responsibility for them by making public apology. There were unthinkable atrocities which, among other things, included human vivisections conducted on Chinese prisoners and forced prostitution of Korean women to supply the "needs" of the Japanese army. To this day there is a guilty silence that prevents open dialogue about the sins of the country that might lead to healing of the communal wounds. Human rights are now considered imperative, but the lack of them in days gone by cannot be discussed. The taboo historical subjects are expunged from textbooks, perpetuating the shame of national crimes to successive generations.

In tragic parallel, Adventism has chosen cover-up rather than discovery regarding the sad distortion of truths regarding the Investigative Judgment and predilection for law over grace. Because of the culture of secrecy its people are paralyzed in their ability to engage in open dialogue regarding their false foundations. Even in the most liberal communities the searching light of inspection is directed away from sensitive topics that may expose the murky darkness in which Adventism was conceived. Grace has, thankfully, become a more widespread sermon topic, but the lack of that teaching in historical Adventism is not acknowledged. Unfortunately, honest educators have not had an easy path to walk in seeking to lead their students to seek truth. Their efforts to extend truth-seeking to Adventist history and theology have resulted in many terminations from denominational employment.

Adventism's history began with spiritual abuse that has been passed on from generation to generation to the present day... As church leaders continue to preach an amalgamation of grace from the new covenant and law from the old they create a confused gospel of condemnation and death that renders the work of Jesus Christ ineffectual and incomplete. The spiritual offspring which they have spawned do not appear to be any more prepared than the current leaders to call a halt to the unholy marriage of old and new. Until the old is put to rest there can be no freedom from fear.

Those who bear the spiritual responsibility for doctrinal purity refuse to institute the necessary changes for fear of toppling the entire structure of corporate Adventism. They consider it preferable to allow the falsehood and spiritual abuse to continue. Just as in days of old, however, the Lord has been sending prophetic voices to warn that He will not always bear with the spiritual rape of their progeny in order to satisfy their own institutional aspirations. They seem to have weighed slavery to condemnation for their people against their own fears of losing Adventist culture and rose-tinted heritage and have been found woefully culpable!

More and more Adventist pastors and leaders are being confronted with a choice of eternal magnitude: whether to choose the truth of new covenant gospel or to continue in the clearly faulty teachings of the Seventh-day Adventist Church. The choices they make will carry with them the power to bring light and hope or confusion and uncertainty to themselves, their families and their flocks. Even silence at the point of decision makes them collaborators in the cycle of spiritual abuse. How many Adventist leaders will hear these words from the Lord? "'Woe to the shepherds who are destroying and scattering the sheep of my pasture!...Because you have scattered my flock and driven them away and have not bestowed care on them, I will bestow punishment on you for the evil you have done...I myself will gather the remnant of my flock out of all the countries where I have driven them and will bring them back to their pasture, where they will be fruitful and increase in number. I will place shepherds over them who will tend them, and they will no longer be afraid or terrified..." Jeremiah 23:1-4 (NIV)

Background of "Custer's Last Stand"

Lt. Colonel George Armstrong Custer had gained renown during the 1800's for his valor in leading American army forces into battle with Native Americans in the "Indian wars". He is remembered best, however for his monumental underestimation of the combined forces of the Sioux and Cheyenne nations in the battle of Little Bighorn in eastern Montana. Custer came with a force of between 200- 600 soldiers, while those who were defending their ancient ways of life had amassed an army nearing 1800 warriors.

Some estimate that within half an hour the defending Native Americans had decimated Custer and all of his soldiers from the Seventh U.S. Cavalry. America tried to redeem the debacle by calling it "Custer's last stand", implying that a brave American army officer had nobly given his life to defend his country against the invading savages. The over-confident, short-sighted Custer was transformed into an icon of bravery and courage. Truth, however, was much less complimentary. The Native Americans were, in fact, making a last stand to defend a way of life that went back many centuries against newcomers who were trying to eradicate them from the face of the Earth. The Americans had corralled them onto reservations with the arrogant claim of generosity–giving them back a fraction of the land that was theirs to begin with. The European immigrants had brought with them disease, suffering and death. With the confiscation of their lands went the very commodity that constituted their identity.

What Are the Parallels?

Historical revisionism has plagued Adventism from the beginning. Just as Custer's defeat was recast as a heroic stand against encroaching evil so was Adventism's erroneous date-setting for the Second Coming reborn as the Investigative Judgment, spawning "The Great Advent Movement". Adventism's last ditch strategy was to turn the "Great Disappointment" into a glorious new truth. But just as in many other distortions Adventist teaching has redefined the word "truth" to stand for error. The words of God will stand against them as He searches their motivations and continued cover-up of His truth. "So justice is driven back, and righteousness stands at a distance; truth has stumbled in the streets, honesty cannot enter. Truth is nowhere to be found, and whoever shuns evil becomes a prey. The LORD looked and was displeased that there was no justice. He saw that there was no one, he was appalled that there was no one to intervene" (Isaiah 59:14-16, NIV) Behind propaganda is the desire to hide the truth with bravado.

Perhaps you, too, have believed the myths about Adventism—its noble, heroic heritage, its moral code, its last-day prophet. Perhaps you have taken comfort in the culture that appears to have been prospered by God and believe that the whole package is of great worth. Perhaps you have determined that you will not cheaply throw away this pearl of great price. Take another look. The "moral code of great worth" (the law) is Adventism's "bushido", Adventism's ancient stronghold that has brought unexpected bondage and immorality. The history of "Adventism's Stand" in refusing to jettison the failed 1844 prophecy has led to numerous doctrines that do violence to the gospel. Within those doctrines hides a stubborn defiance against repentance for willfully covering up the haughty legacy of pride, control, power and an institution built on false prophecy.

Those who "settled" and "won the West" were called "pioneers". Their expansionism came at the expense of generations of native peoples who were dispossessed of their land, gold and security. In the same way, the Adventist pioneers set in motion the conquering of frontiers by dispossessing their adherents of their God-given promised land, their spiritual gold, and their security of salvation. In exchange, the false shepherds have deluded themselves into believing that they have been faithful in protecting the flock while pursuing their ambitious desires for advancement and honor.

Today the legacy of Adventism's General Custers (Ellen & James White, Hiram Edson, Uriah Smith, etc.) continues to lead the "soldiers" of Adventism toward spiritual death. The slow march continues under the weight of condemnation and the banner of the law. New generations of Adventists are marching to a battle in which they are grossly outnumbered, against sin which they cannot defeat. The marching orders continue to tout the glory of the Adventist "stand" while leaders and followers, alike, march blindly to a defeat of epic proportions.

A Game becomes an Endgame

What kind of self-deception could lead the Adventist Church to camouflage its errors as truths taught by God? Since the beginning, honest-hearted people have been attempting to bring about full disclosure and elimination of teachings that cannot stand in light of scripture. In a very short time more than 100 Adventist pastors left the church because they could no longer maintain spiritual integrity within its constricted borders. Exposure of the fallacies in teachings such as the Investigative Judgment, the state of the dead and the Sabbath have become so public that most students of the Bible can no longer pretend to believe them. Even so, the church will not repent of or renounce them.

Do they believe that they can fool God and cover up the falsehood? Is there no fear of Almighty God as they strut around in scanty, self-fashioned grape leaves? God has declared by Himself that He will expose everything for what it is. This is a game that will become an endgame. Any effort to dodge or maneuver around the cherished idols will make the fictional battle in the Last Samurai look possible, and Custer's last stand seem hopeful. God will continue to "strip us bare" of our see-through leaves until we see how foolish our foolishness really is as He holds out His royal robe of holiness and entreats us to make the exchange.

Time for Truth

When is the right time for truth? Jesus said, "I am the truth and the life." He dwells outside of time and transcends it. There can be no Earth time that is not the time for truth. Yet many would evade their mandate from God to stand for truth at all times by alleging that such a position is equivalent to religiosity. Because "doctrine" in Adventism has equaled legalism many SDA pastors and officials have hidden under the subterfuge of "grace" as a way of side-stepping truth. Sound doctrine is Jesus. Jesus is truth and every revelation of "true truth" glorifies and magnifies His name. Let the strongholds fall and Jesus will shine all the brighter.

Perhaps you feel like the last Samurai… Perhaps you feel like Lt. Colonel Custer… Only God knows what is going on in your heart. But God is speaking in love to all of His children bound in the web of Adventism's cover-up of the truth. He wants to lift the veils that cover your heart so that you can have "ears" that "hear" the Truth of the new covenant gospel.

My prayer is that the Lord will speak to you through the pages of this book in a way that will touch your heart and cause you to take a stand for Truth in the face of all opposition. I pray that you will walk humbly in love towards those who will be offended by your decision to step outside of the endless cycle of deception. I pray that you will have the courage to let go of "Adventism's ancient stronghold" and grab hold of Jesus Christ, your Scepter of authority, as Esther did when she ventured into the king's court on her own initiative. I'm sure she had some anxious moments as she walked towards the king's court knowing that the fate of the entire Jewish nation hung in the balance. But King Ahasuerus lovingly extended the scepter of His authority to her guaranteeing that she had been accepted into his favor. Her request need only be spoken. When Esther touched that scepter, a symbol of the King's authority, every power it represented was at her disposal.

In a similar way today, when we come to the Father in Jesus' name, our promised Scepter, our access to God's throne room, is assured by open invitation. "Let us come boldly to the throne of grace…" (Hebrews 4:16). We don't need to have any anxious moments because we have a Savior who is able to "sympathize with our weaknesses" (Hebrews 4:15) and by whose omnipotence our most demanding obstacle may be faced.[1]

Just as Jesus Christ commanded situations to change by His authority, so we can command obstacles to move by the authority He has extended to us. When Jesus told His disciples to ask anything in His name, He used a Greek expression that also can mean, "Make a claim based on my name.[2] I believe that God is calling forth Esthers on behalf of Adventism to bring about miraculous change.

Is it possible that exercising our authority in Jesus' name, our Scepter, may go beyond merely asking God to grant a particular request, but commanding a given situation to change in Jesus' name simply because Jesus Christ has already given us authority?[3] Remember the incident when the disciples saw the fig tree that Jesus had cursed and were surprised that it had withered? What was Jesus response? He said, "Whoever says to this mountain, 'Be removed'… and does not doubt in his heart… he shall have whatever he says" Mark 11:23).

Therefore, because of Jesus Christ's triumph over death and through the power of His name, I take the authority He has given me as a child of the King, and I speak boldly to this "mountain" of offense that has caused generations of children to be spiritually abused, "Ancient stronghold of Adventism, fall down in Jesus' name! Be uprooted from your very foundations and collapse into the sea!"

Endnotes: Chapter 12

[1] Dick Eastman, Jack Hayford, *Living and Praying in Jesus' Name* (Tyndale House Publisher's, 1988) 44.
[2] Ibid., 45.
[3] Ibid., 45.

Ellen White's Arian views, along with unorthodox SDA views in the Clear Word Bible, reveal that historic SDA beliefs are still alive and well within the church.

Appendix A: Chapter 9
ABERRANT VIEWS OF JESUS

In my research I was amazed to discover that most of the early SDA pioneers, including Ellen White, advocated Arianism, a 4th century heresy that denied the divinity of Jesus Christ. Briefly, this altered view of Jesus Christ teaches that only the Father is truly God, because the Scriptures tell us that Jesus is created or begotten of the Father. Then later God created other things through him. In essence, Jesus was only a lesser god, whose preeminence over the angels was conferred to him by the Father. Thus, believing that "there was a time when Jesus was not" denies His divinity.[1]

Ellen White often called Jesus "The Son of God" at original creation. The truth is that before Jesus came to this world He was Yahweh, the Word at creation (John 1:1-3; Hebrews 1:10). The Scriptures reveal that He didn't become 'Son of God' and 'Son of Man' until His incarnation (Hebrews 1:5, 6) when the Father said, "I will become to Him a father, and He will become to me a Son" (Luke 1:35). Most of us who have read these views of Ellen White have not seen them as the Arian views they actually reflect.

The following statements taken from Ellen White's writings show that she continued to hold onto this Christ-debasing view.

- "…yet, Jesus, God's dear Son, had the preeminence over all the angelic host. He was one with the Father before the angels were created. Satan was envious of Christ and gradually assumed command, which devolved on Christ alone… The great Creator assembled the heavenly host, that he might in the presence of all the angels confer special honor upon his Son… **The**

Father then made known that it was ordained by himself that Christ, his Son, should be equal with himself"[2]

Clearly the above quotation implies that "he (Jesus) was not equal to the Father before that time," for Jesus' command was only 'devolved' or handed-down from the Father. His equality was 'conferred' or positional equality rather than being equal by nature, as necessary for True Deity (Galatians 4:8).[3]

- "There was one who perverted the freedom that God had granted to His creatures. Sin originated with him who, **next to Christ, had been most honored of God** and was highest in power and glory among the inhabitants of heaven. ...And coveting the glory with which **the infinite Father had invested His Son**, this prince of angels aspired to power that was the prerogative of Christ alone."[4]

Ellen White sees Christ as God's most honored creature—one in whom the infinite Father has invested with His power and glory. Is she suggesting that there was a time when Christ didn't have this power and glory? Next highest in line to power and glory was Lucifer. So where does this leave the Holy Spirit, third member of the Godhead? Is she implying that the Holy Spirit is fourth highest in honor, power and glory? This is blasphemous!

- **"The King of the universe summoned the heavenly hosts before Him, that in their presence He might set forth the true position of His Son** and show the relation He sustained to all created beings. **The Son of God shared the Father's throne, and the glory of the eternal, self-existent One encircled both**.[5]

Referring to God, she says that He is King of the universe. What kind of king then is the Son of God? The true position of the Son is to share the glory of the eternal, self-existent One. This sounds like the Son of God is NOT eternal!

- "Yet the Son of God was exalted above him, as one in power and authority with the Father. He shared the Father's counsels, while Lucifer did not thus enter into the purposes of God... He (Lucifer) worked with mysterious secrecy, and for a time concealed his real purposes under an appearance of reverence for God. ...The **exaltation of the Son of God as equal with the Father was represented as an injustice to**

Lucifer, who it was claimed, was also entitled to reverence and honor.[6]

This quotation seems to suggest that Ellen White's god is not omniscience (all knowing) as is the God of the Scriptures. She says he (Lucifer) worked with mysterious secrecy, and for a time concealed his real purposes under an appearance of reverence for God.

- "The Sovereign of the universe was not alone in His work of beneficence. He had **an associate—a co-worker** who could appreciate His purposes, and could share His joy in giving happiness to created beings... Christ, the Word, the only begotten of God, was one with the eternal Father—one in nature, in character, in purpose—**the only being that could enter into all the counsels and purposes of God.**"[7]

At first Ellen White describes Jesus as being one with the Father—having the same nature, character and purpose. This sounds biblical. But then she states that Jesus was the only one who could enter into the councils and purposes of God. Where does this leave the Holy Spirit? Since Jesus is God, He didn't have to enter into the councils and purposes of God. He *is* God.

Then she calls Jesus an associate—a co-worker who could appreciate God's purposes. Doesn't this sound like two gods working together? But Isaiah 43:10 says, "Before me no god was formed, nor will there be one after me." So does that mean that this associate and co-worker was not God? So how can this co-worker be one in nature, character and purpose with God if he is not God?

- "Grief, indignation, and horror filled the heart of Moses as he viewed the hypocrisy and satanic hatred manifested by the Jewish nation against **their Redeemer, the mighty Angel who had gone before their fathers.** He heard Christ's agonizing cry, "My God, My God, why hast Thou forsaken Me?" (Mark 15:34). He saw Him lying in Joseph's new tomb" (Patriarchs & Prophets. P. 476).

- **"This angel was the angel of God's presence** (Isaiah 63:9), the angel in whom was the name of the great Jehovah (Exodus 23:20-23). The expression can refer to no other than **the Son of God**... He was revealed to them as the Angel of Jehovah, the Captain of the Lord's host, Michael, the Archangel."[8]

Ellen White boldly labels the Son of God as the angel of Jehovah's presence, Captain of the Lord's host, and Michael, the Archangel. It is obvious that Ellen White did not consider the Son of God to be God Himself. If she did, then why would she say that the Son of God was one with the Creator of the universe when it is Jesus who *is* the Creator?

Jesus is Michael the Archangel

In recounting her 'vision' of December 1844, Ellen White speaks of Jesus and herself as "winging our way upward..." Seeing this statement in the light of her calling Jesus Michael the Archangel, one is led to believe that she really did view Jesus as an angel!

Most Christians are surprised to discover that SDAs teach that Jesus is Michael the Archangel. If the SDA church were to admit that she was in error, they would be forced to reject her as a true prophet. So the SDA church has to hold on to both teachings—that Jesus is both God the Son and Michael the Archangel.

It makes a great difference who Jesus really is. The real Jesus is not an archangel but the God-man Christ Jesus. Sadly, the SDA Bible Commentary appeals to her writings as their final authority and says that Jesus is Michael the Archangel that stands up in Daniel 12:1, signifying that Jesus has ended His mediation for us.[9]

Clear Word Bible promotes aberrant theology

What's more, in order to make these aberrant views of Jesus' identity appear biblical, the Clear Word Bible that has been heavily promoted by SDAs since 1994 continues to support Ellen White's Arian views (http://www.watchman.org/reltop/clearwordbible.htm). Clearly, these aberrant views of Jesus Christ that do not support His full Deity need to be exposed and renounced as heresy. Instead, the corporate church has covered up these erroneous beliefs and unorthodox positions by translating them right into the text of the SDA Clear Word Bible. A number of them are listed below.

- (Adds to original text) "... God is speaking with His Son of making man; then of man's fall into sin" (Genesis 1:26; 3:22).
- "Next I saw a mighty angel come down from heaven... (adds) Then I knew it was the Lord Jesus" (Revelation 10:1).

- "Then this mighty angel (adds) the Lord Jesus..." (Revelation 10:5).
- "Go and take the little open book out of the hand of the mighty angel... so I went up to the Son of God ..." (Revelation 10:8-9).
- "When Christ descends from heaven, (adds) He as Michael the Archangel will give a shout..." (1 Thessalonians 4:16).
- "... (Adds) the Lord Jesus Christ, also called Michael the Archangel..." (Jude 9).
- "... before Abraham was I AM" changed to "I existed before Abraham was born" (John 8:58).
- "...By Him all things were created" changed to "through him the Father created" (Colossians 1:16).
- "... that in all things He might have pre-eminence" changed to "... therefore He is worthy to be given first place" (Colossians 1:18).
- "I and My Father are One" changed "I and my Father are so close we're One" (John 10:30).

The dilemma that the SDA church faces today is that they cannot make Ellen White's aberrant views of Jesus Christ's identity harmonize with Scripture. Although the SDA church today holds the True Deity of Christ in their statement of faith (SDA Believe #4), it is out of harmony with the 1903 statement of Ellen White that said, **"The man Christ Jesus was not the Lord God Almighty"** (Letter 32, 1899; ms 150, SDA Bible Commentary, vol. 5, p.1129).[10]

But the Scriptures identify Jesus Christ as the "same, yesterday, today and forever" (Hebrews 13:8), and since He as "the man Christ Jesus" is our mediator in heaven today (1 Timothy 2:5) then **He has always been the Lord God Almighty** for it's impossible for Almighty God to ever lay aside His full deity!" That is why Paul says of Jesus Christ, "In Him is dwelling all the fullness of Deity, bodily" (Colossians 2:9). The fact that Ellen White failed to recognize Jesus as 'the man Christ Jesus' (1 Timothy 2:5; Hebrews 7:24-25) and that 'in Him dwells all the fullness of the Godhead in bodily form' (Colossians 2:9), could have been the reason I had seen a fuzzy film covering the cross.

Not until the turn of the century did Adventism begin to move out of Arianism to espouse Jesus' full deity, and subsequently, the Trinity. But this was hard to do, in light of Ellen White's statements upholding

Arianism for over 50 years.[11] Although the corporate SDA church has claimed to believe God's Word is their final authority, unfortunately in practice, Ellen White's writings are the filter through which they interpret God's Word. In essence, many SDAs defend and uphold Ellen White's interpretation of Scripture rather than letting the Scriptures speak for themselves.

Christ has a Fallen Nature

This is most clearly seen in the way they have tried to make Ellen White's writings, agree with Scripture, particularly regarding the human nature of Jesus Christ. From its beginning the SDA church taught "when God partook of humanity, He took, not the perfect, sinless nature of man before the fall, but the fallen, sinful, offending, degenerated nature of man after the fall of Adam. The inclinations and tendencies to sin that are in fallen man's flesh were in His flesh; but that, by complete dependence upon His Father, His mind held its integrity and never by a shadow of a thought responded to the weakness or sinful cravings of the flesh."[12]

Comments like the following reveal that Ellen White, along with SDA forbearers, was in error and confused over the human nature of Jesus Christ. They believed that Jesus took on the sinful nature of Adam *after* he fell. Consider the following statements taken from Ellen White's writings, along with early pioneer writings.

- **"He (Jesus) took upon His sinless nature our sinful nature**, that He might know how to succor those that are tempted."[13]
- "Clad in the vestments of humanity, the Son of God came down to the level of those He wished to save. In Him was no guile or sinfulness; He was ever pure and undefiled; yet **He took upon Him our sinful nature."**[14]
- "Though He had no taint of sin upon His character, yet He condescended to connect our fallen human nature with His divinity. By thus taking humanity, He honored humanity. **Having taken our fallen nature, He showed what it might become, by accepting the ample provision He has made for it,** and by becoming partaker of the divine nature."[15]

In 1895, after Ellen White heard a sermon that W. W. Prescott gave in which he made 25 statements that Christ took our fallen human nature, she expressed grateful appreciation for the lecture.[16] This heresy was the accepted teaching of the SDA church as it appeared in periodicals, Sabbath School Lesson Quarterlies and books published by the denomination up until 1949.

Other SDA leaders, besides Ellen White, felt that this view of Christ's human nature in no way denied the church's stand on the complete Deity and absolute sinlessness of Jesus Christ. In 1921 the church published a book by Carlyle B. Haynes that stated that SDAs believe and teach, "**There really was no need for Christ to come at all unless He was to take such flesh.**"[17] This false teaching regarding Christ's human sinful nature continued to go into thousands of homes through the efforts of colporteur evangelists who sold Bible Readings for the Home Circle. The following quote is taken from the 1942 edition of this book, under the heading, "A Sinless Life," p. 174, 1942.

"**In His humanity Christ partook of our sinful, fallen nature. If not then he was not** 'made like unto His brethren' was not 'in all points tempted like as we are' did not overcome as we have to overcome, and is not, therefore, **the complete and perfect Savior man needs and must have to be saved…**"

Christ has a Sinless Nature

In 1949 when a new edition of "Bible Readings" was published, the above statement that says "in His humanity Christ partook of our sinful, fallen nature…" was omitted because it was recognized by some as being out of harmony with SDAs "true position."

However, further checking back into the "Bible Readings" from 1915 we find that the above heresy correctly represented the "true position" of our early forbearers, and was repeatedly found in the writings of Ellen White. The change had been made because this particular point of contention in SDA theology has drawn and continues to draw severe censure from Bible scholars both from inside and outside of the denomination.[18]

So during the period between 1940 and 1955, the words, "sinful" and "fallen" with reference to Christ's human nature were, for the most part, eliminated from denominationally published materials. Phrases such as "sinless human nature," "nature of Adam before the fall" and "human nature defiled" replaced the former heretical terminology. They have been interpreted to mean that the human nature of Christ was "sinful," "fallen," or "degenerated," only in the sense of the weakness and frailty of the human organism. It was stated that these weaknesses were borne vicariously, not innately and intrinsically as a part of Christ's human body.[19]

False Reasoning Exposed

The reason the SDA church can say that Christ "in His humanity partook of our sinful, fallen nature with the possibility of yielding to temptation" in one breath, and then turn around and say in the next breath that He had a sinless and unfallen nature is that "it agrees with revelation and reason". 'Revelation' means the authoritative writings of Ellen White.

Since Ellen White continues to be seen as a true prophet by the corporate SDA church her views have to be upheld even though they are often contrary to Scripture. By using false reasoning techniques, the leadership of the church continues to 'reason' Ellen White's views into the Scripture passages in order to uphold her anti-Christian statements.[20]

Let's consider the truth of Romans 8:3 for a moment. The Scriptures say that Jesus "was made in the likeness of sinful flesh". The SDA church contends that this Scripture is saying that Jesus had "sinful flesh or a sinful human nature" or "fallen human nature" (see SDA Believe… p. 46; Bible Readings, p. 174; & Answers to Questions on Doctrine, p. 391). However, when God made Adam 'in the likeness of God' this didn't mean that He made him in the nature of God. A statement of similarity does not show equality, but rather infers inequality, even though similarity exists. Thus, 'made in the likeness of sinful flesh' doesn't mean 'born in sinful flesh'.[21]

Another Scripture that SDAs have used to support their false reasoning is Hebrews 2:17 which says that in all things He was made like His brethren. SDAs contend that 'all things' includes a 'sinful human nature'. If this is so, then He must have also been a sinner in order to be like us in all things. 'Things' speak of 'tangibles', concrete substance, such as physical attributes. It doesn't describe in-tangibles or abstractions, such as one's state of being or condition of sinful nature. Jesus was not like us in His state of being, because He was sin-less.[22]

Traditional Adventism has also taken Hebrews 2:14 that says Jesus "partook of flesh and blood" and used it to prove that Jesus had a sinful human nature. However, it only means that Jesus became ONE of humanity, having our material substance of 'flesh' and 'blood'. The Scripture does not mean or even imply that He had 'a fleshly carnal nature'.[23]

A familiar Scripture that has been greatly misunderstood because of the KJV rendering of this verse is Hebrews 4:15 which says that Jesus "was tempted in all points as we are, yet without sin." Properly rendered in the Greek, the verse says, "He was tested in all points as we are, **apart from sin**". "Tested" in this verse means "He was proved"— it does NOT mean 'tempted to sin' for God *cannot* be tempted to sin! It means 'to test, prove, in a good sense. In all the temptations that Christ endured there was *nothing in Him* that responded to sin. There was nothing within Christ to draw Him into sin, such as we have with our own fallen, sinful, human natures, which He didn't have.[24]

Christ's sinless, unfallen, human nature put Him on an infinite vantage ground. His deity, with His sinless and unfallen human nature gave Him an advantage over Adam, because Adam had no divine nature and so was still able to be tempted and to sin. Jesus' deity was *God's surety that 'He will not fail or be discouraged'* in His mission.[25]

Historic Beliefs given respectability

In 1957 Leroy Edwin Froom, an SDA church historian, used his vocabulary skills to doctor historic SDA beliefs so they would be received by other Evangelical Christians. In his book, "Questions on Doctrine" he skillfully explained away the fact that Ellen White used words like "sinful," "fallen," and "deteriorated human nature" in referring to Jesus Christ's human nature by making her say that Christ took our nature "vicariously" as our "substitute."[26]

He further sought to change the historic SDA beliefs that had advocated Arianism particularly the following four leading charges that Walter Martin complained were commonly brought against the SDA church:

(1) the atonement of Christ was not completed at the cross;
(2) salvation is the result of grace plus the works of the law;
(3) the Lord Jesus Christ was a created being, not from all eternity;
(4) Jesus Christ partook of man's sinful nature at the incarnation.[27]

In order to give respectability to the reinterpretations he had concocted in his book, "Movement of Destiny" (1971), Froom twisted the words of Ellen White in order to support his contention that she agreed with his version of the human nature of Christ.[28] Here is an example of how he distorted what she originally had written.

Under the title line, "Took Sinless Nature of Adam before Fall," nineteen statements purporting to support its conclusion followed this heading. Within each statement was a tiny fragment from Ellen White's writings. But as you look at the context in which she wrote these quotations, not a single one of them says that Christ took the nature of Adam before the fall, and some of them say exactly the opposite! Three fragments are taken from the same paragraph in Ellen White's writings which opens with an unequivocal statement that Christ took the fallen nature of man!"[29]

In 1983 after the book, "Questions on Doctrine" went out of print (1980), Walter Martin addressed the 1983 General Conference with the following critical question, but it was never answered: "Do you regard the interpretation of the Bible by Ellen G. White to be infallible, that is, to be the infallible rule of interpreting Scripture? For instance, if an issue comes up where you are debating something and Mrs. White speaks on it, is that the infallible voice?"[30]

Given Adventism's history of trying to play both ends against the middle, this question may never be answered. To answer "Yes" would deny the repeated statements that the Bible alone is used as the source of SDA doctrine. For many in the church to answer "No" would deny the "Gift of Prophecy" that many still claim was given to Ellen White for the purpose of leading the SDA church further into the light of the "present truths" revealed through her.

It is interesting to note that the new annotated "Questions on Doctrine" affirms that the SDA church has never modified its doctrines. This new volume indirectly affirms Adventists' dependence on Ellen White by supporting all of the church doctrines and traditional interpretations.

Labeled a "Cult"

According to the October 1985 issue of "Adventist Currents," Dr. Walter Martin stated that the label "cult" may again apply to the SDA church, or perhaps it should never have been removed as it was becoming apparent that he had been deceived by a well-meaning minority of men in the leadership of the church in the 1950's. "If Seventh-day Adventism depends upon Ellen White's reputation rather than upon the gospel of grace alone, its classification as a cult will be well earned before the next twenty years has passed" (quotation from above issue of "Adventist Currents" that was taken from an interview with the Review editor on the John Ankerberg Show).

This strong rebuke caused the leadership of the SDA church to publish a new Adventist doctrinal book in 1988, entitled, SDAs Believe. In Chapter 4 of this book a strong attempt was made again to please all sides on the issue of the human nature of Jesus Christ. "The Bible portrays Jesus' humanity as sinless. His birth was supernatural. The Holy Spirit conceived him. As a newborn baby He was described as 'that Holy One,' He took the nature of man in its fallen state [that is, He took our fallen nature], bearing the consequences of sin, not its sinfulness [that is, He did not take our fallen nature]. He was one with the human race, except in sin."[31]

Amazingly, two diametrical opposed positions are presented within the same quote and accepted as truth. These statements talk about the actions of Jesus as though they were the nature of Jesus. Sadly, this is a classic example of cult double-talk![32]

George R. Knight, an accomplished professor of history at Andrews University (the SDA Theological Seminary in Michigan), makes the following admission in 2003. He states that "Questions on Doctrine" qualifies as the most divisive book in SDA history. Although it was published to help bring peace between Adventism and conservative Protestantism, its release has done more to cause theological division within the SDA church than any other in its history.[33]

Pressure to return to Historic Beliefs

In the November 5, 1992 issue of the "Adventist Review," a 16-page booklet, entitled, "Issues," addressed the doctrinal changes that had occurred 30 years earlier, along with a plea of tolerance from those who wanted to return to the historic beliefs of Adventism. The reason given was that the SDA church had never decided what it believes on the four controversial points that Froom sought to change in order to get the approval of Walter Martin and the evangelical community. Consequently there is still much debate as to what Adventists believe. Even though from the 1960s through the 1980s future leaders were being initiated in their colleges into the new teachings regarding Christ's sinless human nature, these new teachings came with much struggle.

During the 1990s those voices advocating a return to historic SDA beliefs were strongly felt. Ellen White's Arian views, along with unorthodox SDA views in the Clear Word Bible, reveal that historic SDA beliefs are still alive and well within the church.

It seems apparent that the SDA denomination today is witnessing a resurgence of anti-Trinitarianism and semi-Arianism errors that are based on what its early forbearers believed—not on what the Word of God teaches. Jan Paulsen, President of the worldwide SDA Church gave an address to church leaders in May 2002, confirming that there has been no change in the historical SDA position with regard to doctrines that have been at the heart of Adventism. In essence he said that it is vital that Adventism keeps its separate identity as the historical remnant gathering the faithful remnant from all corners of the earth to the purpose of God.[34]

Speaking on behalf of the corporate SDA denomination as he gave this address to 45 church leaders gathered to consider the topic, "Theological Unity in a Growing World Church," Paulsen said, "Being SDAs has direct bearing on our salvation. I would risk my whole spiritual life and salvation were I to leave what I am now and join any other community."[35]

In effect Paulsen stated that the SDA church is not an evangelical church. Without admitting openly that Ellen White is the final voice and authority in doctrinal matters in the church, he and others unabashedly refer to her to find support for those beliefs from the Bible. Although the leaders of the SDA church in 1956 tried to get the approval of the evangelical Protestant world by creatively rewording their fundamental beliefs about the nature and identity of Jesus Christ, the "Annotated Edition of Questions on Doctrine" reveals that the church never really changed its historical positions. Although they make symbolic gestures to other Christian groups, they do not interact spiritually as members of the body of Christ.

Endnotes: Appendix A

[1] Elmer Wiebe, *Who is the Adventist Jesus?* (Xulon Press, 2005) 27.
[2] White, Spirit of Prophecy, Vol. I (Battle Creek, Michigan: Steam Press of the Seventh-day Adventist Publishing Association 1870) 17-18.
[3] D.F. Streifling, *Did Ellen G. White teach A Different God?* http://www.ellenwhiteexposed.com/egw68.htm
[4] Ibid., 35.
[5] White, *Patriarchs & Prophets* (Battle Creek, Michigan: Seventh-day Adventist *Publishing* Association, 1864) 36.
[6] Ibid., 37.
[7] Ibid., 34.
[8] Ibid., 761.
[9] Quotations from *Desire of Ages*, p. 379; p. 99; *Prophets and Kings*, p. 572; and *Spiritual Gifts IV* a, p. 158 support Jesus being Michael, the Archangel.
[10] Francis D. Nichol, *SDA Bible Commentary, Manuscript 140, Vol. V* (Hagerstown, Maryland: Review & Herald Publishing Association, 1953) 1129. Book revised in 1980.
[11] Streifling 35.
[12] Wiebe 35-36.
[13] Ellen G. White, *Medical Ministry* (Mountain View, California: Pacific Press Publishing Association, 1963) 181. L. E. Froom, *Questions on Doctrine* (Hagerstown, Maryland: Review and Herald Publishing Association, 1957) 654-656.
[14] *Review and Herald* (Hagerstown, Maryland: Review & Herald Publishing Association, Dec. 15, 1896).
[15] Special Instruction Relating to the Review and Herald office and the work in Battle Creek, May 26, 1896, p. 13.
[16] Manuscripts 19, 23, 47 and 52, 1895; Letter 2, 32, 83, and 84, 1895. This sermon was printed in the January 6 and 13 issues of the *Bible Echo*, SDAs Australian Journal.
[17] Wiebe 46.
[18] Ibid., 50.

[19] Ibid., 36.
[20] Ibid., 255.
[21] Ibid., 255.
[22] Ibid., 256
[23] Ibid., 256.
[24] Ibid., 256-257.
[25] Ibid., 257.
[26] Ibid., 58.
[27] L. E. Froom, *Movement of Destiny* (Hagerstown, Maryland: Review and Herald Publishing Association, 1957) 466.
[28] Wiebe 61.
[29] Ralph Larson, *Documentary Fraud,* FF-26, p. 2. Now in Doctrinal History Tract book.
[30] Wiebe 66.
[31] *Seventh-day Adventists Believe: A Biblical Exposition of 27 Fundamental Beliefs* (Hagerstown, Maryland: Review & Herald Publishing Association, 1988) 49/1:1-2.
[32] Wiebe 68.
[33] *Adventist Review* (Hagerstown, Maryland: Review & Herald Publishing Association, November 1992) 47. Originally a 16-page booklet entitled, "Issues".
[34] Wiebe 212.
[35] Read the whole article at the following link: http://www.adventistreview.org/2002-1524/story3.html.

By ignoring the doctrines and history of Adventism, evangelical Christians give assent to its abuses and influence while ignoring the victims of its mutilated gospel.

Appendix B:
ASSISTED SUICIDE - A WORD TO EVANGELICAL CHRISTIANS

While making some editorial changes in the Epilogue, the Lord gave Ramone some further insight into the two words I had received ("Last Samurai" and "Custer's Last Stand"). I pray that you will hear God's call upon your heart for intercession as you read the following message.

"Do not be hasty in the laying on of hands, and do not share in the sins of others. Watch your life and doctrine closely. Persevere in them, because if you do, you will save both yourself and your hearers. My brothers, if one of you should wander from the truth and someone should bring him back, remember this: Whoever turns a sinner from the error of his way will save him from death and cover over a multitude of sins" (I Timothy 5:22, 4:16, James 5:19-20).

I believe the Lord has another message in calling our attention to the film, "The Last Samurai." Not coincidentally, the fate of Lt. Colonel Custer is notably mentioned three times in the film. What is the connection, and does it have something to do with why the Lord brought up these two words?

In short, the connection is *intercession*. We are called as intercessors, spiritual wombs and spiritual midwives for those who do not know Him, and even for those who do know Him but remain in bondage. He is calling us to intercede for His deceived children in Adventism. He is calling evangelical Christians to intercede for those caught in the bondage of Adventism. This is a word for you, if you are an evangelical Christian or an ex-Adventist who has become a mainstream Christian.

The film "The Last Samurai" is not only the story of a fictional Japanese warrior based loosely on a real samurai rebellion. In fact, the film's story centers on an American military officer who has been "exported" to Japan to help the country's military. Because the army was sent out prematurely without sufficient training or experience, it was quickly routed by the samurai rebels. The American military officer was captured by the samurai and spent the winter with them, conversing frequently with the samurai leader. In one exchange, the officer mentioned Custer's last stand with disgust for his arrogance, carelessness, and disregard for the lives of his 200 soldiers. Conversely the samurai warrior had great admiration for the glory of Custer's death.

While with them, the American began to learn their "code" and way of life. By the time he left their camp, he had become their friend and ally. By the end of the film, he has chosen to fight alongside them. When the battle will certainly be lost, the officer and samurai leader speak of Custer and go forward into certain death together. The officer has now come to see in Custer the samurai's way. When the samurai leader lies dying on the battlefield, his samurai rebels all slain, the American officer "assists" the samurai in his honorable death and helps him commit suicide (hari-kiri).

The American officer is symbolic of evangelical Christians who have begun to partner with Adventists, either ignorantly or in spite of knowing about the grave errors in Adventist theology. For whatever reasons—keeping peace, unity at all costs, moving "forward", not being sectarian, etc.—many Christians have chosen to turn a blind eye to aberrations of the gospel in Adventism. Many Christian leaders have chosen to turn a deaf ear to the bleating of the wounded sheep from Adventism or discount them as malcontents. They have spent time alongside Adventist leaders who do not expose to them the carefully guarded inner secrets. The well-meaning evangelicals are often unable to see because they have no reference point from which to relate, just like the samurai could not know what it felt like to be a woman or lower-class citizen. Their conclusions are based on the pleasing personal qualities of the Adventists themselves, and not on the truths of Scripture. If, perchance, the Adventists they work with seem open-minded then it becomes easy for Christians co-workers to assume that Adventism is OK after all.

Adventists have become skilled at covering up the more objectionable beliefs of their religion so that they are hidden from view. They use the same words that Christians use, but, unbeknownst to others those words do not carry the same meanings. Use of the correct language can lull their Christian contacts to believe that they are in the same army, fighting for the same cause while nothing could be further from the truth. So, evangelical Christians who should be interceding to break off the heavy burdens of Adventists have instead become "assistants" to spiritual deadness. By ignoring the doctrines and history of Adventism, evangelical Christians give assent to its abuses and influence while ignoring the victims of its mutilated gospel.

The patina of good things in Adventist culture evokes *admiration* for such things as its "health" message, "Sabbath" day principle, missions, school systems, institutions, medical centers, excellence and intellectualism. Well-intentioned evangelicals defend Adventism (as Walter Martin tragically did) and become offended by those who point out Adventism's errors. The experiences, wisdom and cries of former Adventists are often ignored in the name of "unity" and "diversity". But I would propose that unless one has lived the life of Adventism and been freed from its grip it is nearly impossible to understand the paralyzing effect it has on the spirit. Its end effect is to nearly extinguish knowledge of the gospel or the certainty of one's salvation. I would plead with you to listen when an ex-Adventist tries to express the hopelessness of being Adventist.

Like the American officer in the samurai movie, the Christian community is seduced. They have not persevered in a vigilant defense of sound doctrine. Instead of calling Adventism to accountability for their refusal to embrace the gospel alone, Scripture alone, and Christ alone, they have embraced them, thereby allowing them to be robbed of the power of Truth. They have supported, helped and defended Adventism's continuing rejection of new covenant living as their people wither from useless attempts at perfection.

I feel the Lord saying—

My children, I called you to intercede for the weak, for the poor, for the oppressed, for the fatherless, for the widow. I called you to set the captives free, to give sight to the blind in the name of My Son, and to heal the lame who could not walk from the weight of their burdens. I called you to preach My gospel, the

good news of freedom and complete, fulfilled Sabbath-rest in My Son. I called you to proclaim the good news of a New Covenant, based on better promises and My own enduring faithfulness.

Before you, stand the people of Adventism who have toiled under the bondage of their own works… under the weight of an old covenant which I did not give to them, but to Israel of old. Open your eyes and see those who are suffering from a generational cycle of spiritual incest that rejects My Son's righteousness alone as sufficient for their salvation.

Why have you partnered with them and not called them to repentance and life in Me? Many of you have fought hard in the United States against medically assisted suicide, but you have been assisting the spiritual suicide of Adventist children, leaders and members! You have helped them hold onto a millstone instead of cutting them free to fly with you in My new covenant. You have helped them remain in the cycle of abuse by refusing to call them to repentance and accountability by facing the abuses of Adventist history and teachings. You have fought against medically assisted suicide because it is against the law of your land, but you have not fought against spiritually assisted suicide that is against the law of My Spirit of life! Now I call you to repent, receive My heart, and speak my truth.

"Unity" based on compromise is not what Jesus spoke of in John 17. Only a unity based on the solid foundation of Jesus' all sufficiency will answer His prayer. In the name of Jesus I call you to seek true unity that brings life, freedom and release. I believe that Jesus is calling you to receive His heart for Adventists, to receive His words for them, and then speak them out, even when they are difficult words of repentance or rebuke. His words always give life even if they appear negative to your natural eyes. Do not water down His word! Do not water down His choice wine! Do not neglect His holy covenant and consider it irrelevant, for it is the blood of this covenant that sets you apart as His. It is the blood of this covenant that He has given to set you free from the weight of your sins under the old covenant. Do not stand by while His captive children in Adventism suffer from the weight of the old covenant and their abusive heritage. Do not build unity based on distortions of the Son's blood and all-sufficient righteousness, for

unless He builds your unity, you do labor in vain. Do not share in the abuses and assisted-suicides of Adventism, or He will come and fight against you with the sword of His mouth. His children must be set free. He says to us all "I am the Lord. I am the true shepherd". Amen.

Bibliography

Anderson, Dirk. *White Out: An Investigation of Ellen G. White*. Glendale, Arizona: Life Assurance Ministries Publications, 1999.

Bevere, John, *The Bait of Satan: Living Free from the Deadly Trap of Offense*. Charisma House, 2004.

Miller, Walter H. B. *Bible Echo*. Melbourne, Australia: The Echo Publishing Company, Limited, 1890.

Blanco, Jack J. *The Clear Word Bible*. Hagerstown, Maryland: Advent Design, 1994.

Blue, Ken. *Healing Spiritual Abuse*. InterVarsity Press, October 1993.

Brinsmead, Robert D. *Verdict*. Fallbrook, California: Verdict Publications, June 1981.

Canright, D. M. *Life of Ellen G. White Seventh-day Adventist Prophet—Her False Claims Refuted*. Cincinnati, Ohio: The Standard Publishing Company, 1919.

Eastman, Dick. Hayford, Jack. *Living and Praying in Jesus' Name*. Tyndale House Publisher's 1988.

Froom, L. E. *Movement of Destiny*. Hagerstown, Maryland: Review & Herald Publishing Association, 1971.

Froom, L. E. *Questions on Doctrine*. Hagerstown, Maryland: Review & Herald Publishing Association, 1957.

Larson, Ralph. *Documentary Fraud*. Now in Doctrinal History Tract, 1988.

Nichol, Francis D. *SDA Bible Commentary*. Hagerstown, Maryland: Review and Herald Publishing Association, 1953.

Ogilvie, John Lloyd. *Silent Strength for my Life*. Harvest House Publishers, August 1990.

Paxton, Geoffrey J. *The Shaking of Adventism*. Wilmington, Delaware: Zenith Publishers, 1977.

Ratzlaff, Dale. *Sabbath in Christ.* Glendale, Arizona: Life Assurance Ministries Publications, 2003. Originally called, *Sabbath in Crisis.*

Ratzlaff, Dale. *The Cultic Doctrine of Seventh-day Adventists.* Glendale, Arizona: Life Assurance Ministries Publications, 1996.

Review & Herald. Hagerstown, Maryland: Review & Herald Publishing Association, 1896.

Seventh-day Adventists Believe…A Biblical Exposition of 27 Fundamental Beliefs. Hagerstown, Maryland: Review & Herald Publishing Association, 1988.

Sheets, Dutch. *Intercessory Prayer: the Lightning of God, Course Syllabus.* Publisher: Dutch Sheets, 1986.

Streifling, Dr. Verle. *Did Ellen G. White teach 'A Different God'?* http://www.ellenwhiteexposed.com/egw68.htm.

The Fundamental Beliefs of Seventh-day Adventist. Review & Herald Publishing Association, 1980. Also see: http://www.adventist.org/beliefs/fundamental/index.html.

White, Ellen G. *The Desire of Ages.* Mountain View, California: Pacific Press Publishing Association, 1940.

White, Ellen G. *The Great Controversy.* Mountain View, California: Pacific Press Publishing Association, 1950. Revised edition first published 1911.

White, Ellen G. *Spiritual Gifts, Vol. 4.* Washington, D.C, Review & Herald Publishing, Association, 1945. Published four volumes 1858-1864.

White, Ellen G. *Prophets & Kings.* Mountain View, California: Pacific Press Publishing Association, 1943.

White, Ellen G. *Testimonies for the Church.* Mountain View, California: Pacific Press Publishing Association, 1882. Nine volumes published from 1885-1909.

White, Ellen G. *Adventist Review and Sabbath Herald,* 1897

White, Ellen G. *Medical Ministry.* Mountain View, CA: Pacific Press Publishing Association, 1963.

White, Ellen G. *Spirit of Prophecy, 4 Volumes.* Battle Creek, Michigan: Steam Press of the Seventh-day Adventist Publishing Association, 1870.

White, Ellen G. *Patriarchs and Prophets.* Battle Creek, Michigan: Seventh-day Adventist *Publishing* Association, 1864, 1890.

White, Ellen G. *Sketches from the Life of Paul.* Battle Creek, Michigan: Review & Herald Publishing Association; Oakland, California: Pacific Press, 1883.

Wiebe, Elmer. *Who is the Adventist Jesus?* Xulon Press, 2005.

"Wikipedia" encyclopedia online: http://en.wikipedia.org/wiki/Golden_plates.

Note: You can find the Ellen G. White books listed above on the official website of the SDA White Estate at http://www.whiteestate.org. You may also want to check the following website that shows the many self-contradictions in Ellen White's writings, along with the contradictions between her writings and Scripture at http://www.ellenwhiteexposed.com/.

Other Helpful Website Resources:

http://www.gentlybroken.com/
http://sabbatismos.com/
http://www.forthegospel.org/
http://www.lifeassuranceministries.org/
http://www.ratzlaf.com/
http://ex-sda.com/
http://www.exadventist.com/
http://formeradventist.com/
http://www.nonsda.org/
http://www.truthorfables.com/
http://www.oneflockministries.org/home.html
http://art-for-jesus.blogspot.com/2008/08/artists-statement.html
http://sound-the-trumpet.blogspot.com/2008/01/adventisms-package.html

Made in the USA
Lexington, KY
20 November 2010